On The Seventh Day She Rested

Lynne Farr

CREATESPACE.COM

On The Seventh Day She Rested is a work of fiction. Names, characters, places and incidents are either the products of the author's imagination or are used fictitiously. Historical and scientific certainties may change.

© 2014 by Lynne Farr
Cover design by Patti Millington

ISBN-13: 978-1499272123
ISBN-10: 149927212X

Library of Congress Control Number: 2014909723

Printed in the United States of America

Contents

In The Beginning . . .   1

Day One: And L. A. Was Without Form And Void, But Lo! There Was Beverly Hills   3

Day Two: And There Was Light   30

Day Three: And Behold! There Were Bucks To Be Made Out of Everything   68

Day Four: And There Was Power   112

Day Five: Yea, Verily, And There Was Glory   145

Day Six: And It Came To Pass That She Got It All   182

Day Seven: And On The Seventh Day God Ended Her Work Which She Had Made, And She Rested From All Her Work Which She Had Made   219

Acknowledgements   242

Also by Lynne Farr

Off The Grid Without A Paddle
Off The Grid And Over The Hill
Off The Grid: What's Cookin'?

For Dorothy, Irene, two Connies, and Ruby-uh-Joan

In The Beginning . . .

In the beginning, give or take a few billion years; after the dinosaurs but before Exxon; after pterodactyls but before ground-to-air missiles; after asparagus but before agribusiness; wanna-be humans showed up on Earth. There's still debate over how they arrived but we know they weren't driving Rolls Royces. In those days, if science has it right, most people travelled by tree.

What a picture for the family album: our acrobatic antecedents bounding gracefully through triple-canopy forest, pausing occasionally to nest, and nap, and pick bugs out of each others' fur. When they got hungry they'd eat: a leaf, a fruit, a stem, a root. There was sweet water to drink unless too many white rhinos lived upstream. No non-degradable waste blighted the landscape, though sometimes a blight blighted it. When it rained, and they say it rained a lot, personal hygiene improved and living rooms got greener, but no one viewed raindrops as pennies from heaven. There was nothing to buy or pay for. You just took what you needed and left something for the next creature.

Not only were there no pennies, there was no heaven. And no hell. There was no God with a capital "G." All that came later when things got complicated.

Since television hadn't reached the suburbs yet, proto-people had to entertain themselves. They'd make animal shapes out of the clouds, or admire a butterfly ballet. For comedy, they could watch the little kids trying to swing from branch to branch, near-missing. At night they studied a billion stars and the moon which was always changing.

Then, once a year, came the irresistible urge to merge, a passtime which proved so pleasurable they decided not to wait for spring, the way the neighbors did, but to engage in it more often.

It was a nice life. Sure, once in a while, a sabertooth tiger might climb your tree and pick off the weakest of your siblings, but you pretty much learned to flow with it. Not that you didn't keep a wary eye out for striped cats with big teeth, but nobody tried to sneak out of dying the way we do today with our organ transplants, our life support systems; our drugs, drugs, drugs. Face it, sooner or later we're all going to be dinner. Back then, they understood this sort of thing.

Which brings us to Him, and Her, and which one of them chose to opt out of a perfectly balanced eco-system.

Was it Her? "These kids are eating us out of house and home. We need a bigger better tree."

Or was it Him, the big ape, turning his nose up at a twigful of tender greens: "I'm sick of salads. I'm in the mood for a steak tonight."

Maybe it doesn't matter who said what.

Then again, maybe it does.

For Ages, we've been blaming their exit from Eden on Her and some talking snake, a possibly undeserved defamation with far-reaching, less than positive, social consequences.

It's a story overdue for a rewrite. But since neither He, nor She, nor their children, nor their children's children, nor their children's children's children's children took the trouble to record their dialogue, we'll have to dig for the truth.

For now, let's just say, one Darwinian day, somebody turned to somebody and said, "Okay, Kid, let's make tracks."

And somebody said, "Where we goin'?"

And somebody said, "This time I want it all."

And somebody said, "Sounds to me like we're talkin' Southern California."

Day One: And L. A. Was Without Form,
And Void, But Lo! There Was
Beverly Hills . . .

1:1

Mr. and Mrs. Isaac Newman and family live in a much bigger, much better tree.

Their home, some would say mansion, dominates one and a half acres of prime Benedict Canyon bottomland, sheltered by hills and blessed with a twenty-four karat climate which makes the change of seasons unremarkable. Uncertainty over rain has been offset by sprinkler systems which keep the Newman property evergreen and hinting at its hidden talent for growing things to eat.

Zack Newman missed the hint and bought the place for its proximity to the Beverly Hills Hotel, which was exactly two minutes by Rolls Royce away from his new front door. Now he'd no longer have to rush to those Polo Lounge breakfasts where he consummated deals for well known actors, actresses and comedians. Zack managed the stars – the Hollywood ones. Unfortunately, no sooner had he moved in than the Beverly Hills Hotel went under in the double-dip recession of 1980 through 1982, dragging real estate values in the neighborhood down with it. But that's another story. No, it's not.

The house, before he paid too much for it, was listed as "Prestige Mediterranean-style Villa, 4 + mds, 5 ½ ba, frml dning, slrium, dn, 3 frplcs, pl, cbna, rm fr tns ct, must be seen to be appreciated."

This was true. You had to see the two-story entry hall with its sweeping staircase and twelve-tiered crystal chandelier. The frplc in

ON THE SEVENTH DAY SHE RESTED

the living room featured rare Greek marble. The master bathroom had gold-plated fixtures and two bidets.

But it wasn't quite perfect. The chandelier in the front hall made Zack think of his deceased mother for whom he had an unresolved dislike. He wanted it replaced with recessed lighting to give the entry a different look. The dining room was obsolete, he said, and could better be used as a game room. The kitchen cried for remodelling. The master bedroom needed help.

Zack's third wife was glad he bought the 4.9 million dollar fixer-upper. It would give her something to do.

Mrs. Newman, who had once been Mrs. Best, and before that Miss Johnson, had an imposing given name. It was Demeter, a name which ran in her mother's family, but which was, perhaps, too lofty for the small town of Paradise, Texas, where she was born and would spend her early years, and, too, undescriptive of a fragile, fair-haired, blue eyed, button-nosed baby.

A nickname was needed. Demeter – Demmy? Not that, she'd have trouble in school. She'd get Dimmy and Dummy. Then Dede? No. Mimi? Nah. Meaty? Ha ha. Terri? No. What're we gonna call our l'il honey?

Honey Johnson Best Newman had a flair for design and a feel for antiques. Nevertheless, Zack insisted she hire the obligatory decorators to make the big house at the foot of Benedict Canyon liveable. So it was they who picked the pool table, planned the appliances, suggested the solarium as the spot to eat in, redid the kids' rooms: high tech for the boys, gingham for the girl – it might have been Honey's idea to go for the mint green watered silk upholstery in the den.

They also did up the master bedroom, selecting the giant Elizabethan four-poster bed with carved head and footboards, which governed the all white sanctuary, as suitable for the 6'- 3" 250 lb. owner of the house, though it dwarfed his current mate. They hunted down the inlaid Spanish chest to house the stereo, the only other piece of furniture in the 18' X 18' room. They designed the quilted canopy over the bed, the carelessly pulled curtains which surrounded it; chose the snowy linens. And it was they who decided that a fifteenth-century oil painting of Adam and Eve being banished from the Garden of Eden would provide the one splash of color on the blank wall opposite the four-poster that was needed to finish the room.

Zack was less than thrilled when he got the tab.

"*NINETY-TWO* thousand dollars?" he beefed.

"Furniture's expensive," said his wife

"We have two pieces of furniture in the entire bedroom."

"The linens are from Porthault," Honey countered. "They're handmade. That chest belonged to the Duke of Aragon."

"I don't care if it belonged to the Duke of Earl. For God's sake, Kid, Valerie Wexler furnished a twelve room house for three sixty-five."

She, crestfallen, quoted her designers: "Sure! If you want to live with reproductions."

***

"Zack, Zack. Can you roll over?"

"Fmrnnnnnnnfnf."

"Please? Roll over, okay? You're snoring."

Honey was wide awake in their newly decorated bedroom and it was only 5:30 in the morning.

That other decorator, dawn, was already gussying up Los Angeles; gilding the towers of Century City, tie-dying a pink streaked morning sky, backlighting a tree with a gnarled trunk and lacy grey-green leaves which grew near the swimming pool in their backyard.

Honey, meanwhile was doing her best to blot from her conciousness the painting of a similar tree occupying the wall opposite the end of her bed: the one with the lightening bolts aimed at it, and a smug snake in it, and two accursed, evicted humans slinking out from under it, clutching their private parts.

She'd called the interior designers again yesterday and asked them to take the painting away. She'd told them to start with that she didn't care for it, but they'd talked her into trying it for a while. Then they billed Zack, who paid, and now they didn't want to take it back.

No. They weren't the ones who had to wake up every morning to the hand of God zapping people: pitiful, almost lifesize, guilty, naked people, who were also the last thing you saw at night before you went to sleep. *If* you went to sleep.

She turned to regard her husband, with his playful but pragmatic brown eyes shuttered, his greying hair tousled on the pillow, his tanned face displaying its strengths against the pure white of the Porthault bed linens. One hand was flung over his head, and the other, held close to his chest with one finger pointing, twitched as though he were conducting a meeting in his dreams. His mouth, which was usually turned up pleasantly at the corners, was slackly agape, and resonating the glottal sounds of a sink drain impeded by a hair ball.

If only his snoring had some rhythm to it, she could have used it like the sound of the ocean to rock herself back to sleep. But Zack had no internal metronome. After an ill-timed silence, he'd come up with some long strangulation, short snort, snuffle, gurgle or gleep to grate on her nerves.

She couldn't remember when she'd had a good night's rest. She'd tried getting him to sleep on his stomach. She'd tried earplugs. Nothing worked. So, often she lay awake, as she was doing now, worrying her diamond wedding band around on her finger, picturing herself behind the wheel of a forty ton Mack truck wailing over Mulholland Drive.

With drifting mists and the switchback road demanding her concentration, Honey downshifted and flicked her lights to high beam. As she turned a corner, there was Zack, unaware, defenseless, frozen in the glare. Her mauve snakeskin sandal hit the accelerator and . . .

She never made it to the point where he was flattened like Wile E. Coyote. She was always shocked back to reality at the point where she booted it, offended by her latent violence; horrified.

Why would she want to hurt this hardworking, outgoing, generous man? Everybody loved Zack. And Zack loved everybody. He loved her kids. He loved her parents. He loved her, she guessed. Although he almost always slept with his back to her these days, whereas before he used to curl himself around her with his warm hand moving over

Day One: Lo! There Was Beverly Hills

her breasts. She would reach down and there would be what he called "the big snake" getting hot and hard and . . .

Honey got up.

One time her ex-husband, Roger, told her she was sexually repressed. He said it took an Act of Congress to make her come. He'd actually made an appointment for her with some swami in Malibu who, he claimed, could make her have multiple orgasms just by thinking about it. This was the sort of thing that Roger Rolfing/Primal Scream/est, Roger good/better/Best could be expected to do. Something to make her feel inadequate.

She'd only pretended to keep the appointment. She knew where she'd left her lost passion: in the cramped front seat of Eugene Green's used turquoise and white Nash Metropolitan automobile, parked a half-mile west of Benedict Canyon on the tortuous lovers' lane which figured so prominently in her waking nightmare. She knew on which high-breasted, summer's almost over, city lights shimmering like a mirage below Mulholland, night she'd left it behind. She knew to the instant in time: 11:15 P.M. She'd checked her watch in the midst of ecstasy because she didn't want to catch hell from her parents.

As for Roger, the love expert, he was only in love with himself. He'd probably have liked it if she'd named both twins after him. And what did his endless psychic experimentation do for him? What he referred to as "expanding his parameters," did it make him think twice about dumping his family? If it hadn't been for Zack . . .

She put on her robe and slippers quietly so as not to wake her husband. He needed his sleep.

She slid into the bathroom, tiptoed past the two bidets, brushed her teeth with her automatic toothbrush, popped her daily birth control pill, though why she bothered . . .

What day was it? Monday? Tuesday? She ought to make a hair appointment with LaVie. That would get her mind off things.

Her bangs were deadly, she decided, her blonde hair too straight. She should try something new, something now.

Get frizzy curls. Become a brunette.

Honey shrugged.

She could shave her head bald, dye herself blue and turn cartwheels. Nobody would notice.

No. That was wrong. Her kids would notice. She could guess their reactions: the usual, teenaged, mortified, "Oh, Mom!"

When Honey was a teenager, thirteen or fourteen, back in Texas, she told her mother she couldn't wait to be forty.

"Why would you wish that on yourself?" her mother had smiled.

"So people will take me seriously," she answered.

Last May 23rd she'd turned thirty-eight. On close examination she could find a couple of crows feet, a suggestion of frown lines, slight circles under her extravagant blue eyes, but nothing to suggest that she had lived this many years, had chewed, swallowed, digested life; had accomplished anything at all; some sign that she was, as Roger might have put it, "a woman of substance." There was nothing to command the respect that she'd imagined would automatically arrive with maturity.

Or, at least, with motherhood. But could she even say she'd been a great mother?

Dear Honey – the world did not yet know her by her real name, the name of a goddess who would soon play her part in the rewrite.

1:2

The Newman's' housekeeper, Jelia, an undocumented immigrant to the United States from Central America, was singing a song from home, quietly, so as not to wake the sleeping household, as her employer wandered into the kitchen. Unaccustomed to visits from the lady of the house at 6:00 AM, the maid was startled.

"Ay, Meesis! You escare me!" said Jelia (at the Newman residence her name always came out "Hey Ya"). "How come you come? Ees too much early. I no make coffee yet."

"That's okay, I'll make it," said Honey apologetically.

"No, no. I make." Jelia had her own routines and didn't much like anybody mixing in.

Resuming her Guatemalan ditty, she set the coffee beans to grinding in the Compu-Kitchen food processor – slices, chops, grinds, blends, purees, juices, juliennes.

"Then why don't I start the toast? The kids'll be up soon."

"No, no, Meesis. I do." This was said with a certain firmness, backed up by her bulk.

Humming again, she pushed a button, causing freshly ground coffee to find its way into its companion six-cup brewer, got the eggs and the Sizzlean out of the programmable refrigerator – makes its own filtered water, ice cubes, and crushed ice. She removed a loaf of newly baked rye bread from the bread machine and sliced it with the electric knife, simultaneously defrosting a package of hash browns in the microwave oven.

"Why don't I set the table?" said Honey.

"More better you beat it," advised her housekeeper.

Honey took the steaming mug of coffee that was offered, and beat it into the garden. Everyone took Jelia seriously. And she was only twenty-three.

Honey flip-flopped, in her pink terrycloth slippers, across the emerald lawn, past the pool, towards the gazebo. It was late January, a time for planting spinach, lettuce, cucumber, and pea in Southern California, and for harvesting cabbage, kale, and Honey's childhood favorite, rutabaga. But there were no edibles on the Newman estate, just a profusion of flowers, which could have used some weeding, and hedges, which had little sprigs of greenery sticking out of their formal shapes, and the grass, which was looking longish, and that tree, the one she didn't know the name of.

Grass needs cutting, she noted absently, her mind still on Acts of Congress and used dreams of a turquoise and white Nash Metropolitan; the night the Nash broke down at the beach and neither she nor Eugene Green had money for a towtruck; how they walked home, singing "Ain't No Mountain High Enough," which they never got all the way through because he stopped to kiss her under every streetlight.

For the hundred millionth time she wondered whether he, her decent, quick to laugh, radically hopeful, curlyhaired Gene was alive.

For the hundred millionth time she wished he could know their child.

"Must find a gardener," she said aloud, pushing away pervasive sadness, pulling herself back to the present. The gardener who came with the house had quit two weeks ago when she suggested he try not to drip lawn mower oil on the brick walkway between the pool and the wet-bar. Whoever took over would have to know all about feeding and watering and what to plant where, when. She couldn't just hire a yard man and direct him. When it came to nature, Honey didn't have a clue.

"This garden's going to pot!" she added with a vehemence not warranted by the content of her sentence.

"What, Kid?" said Zack, sleepily, coming out the side door in his bathrobe, rubbing his eyes against the brightness of the day.

"We've got to get a gardener!" said his wife.

"Yes, we do, but it's nothing to cry about, is it?" said Zack.

"Cry? What are you talking about?"

"Those two wet things coming down your cheeks."

"Oh," she said, and hurried back into the house.

***

Sunny: a word to describe the ambience of the curved steel and glass-paned potential greenhouse where the Newmans were having breakfast, the side-upness of the eggs served by Jelia to every member of the family, but not the mood of Mrs. Isaac Newman, that hothouse tomato.

And yet she was doing her best to be there for the one meal she and her children and Zack, on busy weekdays, could count on sharing, that is, unless Zack was doing business at that new hotel on the Sunset Strip.

Her husband was sampling channels on the solarium TV, dividing his attention between a network morning show on which a six-figure client was promoting an upcoming film, and an entertainment channel, which was airing clips from the popular prime-time television soap opera, *Inheritance*, produced by Norman Nathanson.

On that show, which so cleverly updated the prerequisite themes of sex, greed, and violence with socially redeeming ecological subplots, Zack represented actors playing three of the leading roles: Bianca (she's battling to save the ozone layer), Matt (he's raising funds for the rainforest), and the cute blonde poolman in the tight pink satin jogging shorts (who's fighting for the white rhinoceros).

In mid-perambulation, Zack held for a moment on a religious channel which he'd stumbled on by mistake. Reverend What's-His-Name was claiming AIDS was a plague from God to punish the wicked.

"I guess He ran out of locusts," Zack laughed.

"I guess so," his wife replied dully.

"That was a joke, Kid," said Zack.

"Heh heh," Honey reacted, loyally but too late.

She picked at her hash browned potatoes as her husband switched channels to the news.

"Births to single teenaged mothers have reached ungodly proportions," a politician stated. "We in government are joining church officials in calling for a return to family values."

This time it was Honey who changed the channel and kept on changing it until Zack could again watch himself make money.

Sean, one of her two gangly fourteen year old sons was scraping the bottom of the Sue Bee jar.

"We're out of honey," he said. He directed the statement to his mother but she didn't seem to catch it.

"I said, we're out of honey, Honey," he repeated, sending Brian, his twin, into a cracked-voiced giggle.

"I'll pick some up today," his mother answered.

"Hey Ya could do it," interjected the twins' half-sister, Corinne, brushing unruly blonde curls away from her face, "if we taught her to drive. I think it's criminal we haven't."

Corinne, twenty, a sophomore student of sociology, was acutely aware of the inequities in the world.

It was her opinion that Jelia, a virtual prisoner of the house, might never escape her status as a member of a growing, inadequately educated, soon to be unemployable underclass. How was she going to learn English if she never got to go anywhere? How was she going to improve herself?

"Why don't you improve yourself," said Sean, "and learn a little Spanish."

"Corie can speak Spanish," Zack teased. "She knows how to say Ro-day-o Drive."

The object of Corinne's concern came in to clear the plates and was heard to mutter "*O Dios ayudame*," as she noticed that some of Brian's egg yolk had found its way onto his hand-wash-only organza placemat.

"You see?" said Corinne, "She's praying to God to get her through one more day with this family of exploiters of the disadvantaged."

"I'm praying you'll lighten up," said Sean.

"Corie's right about one thing," Brian put in, as their housekeeper cleared away the breakfast dishes. "The days of personal servants are almost over. It'll be robots and computers in the future." He turned to Honey and predicted dourly, "That electronic kitchen you put in is the beginning of the end."

Honey followed their housekeeper out to the kitchen.

"Hey Ya," she ventured, "were you really praying to God to get you through one more day with us?"

"No, Meesis."

"But you were talking to God."

"Si, I say 'Help me get egg out of placemat.'"

"Who is God, anyway?" said Honey, surprised she should ask.

"God, Meesis?" answered Jelia, equally surprised, as she scraped Sean's untouched hash browns into the garbage disposal. "Ees Hombre Upstairs. You know. He make everything happen."

"Yes, of course," said Honey thoughtfully. "Could you ask Him what He's done with Gene Green?"

***

Day One: Lo! There Was Beverly Hills

Did they have potatoes in the Garden of Eden? Hash browned or otherwise?

Some say they had apples, and that Eve took a bite of one, though that may change in the rewrite.

But you don't hear much about potatoes, or spinach, or lettuce, or peas. Or rutabagas, for that matter.

***

When the sun's on its way up in Beverly Hills, it's going down in Sri Lanka. So it was through long shadows that a solitary man named Sah padded barefoot down the path he had worn through primeval forest, returning to his version of home.

Simians screeched in the treetops, birds chattered, bugs buzzed, but for nearly two decades this Buddhist monk had been personally silent, dwelling apart from other humans in a cave in the Sri Lankan hills, with nothing more than a bowl, a blanket, and a piece of cloth to cover himself.

Once every two weeks a fellow renunciate from his monastery would bring him food, a meager supply of rice and vegetables, and, once a month, soap and a new razor blade for shaving his face and head, but always when Sah was away from his hard rock domicile, out walking in contemplation, as he was now.

Heel goes down, arch down, ball of foot down, toes down, as other heel lifts, arch lifts, ball of foot lifts, toes lift; he walked slowly, mindfully, breathing in rhythm with his steps.

Where was he going? Here. For a moment he became part of the path, part of the jungle, part of the coming night. But then, remembered sounds of the monastery intruded on his concentration.

The evening chant was droned in Sanskrit, repeating: "Awaken! Awaken! Awaken! Awaken!" The striking of a wooden block, *BOK!*, as punctuation to the admonition always thrilled him, but he let the memory go, together with his longing for the comfort and company of friends. He brought his mind back to putting one foot in front of the other.

ON THE SEVENTH DAY SHE RESTED

Just walking. Walking, he meditated. Just breathing. Breathing. In the low light he stepped on a stone with a sharp edge, so he mentally included, "Ow!"

***

Heel down, arch down, toes down – in Mrs. Isaac Newman's case, walking produced the staccato click of high heels on pavement; mauve snakeskin strappy spikes on the sidewalks of Rodeo Drive.

Rodeo was still feeling the pinch of back to back recessions. For Rent signs in shop windows and placards shouting *SALE 50% OFF* announced the desperation of some. But the international corporations, Gucci, Hermes, Van Cleef and Arpels, stood firm with their thirteen thousand dollar handbags, their sapphire-eyed frog brooches, understanding that the people of Beverly Hills have to cut down on extras when times get tough, but they'll always buy the things they really need.

Honey, inappropriately, didn't need anything. Having earlier completed her condiment assignment, she wandered Rodeo aimlessly, lacking the zeal with which she'd formerly zero'd in on every known knick-knack for the kitchen, or the ideal arrangement of silk spider lilies to put on the living room coffee table (which the decorators had removed when they took pictures of the house).

There was no point in buying clothes. One pair of slacks, tried on in Saks, had convinced her she'd better drop that spare tire she was carrying before adding another thing to her overflowing closet. Something for her husband? He didn't believe in clothing. Three XXL jogging suits and a tuxedo constituted Zack's wardrobe. Her children, now that they were older, liked to shop for themselves.

For most of her adult life, Honey'd had that born-to-spend aura that a Beverly Hills vendeuse can spot a mile away, but today she had an inability to concentrate on their wall-to-wall goods, so the salesgirls kept their distance, deferring to her "just looking around." After she left without increasing their commissions, they'd talk about the miserable state of these burned-out, shopped-out Beverly Hills beauties who had nothing to do but spend their husbands' money.

"What's her problem anyway? I hear his net worth is over a hundred million."

"Zack Newman's not in that league. You're thinking of Norman Nathanson."

"I hear he buys her diamonds as big as headlights."

"That's Norman Nathanson."

"I hear he brings in snow at Christmas and puts it in their backyard."

"Norman Nathanson."

"Well, she still doesn't look happy. Anyway, are you watching *Inheritance* tonight? Is Bianca going to sleep with Matt or is she too worried about the continued manufacturing of chlorofluorocarbons?"

Honey wasn't at all happy, though she wouldn't have said so. She would have described herself as a little edgy, a little emotional. "Farmischt," to use Zack's expression.

With nothing to attract her interest, she found herself thinking of God again: aiming His thunderbolts, making off with Eugene, dooming people with plagues.

"What a Guy," she said to no one in particular, "What a Guy."

But if AIDS was a punishment, why didn't everyone who abused sex or drugs come down with it? If AIDS was a plague, what in heaven's name was cancer? And what about babies with AIDS? What had they ever done to Him? Still, if Reverend Someone-Or-Other said "plague," plenty of people were going to believe it.

If God causes everything to happen, then it's His fault there's nothing to buy, she decided, leaving one more store with no package under her arm.

"And it's His fault teenagers get pregnant!" she announced to an astounded passerby.

Without an errand, she was little more than a stranger on a street of strangers, the few who smiled at her marking themselves as tourists.

She did run into one person she knew, Liz Macavoy. But since Liz and Melvin divorced, Liz ran with a Bel Air crowd.

Nowadays, she and Honey had little in common. Had Liz heard from their mutual friend Karen? Yes. She was loving Atlanta. Too busy to stay in touch.

Honey hiked up her handbag and kept moving. It hadn't rained once this winter. And, though this day, too, continued golden, there was something bleak about Rodeo Drive.

There'd been a time when she'd thought of Rodeo as the end of the rainbow. To a small town teen from Texas, the main street in Beverly Hills was a giant step up from Main Street back home, with its hardware and feed store, its post office, its pharmacy, its doctor and dentist offices, its funeral parlor, just down the way from its white clapboard grange, where people held meetings, and dances, and talked about their crops, and had harvest festivals where they were always giving and getting vegetables.

An exchange of produce happened often in Honey's home town. Apparently, it was a satisfying thing to do. Back there, you got to know your neighbors, friendship was lifelong. And one way to show it was to give fresh-from-the-garden things to one another.

Honey wondered what would have happened if she'd walked up to Liz Macavoy, bustling out of Giorgio Beverly Hills, and handed her a rutabaga.

"Hi, here's a rutabaga," she imagined herself saying.

She didn't think Liz would have understood. She didn't think anyone on Rodeo Drive would have understood. She, herself, didn't understand. Why these off-the-wall thoughts on a perfectly ordinary Tuesday? Or was it Wednesday?

Well, it definitely was 4:30. Almost time for her to head home. If she just stopped in to Café Rodeo for half an hour, it would look as though she'd had a busy day.

"I'll have the vegetable nibblies," she said to the waitress, thinking about the five pounds she wouldn't mind losing.

But then, "On second thought, I'll have the blintzes with sour cream, but will you tell them to leave off the powdered sugar?"

"Oh," said the waitress, "you want the diet blintzes."

"Yes," said Honey.

Day One: Lo! There Was Beverly Hills

"Gee," said the waitress, handing her a Kleenex, "Don't take it so hard. All I said was 'diet blintzes'."

"Oh," Honey said. "Am I crying again?"

***

The rest of the week was predictable.

Thursday, after her hair appointment, with her enviable shoulder-length blonde blunt-cut still intact, Honey phoned the decorators one more time about the painting at the end of her bed. They didn't return her call.

Friday's high point was opening the mail, most of which was addressed to Resident. The low point was finding that every gardener on her list was booked – gardening, she was discovering, was a recession-proof profession.

On Saturday, Roger picked up the twins for his alternate weekend; Corie had a school friend over; Zack took a meeting which went late.

"I thought we were going out," his wife complained.

"Believe me," Zack said, "I'm not doing this for me. I'm doing it for all of us."

Honey found herself prowling their bedroom at midnight. On a whim she put on an old Aretha Franklin tape:

". . . just a little respect when you get home. R. E. S. P. E. C. T., find out what it means to me . . ."

She was dancing with the doorknob, stark nude in front of God and everybody, when Zack walked in, gave her a perfunctory kiss, turned the stereo off, complained of a headache, went directly to bed and started snoring.

She got in beside him and revved up her Mack truck. The truck was loaded with rutabagas. Zack was joined by Roger and Gene Green, all three standing stupified in the middle of Mulholland Drive.

The leather seat of the big semi felt cool against her naked back. One bare toe hit the accelerator and . . .

1:3

Vegetables hold the comestible key to a rewrite of the story of the Garden of Eden.

And they're important in terms of Honey's future.

That being so, it might be useful to define what a vegetable is.

Broadly, it's anything having the nature of plants. More specifically, it's a plant that you eat. If you've discovered fire, it can also be a plant that you cook.

Around twelve thousand years ago, someone figured out that it's also a plant that you plant.

Let's see, that would be eight or nine thousand years before people put pen to paper.

But that's another story.

No, it's not.

***

Sunday, sunny again. It was a sun day with fluffy white clouds making animal shapes in the sky, not that Honey paid any attention, although she was out in the garden and had positioned her lounge chair, her iced tea, and her copy of the Sunday paper, to take advantage of the shade provided by the specimen tree which was its central feature.

"Corie, where my pepper sauce?" (Zack.)

"I don't know." (Corinne.)

Sunday. The man of the house was barbecuing.

"How am I supposed to cook for Texans if I don't have pepper sauce? They're gonna say 'That Jew doesn't know from barbecue'."

"I'll ask Hey Ya," Honey's daughter volunteered.

"Good. A beaner should know about hot sauce."

Couldn't he have simply said "Thank you?" Honey tried her hand at a rewrite, knowing perfectly well what was to come next.

Day One: Lo! There Was Beverly Hills

"Hey Ya is *not* a 'beaner'!" Corinne shot him an indignant look. "She's a member of an ethnic minority impacted by poverty."

Sunday. A day for family to be together.

"So ask the ethnic minority, willya?" said Zack.

He just had to get a rise out of Corinne.

And she always obliged him, Honey thought, as her firstborn exhaled audibly and stalked off, while Zack poked innocently at his marinating steaks.

Sunday. Referred to by Honey's mother as The Lord's Day, though Zack viewed Saturday as God's day off.

In her lounge chair under the tree, Honey hid from Sunday behind the weekend paper, but *The Los Angeles Sun* gave no quarter. Despite the good news that the U.S. and Russia were still too broke to be adversarial, its front page was full of the new bad news: worldwide economic mismanagement and thuggery, political self-interest, racial and religious violence, ongoing ecological suicide. She had to turn to page two to get to rape, murder, and child abuse.

Maybe God shouldn't take a day off, she thought. There were plenty of wicked in this world who weren't coming down with any plague.

Subsequent pages featured Acts of God. These earthquakes, volcanic eruptions, hurricanes, wildfires and floods struck Honey as overtly unfriendly. Especially when insurance companies went belly up and didn't pay their claims.

She skipped through the paper hoping to avoid other subjects which made her feel helpless or hopeless: the hungry, the homeless; the endless civil wars; the proliferation game – Who's Got The Bomb?; the miasma in the Middle East where the words jihad or Jehovah could lead people to their deaths for the glory of You Know Who.

Maybe the Home Section, she thought, fleeing her fears of nukes and nerve gas and wars her sons might have to fight.

She was hoping for a nice recipe she could pass on to Jelia. But instead she found another of those unsettling articles on super-women, successful at home and in impressive jobs: a female movie producer, a Wall Street wizard, even a Supreme Court Justice – the days were long gone when you could pat yourself on the back for just being a wife and mother.

Zack interrupted her reading, "When are the goyish hordes arriving?"

The "goyish hordes" – that would be her parents. And Roger Best, her ex, coming to return the twins. She supposed Margo would be with him.

"Any time now," said Honey, her voice fraying.

Although it had been years since she and Roger divorced, she still couldn't get used to the idea that he left her for the deli-girl from Ralph's, deflating her life and the lives of her children over a baby-faced purveyor of cream cheese and dill pickles.

Whom God hath joined together . . . those words had sounded so comforting, so safe, so permanent.

"Is Margo coming?" asked Zack.

"Who knows?" she answered offhandedly, she wished.

"I like Margo," said Zack. "She's the only one in that crowd who knows what a bagel is."

Yes, Margo would know. She knew what a big salami was, too, to quote Roger. He could never resist an opportunity to insinuate that Margo was an expert between the sheets.

And that was but one of her abilities. After she married Roger, she went back to school and earned her Phd. in endocrinology. She was Dr. Margo Best now and had not only a successful but a meaningful career doing hormone research. Margo the deli-girl/seductress could turn out to be the one who found the cure for cancer.

Honey returned to her newspaper article which suggested she conquer her fear of success and re-use her dormant skills to do more. Accomplish! it urged. Aim high! It pressured.

"Zack," she asked, "What would you think if I went back to work?"

"Why? We don't pay enough taxes?" he replied.

***

Jelia handed Corinne the pepper sauce and waited until she was out of earshot before completing her telephone conversation. She was frowning deeply, but kept the frown out of her voice as she accepted the dampening of her hopes and politely rang off.

She was still one thousand dollars short. Until she had the cash, the one she was counting on would not make plans. The money would take months to save and she still hadn't finished paying for her mother's dental surgery.

She took a moment for kitchen pacing, then realized she should be slicing the okra for the Newman family's barbecue. She must keep her mind on what was expected of her. Her job, the source of her funds, was *muy muy importante.*

But what if a robot or a computer took it over? What if the days of personal servants came to an end before she made good on her promises?

She had never heard of a computer that could make a bed or batter and deep-fry a chunk of okra, but just to be on the safe side she declared war on her enemy, this fancy kitchen she'd heard one of the twins describe as the omen of her unemployment.

For openers, she put the electric knife down the garbage disposal.

***

Sunday. A day of rest. But not for Honey.

She had a stiff neck. She felt dizzy. Her stomach was in a knot which she attributed to greasy Southwestern cooking. She hadn't needed that extra helping of deep fried okra. Her mother had taken pains to tell her so. She guessed she'd eaten more cornbread than necessary, too, but that was to spite Roger who kept slapping her hand every time she reached for the butter.

Sean and Brian were like the possessed, spraying celery tonic at each other, chasing each other around the pool, ignoring her attempts to quiet them, a trick they pulled every time their two sets of parents were together, perhaps because they weren't old enough to be capable of more subtle savagery.

Corinne was. Honey heard her refer to Roger as her "ex-stepdaddy."

Honey's mother Rhea, known as "Missy" Johnson, described her charitable work with single mothers as "the Christian thing to do." Then she turned to Zack with an "Oops, sorry, Son." Then she could hardly look at Roger for whom she used to reserve the filial label.

Honey's father, Red Johnson, told the gathering about his latest real estate deal in which all the parties acted "white." His comment made her cringe for Roger's second wife, who was black.

Margo's blackness was not an issue for Honey. That is until Roger whispered, "Who in God's name decided on watermelon for dessert?"

God's name was bandied about a lot at this particular garden party: "Oh, my God." "Thank God." "God knows." The name was freely used. She even heard her father, bragging about his business pact, say, "It was God's will."

But who, exactly, were they talking about?

Zack had his tooth-for-a-tooth, eye-for-an-eye Adonai, a bachelor.

Her mother had her Lord and His Son.

Her dad, whom she'd never known to set foot inside any building with stained glass windows, was apparently a believer in Somebody. It sounded as though Roger was, too.

But they didn't believe in Zack's God. Or Missy's, as far as she knew. Nor Jelia's Hombre, nor the fundamentalists Fellow with His very selective plagues. Nor did they believe in the Muslim's Man, though he was making inroads in America.

Then Whose Will, specifically, was it that Brian and Sean Best only saw their father every other weekend? And Whose Will that Corinne had never seen her dad at all? Whose Will was it that this motley group of parents and step-parents and grandparents was thrown together on a Sunday and expected to feel like family?

The one thing she thought they might all agree upon was that God was a He on high, who did, more or less, what Zack did for his clients: favorably influenced their destinies, brought them luck, and modelled a larger view of life.

Honey looked skyward.

Day One: Lo! There Was Beverly Hills

"Our Father, who art in heaven," she said, loudly enough to startle all present, "You're doing a lousy job."

Her loved ones stared at her. She had to excuse herself in case she started to bawl again.

1:4

Notes on vegetables vis-à-vis the Garden of Eden for consideration in the rewrite:

Okra and watermelon, botanists say, first sprang forth in the heart of Africa. Does this mean they should be left off the list of Eden's vegetables?

What about corn as in "cornbread"? And beans as in "beaner"? Or peppers, sweet or blazing hot? Science says they had their origins in Central America, while potatoes and tomatoes, originated in Peru.

A cornless, pintoless, potatoless, tomatoless, watermelonless, okraless place? A place with no peppers? If that was Eden, it doesn't sound much like paradise.

***

Everything in Zack's Sunset Boulevard, penthouse suite, leather and chrome, corner office was big: big windows, big view, big desk, oversized chairs, opulent sofa with large pillows, massive bookshelves, gargantuan coffee table. It was a big office for a big man whom everyone called The Biggie, not just because of his size but because he was big in the business.

Zack could pick up a phone and get a motion picture made. With one lunch he could create a career. Well, he used to be able to. These days it could take a couple of lunches.

The market was shrinking. With one corporation eating another and half the indies going under, there were fewer places to make a sale. It was harder to know who your friends were. The project better be a sure thing. But for all his complaints about the hassles of show business, how the people who could "green-light" were dreck, how nobody was a mensch anymore, you had to notice Zack was thriving.

"I heard you had a call from our anal favorite," he was saying, blue and red Nikes on desk, executive swivel chair reclining, telephone receiver an extension of his personality.

"Bullshit," he continued. "Allan didn't say that. He said we'd start shooting no later than March 15th.

"These people tell half truths. Like the doctor when he told Allan's father 'It's a boy'." Zack laughed at his own joke. "Hang on a minute willya, Kid? Lemme get the file."

He punched the intercom button for Rayanne, his secretary. "Get Eddie's Vegas bookings. We've got a conflict."

"Sure, Zack," said Rayanne,

"I'm back," said Zack, but the intercom buzzed. "Shit, hold on again, willya?"

Irritated, he punched the offending button. "What is it?"

"Honey's here," Rayanne announced.

"Really?" Zack said. He wasn't expecting her. "Who do I have to fuck to get the Vegas file?"

He was back into his phone call as Rayanne showed Honey in and put the file he wanted in front of him.

"The trouble with Allan is that Allan's into Allan, but we can't afford to piss him off. If he thinks the script needs work, let him potchkey with it. How much harm can he do?" Zack motioned Honey to sit in one of the burgundy leather chairs opposite his desk. "Hold on a second," he said softly. "No, not you. My wife." He flipped open the Vegas file. "Meanwhile, we'll switch your dates with Billy's. Sure. Then I think it would be a nice gesture if we found a part in the picture for him.

"That's why I get the big money. You, on the other hand, get the big money for using the word 'motherfucker' thirty-two times in one sentence. Love you, too. 'Bye, Kid."

Zack turned his attention to his third wife who didn't usually drop in. From the way she was perched on the edge of the chair, he could see it was urgent.

Day One: Lo! There Was Beverly Hills

"I've decided I really would like to go back to work," said Honey.

Oh, that. Her husband's engaging smile belied his reaction. "Doing what?"

"Something meaningful," she told him.

Zacks teeth sparkled, his dimples dimpled, but his eyes glazed over. His clients came to him with this kind of garbage every day. If he let them, they'd meaningful themselves right into the toilet. The only thing meaningful to Zack was the size of the check, but he played along with Honey like he did with his people.

"First things first," he said. "Let's get Rayanne to type you up a resume."

"I've already made one," Honey announced, taking a manila envelope out of her purse. "I was in sort of a hurry because there's this position that needs filling." She held the envelope out to Zack.

"Great," he said, enthusiastically reaching for it. "I'll read this and we'll talk some more tonight."

He stood, signalling the end of the interview, rounded his desk, kissed his wife, and ushered her out of his office.

"See you later, Kid," he said, waving as she crossed his reception area with its deep pile carpet and posters of his clients. He gave an extra little twiddle of his fingers as she opened the heavy mahogany doors and went out.

Then, "Here, Kid." He handed Rayanne Honey's resume. "Read this," he said. "I'm swamped. Fill me in later."

"Uh, get me Billy willya?"

***

Only one page came out of the manila envelope. Rayanne placed it on her desk ready to read: just part of her job as the personal manager's personal manager. Besides her secretarial duties she took Zack's clothes to the cleaners, got him cash from the bank, bought the presents he handed out on Christmas morning from under the Hanukkah bush, stocked his office refrigerator with lox and Louis Roederer.

For years now, she'd also been reading and commenting on screenplays submitted for clients, and making deals for the less important people on The Newman Company's roster.

"What'd we get out of Norman for 'the poolman'?" Zack had asked yesterday. "Four fifty? You did good."

Sure, she did good. But 'the poolman' would never know. You couldn't tell a client that his deal got done by his manager's mistress.

The word R E S U M E was double spaced across the top of the page and centered nicely. She can type, thought Rayanne, though I would have underlined RESUME.

NAME: Demeter Johnson Best Newman

"Demeter?" said Rayanne.

AGE: 38 "Older than I thought."

EDUCATIONAL BACKGROUND included Alamo Elementary, Paradise High School, three years at Beverly Hills High, and an unimpressive two semesters at U.C.L.A.

WORK EXPERIENCE was even less dazzling. Six months the woman had worked in her entire life as receptionist to Roger Best, Attorney at Law, and that was back in the sixties.

Rayanne was shaking her head by the time she got to REFERENCES: Mr. Floyd S. "Red" Johnson, President, Titan Realty, Inc.; Mrs. Rhea "Missy" Johnson, Convener, F.E.E.L. Charities.

"Her parents?"

Ms. LaVie Cleland, Hairdresser, LaVie 'n Rose . . .

"Oh, no," she said.

But it was when she got to the heading POSITION DESIRED that she, again, used the intercom to Zack's office.

He was gruff. Couldn't it wait? Rayanne didn't think so. She rushed the neatly typed page in to her employer who was, as always, on the phone.

"We don't need a contract. My wink is binding," he was saying. "So?" he asked Rayanne with one hand over the telephone mouthpiece.

She told him Honey was losing it.

"In her resume under POSITION DESIRED? It says she wants to be God."

"Jesus Christ!" Zack hung up on his caller.

"Nope. God."

"Get me a shrink," Zack said, sublimating his distress, transforming it into action. "I want the best. Have him at my house tonight no later than six-thirty."

Rayanne demurred. Picking a doctor, shouldn't Honey have something to say about it? It wasn't like buying a birthday present. She wouldn't know where to begin.

"You think I do?" Zack said, revealing his panic. "Look in the Yellow Pages under Viennese!"

***

Zack's home and the life he lived there was only one element of his Eden. He saw it as a sign of his wider achievements. He'd had other homes with other wives. He'd been a millionaire, tapped out, and was rich again. His ability to adapt to change was the secret of his success, the barometer of his Bigness: a Biggie never clings.

Nevertheless, in the den at home by about seven that night you could hear (was it real or imagined?) the faintest scraping of fingernails.

The den, with its flowing ferns and mint green watered silk upholstery was the benign setting Zack had chosen for the promised discussion with his wife.

Hoping to make this God business go away, he limited his part of the chat to the question of whether Honey should go to work at all. His thrust was that she should not.

He tried flattery. She was a topnotch mother, wife, shopper, who could arrange a mean bowl of fake spider lilies, and beat them all at backgammon. How could she consider spending less time with her family who loved her, who appreciated her, who couldn't manage without her?

He tried to keep smiling as his wife responded, in all sincerity, "This is a job that needs doing."

Zack tried "poor me." If she went out and got her hands dirty every day, they'd say he was a bad provider.

Honey just said how pleased she was that her life was finally heading in an upward direction.

He tried bribery. They'd take a cruise, he promised.

But the farthest thing from Honey's mind was a holiday. What she wanted, she said, was to roll up her sleeves and tackle the problems of modern existence. She'd even started composing her own Commandments. Her first was: "Give And Receive Vegetables." She wanted to know how he liked it. She said it worked for the people in Paradise.

This was more than Zack could handle. His wife was definitely over the edge. He opened the door to the game room where he'd parked Dr. Augustus Hess and invited him to come in.

Rayanne had done her utmost. Dr. Hess had a long string of degrees, taught at two universities, ran his own multi-million dollar private hospital. And he charged a fortune, which was Zack's main measurement of the man's worth.

The doctor, a slim, cool, slick-haired individual with smallish black eyes, had already read Honey's resume. After requesting time alone with her, he confirmed she was having a nervous breakdown.

He could treat her as an outpatient, he told Zack, but the most intensive and effective therapy would involve removing her temporarily from the home environment.

"What's wrong with her home environment?" Zack protested. "Look around. She's got it all."

Still, having hired the high priced help, it made sense to trust what was recommended. He only hoped Honey wouldn't fall apart completely when he and the psychologist carted her off to Hess's place.

As it turned out, nobody had to cart his wife anywhere. Dr. Hess simply suggested that before Mrs. Newman re-entered the workforce she might want to brush up on her skills, get prepared, learn and return.

Day One: Lo! There Was Beverly Hills

This made perfect sense to her. She'd go on a sort of retreat. Quite happily she went upstairs to speak with her kids and pack, leaving Zack with The Quack.

Don't think like that! Zack told himself. Think: responsible professional who's going to cure my wife. Signing the insurance paperwork in partial payment for Honey's hospitalization he convinced himself he was doing the right thing. It hardly threw him at all when he noticed that Dr. Augustus Hess was only wearing one sock.

So the guy rushed here, he rationalized.

Later, of course, he'd kick himself, *Goddammit!*, for not spotting a red flag when he saw one.

To his credit, though, Zack never did blame God for any of what followed.

Instead he blamed Rayanne for not checking the doctor out more carefully.

He blamed the doctor for being in the Yellow Pages.

He blamed himself for delegating important decisions to minions.

But, most of all, he blamed Honey for potchkeying with the script of his life. How much damage could she do?

𝔇ay 𝔗wo: And There Was Light . . .

2:1

So, what could you eat in Eden besides the fruit of a tree?

It's a question which raises questions. No one knows for sure where Eden was: Southeastern Turkey? Northern Syria? Egypt? Iran? Iraq, where the Tigris and Euphrates Rivers meet?

Was it in a forest, savannah, lake country, or close to the sea? Vegetables are a lot like real estate buyers. They ask first about the location.

To add to the mystery, there's no telling when Eden was. But if Adam and Eve were sentenced to till the soil, it was late in human history.

Then perhaps a better question to ask of scientists, now that we have them, is: Which vegetables had their genesis in what's known as "the cradle of civilization," the fertile crescent of land lying east of the Mediterranean Sea?

Bingo! Artichokes. Asparagus. Broad beans. Beets. Cabbage. Celery. Yes.

Carrots? Eggplant? Onions? No. They were introduced by invading Indo-Europeans.

But spinach is a probability, as is salsify.

There is absolutely no sign, however, of the original rutabaga.

***

Honey thought she was going to like Dr. Hess's retreat. It was less than an hour from town, in Malibu, on the ocean side of Route One.

Day Two: And There Was Light . . .

Built in the 1950's as a private beach club, it had its own tennis courts, an Olympic pool, rooms with individual patios, and a spacious lounge with a fieldstone fireplace to warm the guests on the foggy nights of early February. The doctor had even left the old beach club sign up, since it was a local landmark.

After Zack left, Hess himself showed Honey around. She was to occupy a small suite done in flowered chintz with a picture window full of the Pacific, where, he said, Sandra Dee once spent the weekend.

He showed her the dining room and the menu. She could order anything from vegetarian cuisine to a burger all-the-way.

Despite the late hour, he invited her to his office with its wall of certificates, sat her down and explained the way things were going to work.

He and Honey would have regular meetings once a day, five days a week. Dr. Hess would not be available on weekends, except in an emergency, but he was usually only a phonecall away.

During her free time she could relax or join the other guests in arranged activities: gardening lessons for example. He'd prefer that she not swim in the pool without some other people present because his lifeguard had quit to become a personal bodyguard to Norman Nathanson.

She said that in her free time she'd probably go shopping on Rodeo Drive. Hess said that ought to wait. She said it couldn't. Going out for God, she'd need clothes. That was when Hess told her that while she was here at the hospital, it would be better if she didn't leave the grounds.

Suddenly, Honey realized that this was an asylum, classy and comfortable, but a loony bin just the same.

Well, they couldn't keep her here. She'd leave. But go where? Not home. Not yet.

And she couldn't go running to her parents. Not again.

She'd go to a hotel. Think things over. Decide where to send her application.

"You can do that here," Hess told her kindly, his somewhat beady black eyes never blinking. "Here, you'll have someone to talk to who not only understands but approves of your ambition."

He took off his shoes and his green and yellow striped sock. Honey noticed he had a box of sand under his desk. He wriggled his toes into it.

"In fact," he said, "let's start with the premise that your application's been accepted; that you already are God."

Her blue eyes widened.

"Don't worry," he told her. "You've got what it takes."

***

Easy for him to say, thought Honey, back in the Sandra suite, drawing the curtains against the roiling Pacific as if to shut out impending responsibility. In her mind she'd only taken things as far as the employment interview: Be well groomed. Don't volunteer too much information. Avoid nervousness by picturing the interviewer in his/her underwear. Now, suddenly and forever, everything she did was going to be meaningful.

She turned on TV. Norman Nathanson's over-the-top hit *Inheritance*. Onscreen, Bianca, who was married to Robert, was sleeping with Matt, while enlisting him in her crusade against CFCs. Meanwhile she had her eye on the cute blonde poolman who was enrolling her in his campaign for the white rhinoceros. In real life, Honey knew, Bianca was married to Matt, and Matt had his eye on the poolman.

She flipped channels, wondering whether God should be watching television. Would it unfairly affect the ratings?

Hoping it was okay, she left the set tuned to a program on scuba diving, narrated by someone with a deep, comforting voice.

She had to agree with Dr. Hess about no Rodeo Drive. She'd never heard of God shopping.

She twirled her wedding band around on her finger. Should God be wearing jewelry?

And if she couldn't begin to answer these trivial questions, how was she going to approach the big ones?

Day Two: And There Was Light . . .

Whose side was she going to be on when people said, "God's on our side?"

How was she going to stop people from killing and stealing and lying?

What was she going to say about coveting thy neighbor's ox, or his rhinos, or his poolman.

God! – Could God say "God"? – she'd only come up with that one dinky vegetable Commandment.

"Under water," said the liquid voice of the television announcer, "the most important thing to remember is to keep breathing."

Involuntarily, Honey took a deep breath, then another. Somehow, she felt calmer having followed his dive advice.

"Keep breathing," she said it again to herself. She decided to write it down.

***

It was this scuba/yoga that enabled her to be soundly asleep by eleven-thirty.

That is, until the music woke her up.

When she tapped on the wall, the rock 'n roll got louder. She had to get up, dress, go next door, and knock twice before anyone even heard her.

"What," said the emaciated, bare chested, twenty-three year old with the two day beard stubble, ripped jeans and blackout sunglasses, who finally appeared.

"I can't sleep," Honey said, just before he shut the door in her face.

She had to knock for some time – Keep breathing – before he opened it again.

"Apparently," she said, "you don't realize who I am."

"Who?" asked the youth, "Joan of Arc? Queen Elizabeth? Grace Slick?"

"If I say the word 'Almighty' will it give you a hint?"

"You can't be God. God's a man."

"Not necessarily," said Honey, drawing herself up to her full five feet five and a half.

"No shit," said the boy, clearly impressed. "Wanna do some lines?"

***

At four AM they were still together.

Lowell, that's how the young man introduced himself, insisted she join him in his quarters, a litterbug's version of her own. Humbly billing himself as an unworthy host for a personage of her stature, he vowed, nevertheless, to do his best to amuse her.

He cleared a path for her through dropped clothing, discarded magazines, and a kickable empty soda can, producing, along the way, a glassine envelope of cocaine and a straw to inhale it with, letting her know, with what he thought was a grin, that he was "in" for substance abuse.

When Honey politely declined to join him, Lowell snorted his illegal snuff alone, saying he was just as glad she didn't do drugs since that meant more for him. He supposed God didn't need them. Mere mortals, on the other hand . . .

He indicated she could take a seat on his unmade bed as he plopped himself on the floor next to a pile of mix-tape cassettes of his favorite music, a television remote control, and a ziplock bag full of assorted additional pharmaceuticals which he extracted from the third speaker cavity of his four speaker boom box.

He refused to tell her his last name. It was a name she'd recognize right away, but he didn't think it was any of her business.

Honey found it hard to concentrate with the blaring of Lowell's blaster, but he wouldn't turn it off. Instead he added visuals, turning on the television set and rapidly changing channels without the sound. The effect was mesmerizing, with his music perfectly underscoring the movement of the images onscreen.

Even so, as the night progressed, she managed to tell him lots of things that were none of his business: how at eighteen, she got pregnant with Corie in the front seat of Gene Green's turquoise and white

Day Two: And There Was Light . . .

Nash Metropolitan; how before she or Gene knew she was expecting, he'd been drafted and sent to Vietnam. She told how all her letters came back because Gene was missing in action; how she finally married Roger and gave birth to the twins; how Roger thought a marriage license was something like a dog license; how here she was in another marriage and it still wasn't like they said it would be in the ads for diamond rings.

Anyway, now that she was God she wanted to make new rules.

"Screw rules," said Lowell, reaching into his bag of illusions.

"You have to have them," said Honey. "So people will know how to act."

Lowell said he'd never heard of any rule that could stop someone from doing exactly what they wanted.

"Thou shalt not this. Thou shalt not that," he scoffed, downing a Quaalude.

Honey found it hard to argue with his pointed presentation. Perhaps, she reasoned, rules would be more effective if they sent a more positive message, like, "What was it my grandmother used to tell me? 'Do the friendliest thing.'"

"Do the friendliest thing," Lowell mimicked in a sweet-old-grandmother voice. But then, removing his dense black sunglasses through which he was having trouble seeing, he added, "I wish my father would try it."

He went back to changing channels and fast-forwarding tapes, chosen haphazardly from the pile in front of him, looking for a promising media pairing.

He had gone through a few bars each of Cheap Trick, The Motels, and Bow Wow Wow, when he finally came to a voice she recognized, Aretha, singing a song she liked: "Respect."

On the soundless TV a couple held hands on a beach at sunset, slow danced on a terrace under the stars, kissed as they lay together on a fur rug in front of a glowing fireplace.

Their movements fit Aretha's music as though it had been planned. But when she sang, "Sock it to me, sock it to me, sock it to me, sock it to me!" the action went to black, and a jumbo sized package of condoms filled the screen.

Honey laughed herself helpless.

***

A Santa Ana wind had blown in off the desert overnight, raising daytime temperatures, even at the beach, into the nineties. Despite its cool rock walls and the breeze from the air conditioner, Dr. Augustus Hess was finding his office hot and debilitating. He closed his mini-blinds and lowered the thermostat. To offset what promised to be a refreshing chill, he selected and put on a full pair of striped socks from the box-full he kept in his desk drawer.

His patient was late. Twenty minutes into Honey's appointment he'd rung her room and she was still sleeping.

Avoidance, thought Hess. She'll come in here rattled and defensive and we can get off to a rolling start.

Except she didn't. She strolled in to his office, greeted him matter-of-factly, and had absolutely nothing to say.

When he asked how her first evening as God had gone, she smiled and said, "Okay."

When he asked her to expand on her resume, she replied that her hometown of Paradise was a nice place, her parents were nice people, her husband was a nice man, she had nice children, a nice house, a nice maid.

Hess probed and questioned but Honey fell asleep again. It had been a long time since she'd stayed up 'til four in the morning having fun.

2:2

What are the odds of peas in paradise? The pea is as old as the hills, as Honey's sweet old grandmother might have put it, so old that it's hard to pinpoint its leguminous origin.

Day Two: And There Was Light . . .

The best that paleobotanists can do is to hang more than one tail on the donkey. They've got tails around the Mediterranean, through the Near East, and beyond.

Annoyingly, the oldest pea unearthed by archeologists, dating from 9750 BCE, was found in a cave on the Burma-Thailand border, some three thousand five hundred miles, as the snake crawls, south-east of the pea's supposed home.

Still, the wild Near Eastern pea has been proposed as Pea #1 on the grounds of chromosomal similarity. (Try saying "chromosomal similarity" three times, fast.)

***

Peas are tricky to grow in Southern California. They need cool, dry weather if they're going to do well. Too much heat wilts them, too much sun browns them out, too much watering invites mildew, but if they mature they have a sweet green taste the like of which can never be found in a supermarket.

The peas in Dr. Hess's hospital garden were just showing two leaves above the ground when the recent blistering Santa Ana winds had hit, but a little extra water and that they'd been planted on the east side of the main building had saved them from nature's insouciance.

Now, barely two weeks into February, they were beginning to climb their netting, putting out curlicue tendrils, pulling themselves out of the darkness, getting used to the light.

The doctor wished he could say the same for Demeter/Honey Newman, but so far she'd refused to deal with reality, to show any honest emotion or trust him with the truth. Beyond her gardening lessons, which seemed to center her, there was no sign of improvement.

It was upon his ability to be patient that Dr. Augustus Hess had built his reputation as the psychologist's psychologist, so he de-socked daily, slid into his sandbox, and waited. Fulfilling his professional role as an unobtrusive observer, he did his best to blend into the background, with only his black eyes darting to register Honey's body language, his hearing finely tuned to tension in her voice. A breakthrough could take months or minutes. There was no predicting the event. It could happen today. It could happen right now.

He prepared himself for the possibility as Honey settled herself on the therapist's couch one more time. But, again, she got to the starting gate and didn't hear the gun go off.

She chattered about her sons' latest good report cards, going over them in proud detail. She talked about her daughter's high marks in college. She talked about her husband's success in business, telling Hess more than he wanted to know about the stars Zack managed.

She said that in this new enterprise of hers, being God, she, too, wanted to strive for excellence.

She went over her Commandments: Give And Receive Vegetables; Keep Breathing; Do The Friendliest Thing. These were final, she'd decided, set in stone, but she was going to need more. Most religions had at least ten Commandments, although ten she thought, was too many to remember. Perhaps, since she was making them Do's instead of Don'ts, she could get away with less.

She wrestled with new notions, complaining that it wasn't easy coming up with universal laws.

She told him she'd been watching a healer last night on one of the religious channels. He'd slap people on the forehead and holler, "Take all you need!" This, she thought, might make a good Commandment because it indicated there was plenty for everyone, enough to go around, which she thought was true, if only some people weren't quite so greedy, but then she started thinking what would happen if people actually followed that Commandment and walked into a store, say on Rodeo Drive, and just took what they needed.

Then she thought maybe this was the whole trouble with the human race, that all we did was take and not give anything back. Especially in terms of love, which she thought some people really took for granted.

Then she figured maybe a better Commandment might be "Pay What You Owe," but Lowell hated that one. He said the idea of owing was bad because it made people feel obligated, the way his father made him feel just because he bought him things, then shunted him off

Day Two: And There Was Light...

to one side of his life, like a white rhinoceros on a reservation. So then she decided maybe a better Commandment might be "Take Off The Price Tags", but that brought her back to square one, the concept that everything belonged to everybody, which just wasn't working for her. So then she thought . . .

"Shhhh!" said an exhausted Dr. Hess, momentarily losing his equanimity.

"Shhhh?" Honey mused. "That might make a pretty good Commandment. I mean, we'd actually have to listen if we ever stopped talking. We'd find out a lot about each other, what we're afraid of, what makes us happy . . .

"I wasn't suggesting a Commandment, though you can use it if you want to. What I meant to say was, we have to stop for today," said the drained doctor.

"What do you mean stop? This is All Important! Y'know, I'm beginning to think this place is a waste of time. You say I'm God? I'm going to act like God." She bounded off his couch and over to his phone. "My ex-husband's a lawyer," she said, beginning to dial Roger's number. "*He'll* get me out of here!"

"Demeter," said the doctor gently, "you signed yourself in. You can sign yourself out anytime you wish."

"Oh," she said. Her belligerence dampened, she placed the receiver back in its cradle and sidled out of the room.

***

The trash compactor and the garbage disposal were both broken, so Jelia made an extra trip to the lane behind the Newmans' house, carrying two bags of garbage like a burro. She heard with satisfaction Corie's cluck of disapproval as she dragged her burden off, knowing she was being viewed as disadvantaged, but at the same time indispensable.

Returning to the kitchen, she began to do the dinner dishes Since the dishwasher was broken – somehow a fork had jammed itself under the washer arm – she put the dirty dishes in the sink, then dropped the food processor into the sudsy water to soak, motor and all.

"How ees you mother?" she enquired of Corinne, who was wolfing down a lukewarm tamale she'd brought home from the AM/PM Minimart.

The tamale was going down like a lump of library paste but Corie felt happy eating it. Delayed at the university, she'd decided to spare the overworked Jelia the trouble of cooking dinner twice. Eating this tamale, she felt, was the act of a socially conscious human being. It also made her feel closer to Jelia culturally.

Regarding her mother, she raised one shoulder, as Jelia, crossing herself twice, re-lit the flame of a votive candle that had sputtered out beside the sink.

"Is that for her?" asked Corinne with her mouth full of ground corn and who knew what else – the label said turkey but . . .

"No, Mees. Tomorrow I see boyfriend, Innocencio. This candle for no having baby."

Corinne let out an exclamation of wonder. Hadn't Jelia heard of the pill?

"I no like," said Jelia.

Corie knew that women from underdeveloped countries were often denied information about family planning. She sketchily outlined alternatives to the use of a hormone pill: diaphrams, condoms. Everybody was using condoms.

"I no like because is wrong," said the housekeeper with religious conviction.

Corie picked a fragment of mystery-meat from between her front teeth. Not wanting to infringe on Jelia's beliefs, she nevertheless felt it her duty to state that this was not a moral issue. It was a practical one. There was AIDS out there.

With a small smile, Jelia thanked her for her concern but was able to assure the slightly younger woman that Innocencio did not have AIDS.

"He no gay-boy, he no shoot drugs," she said, showing her fairly sophisticated grasp of the matter. "He no sick," she added. "He healthy," putting the subject to rest.

Day Two: And There Was Light . . .

Still Corie felt it necessary to press on, with her repast and with the facts. She stated that Jelia was living at subsistence level now. She couldn't afford other mouths to feed. She should be using something to protect herself and if it didn't work, she should have an abortion.

The housekeeper scrubbed at the dishes, but under the water she made an ancient two fingered sign to ward off the evil eye.

"I'd have one in a minute," Corie condescended, feeling she was setting an enlightened example, as she allowed a discreet burp to escape.

Jelia considered whether or not to continue the conversation, but she liked the girl so she said what was on her mind.

"You mother no have abortion," she almost whispered.

Corinne pushed away the last of her tamale, which suddenly made her feel nauseous.

"She carry you in her belly, Corinna. Why you no thank her for you precious life?"

"My 'precious life', as you put it, was a mistake," Corinne said fiercely. "I've never even seen my father. He probably found out she was pregnant and split. So she dumps me on my grandparents, then she dumps me on Roger, then she dumps me on Zack. What do I have to thank her for? Nothing, Hey Ya. You understand? Nada."

"I hope my little ones no feel the same," said Jelia pensively.

"What little ones?"

"The three I got in Guatemala."

***

Whether or not peas got their start in Eden or a good deal further east, they grew wild, then were cultivated, everywhere in the Mediterranean.

Dried fried peas were sold like popcorn at the Roman Colosseum. But there was no corn to pop in the Old World until the Spanish brought it back from the Americas. And there was nary a pea in the New World until the Spanish brought them there.

2:3

February 14th is a rewrite. Long before they named the day for a Christian martyr who died horribly, it was a rite of spring, a pagan feast, a celebration of life and love which the classical Romans adapted from the Greeks, who adapted it from the Minoans, who adapted it from the Carians, who adapted it from the Lycians, who lived in what became a part of Turkey, on the northern tip of the fertile crescent lying east of the Mediterranean Sea.

As the Romans had it, the star of the festival was a stunning single mother whose baby son kept shooting arrows at the hapless inhabitants of heaven and earth, who then ran off together into the bushes.

It was the mom who handed her kid his quiver, calculating that gods and humans, with pierced hearts, and gonads engaged, would be too busy to usurp her power.

What power? Well, that's another story.

No, it's not.

***

Since it's almost always spring in Southern California, and people are constantly running off into the bushes, for Rayanne the date of February 14th simply signaled one more order tacked onto Zack's list of her duties for the day, a list he'd recorded on tape on his way to the office, leaving the micro-cassette in a prominent spot on her desk before he went off to his round of meetings.

She was to:

. Call Honey and get her to phone the schmuck (Roger) to ask if Red and Missy could take the twins to Disneyland on Saturday, part of the schmuck's alternate weekend.

. Tell his accountant to transfer some money into Corie's bank account. "A couple of million should do."

. Find Zack a gardener ASAP. "I've got dead flowers and grass up to my poopik."

Day Two: And There Was Light . . .

. Get a repairman for appliances.

. Tell Honey he'd visit on Friday. They could play tennis. "Ask Hess if I can take her for dinner. See if God eats out."

. "Oh, yeah. It's Valentine's. Do presents."

Rayanne turned off her Pearlcorder and allowed herself a shake of the head. Always The Biggie: with his wife in a sanitarium, and his business going sideways in the endless recession, he was still making cracks, slapping backs, playing the game.

Only she, being in a position to observe him closely, had noticed that the strain was telling. He was taking the occasional tranquillizer, needed a little more sex, to keep that ever-present smile of his in place. Yesterday, he'd fallen asleep, mid-afternoon, in his high-backed leather swivel chair.

Thank God it was Honey who had to live with him. His snoring could wake the dead.

***

During most of February 14th, Honey refused to come out of her room. And, since her tiff with Dr. Hess the previous afternoon, she hadn't allowed anyone in, except for room service. Not even Lowell.

She told Hess's staff she was busy packing, but she wasn't.

She wasn't dressed either. Wasn't up. Was lying in bed, ducking her destiny, unable or unwilling to go out and get on with being omnipotent.

She repeated the packing lie when Dr. Hess came by to check on her at noon, and again, later in the day. So she felt somewhat foolish barging into his office at five o'clock, but she had to yell at somebody.

Hess was getting ready to leave for the day, but he sat back down at his desk, pleased to see her, even if she was ranting.

The reason she knew this was that, in the midst of her tirade, he cheerfully removed his shoes and socks and slithered into his sandbox. She almost paused to rage at him about it, but she had other priorities.

She needed to rage about her ex-husband, *ROGER*, whom she'd merely called to ask about his *ALT*ernate *WEEK*end. But Roger wouldn't come to the *PHONE*. He made *MARGO* say that conversation with her could prejudice any future *COURT ACTION* he might bring to get *CUSTODY* of the *TWINS!*

UNFIT MOTHER!!! That was the innuendo, the implied threat, when he knew, *HE KNEW*, that in every move she'd ever made she'd *PUT HER CHILDREN FIRST!!!* She'd only married him in the *FIRST PLACE* so Corinne could have a *LAST NAME* and a *NORMAL LIFE*, not that she *PARTICULARLY APPRECIATED IT!!!*

Her fury ricocheted around Hess's office, then bounced into embarrassment. But she'd already said it: that Corie was illegitimate, so she might as well admit that her firstborn was five and a half years old before Roger made her an honest woman. She might as well remind Hess that they didn't have the euphemisms "teenage mother" or "single mother" in those days. All they had was the loaded word "unwed." She might as well tell him about the way people looked at her, how they'd made her feel filthy, how, behind her back, they'd whispered "whore."

They had names for Corie, too, she told him bitterly, though with resignation, as she finally sat down hard on his couch. It was out of the ordinary for Roger to take them in. Perhaps he was expanding his parameters even then.

She'd been happy, though. They all were. The twins were born. They bought the house at Broad Beach. Then one day Roger walked in to Ralph's Market to get himself a half a pound of Gorgonzola . . .

"Y'know," she said blinking back tears, "I've never made a decent decision in my life. I'm a failure, a nobody, a nothing. I'm certainly not God."

"Yes, you are," said Hess. "You just lack information. Lie down, close your eyes."

That's what every man I've ever met has said to me, thought Honey, but she did as she was asked.

He told her to let her tension go, to relax and get comfortable.

She supposed she was.

He told her to imagine herself walking down a path in the woods. She would come to a lake which she owned.

Day Two: And There Was Light . . .

On the beach would be a boat with some oars in it She was to get in the boat and row out on the lake.

Not a chance, thought Honey. I'm not going out on any lake in any boat. This is a trick, as usual.

"It's a beautiful day," Dr. Hess encouraged. "The lake is sparkling in the sunshine."

But Honey wasn't rowing. She was still shivering at the tree line, hadn't set foot on the beach. She waited for the doctor to say more, but he was silent.

He thinks I'm rowing, she realized. I'd better row. This is only a mental exercise.

She gingerly boarded the boat, propelled herself out onto the lake. But no sooner had she lost sight of shore than a force five gale began to blow.

With white water all around her, Honey found herself fighting for her life. Five foot waves swamped the gunwales. She tried to bail and row at the same time. Her little craft went around in circles. Frantic, she began to founder and sink. She knew this was going to happen! Why did she get in this killer boat to begin with? This was it! She was going to die! No point in screaming for help, there was nobody else on her lake.

Wait a minute, it was "her" lake, that's what Hess had said. If she owned this lake it could be anything she wanted.

As soon as that thought could penetrate, the lake turned mirror flat. Out of nowhere there were other boats floating lazily by. Total strangers waved at Honey. One said, "Catch!" and tossed her a rutabaga.

Honey giggled and opened her eyes.

"What happened?" asked her doctor, knowingly.

"I remembered it was my lake," she replied. "It was almost too late."

"Uh huh," said Hess.

"But it's never too late, is it?" said Honey, her intuition finally operating.

"No," he answered.

"But this was like a dream. What's it got to do with real life? What's it got to do with being God?"

"I hate to stop now, but I'm teaching a class tonight."

"Oh, no! We're not stopping! This is my lake!" Honey bullied, staying prone on his sofa.

But a moment later, she sat up, saying, "But it's your lake, too, isn't it?"

Hess just smiled.

"Does this mean you're God too, and Zack? And that crumb Roger? And Corinne? And the twins? And Hey Ya?

"I'll see you tomorrow morning," Hess said, emerging from his sandbox. "Unless you'd still like to leave."

"I guess I'll stay a little longer," said Honey.

As she passed his desk on her way to the door, she reached impulsively into his drawer and handed him a fresh green and yellow striped sock.

2:4

What is a rutabaga, anyway, this vegetable which didn't grow in Eden?

It's a Do The Friendliest Thing food: in Honey's home town of Paradise, Texas, three crops will grow in a year.

Golden, globe shaped, it wears a crown of greens and the purple mantle of royalty on its shoulders. Texans eat the tops like spinach, with butter and a dash of pepper vinegar. But it's the root, steady, sturdy, that sings survival because it will last through the winter. You can store the rutabaga, waxed, for long periods and have something to eat in December, or leave it in the ground under ice and snow, dig it up and eat it in the spring.

In Los Angeles, where they don't have winter, they don't value the rutabaga the way it's prized in colder climates, as one of the healthiest of vegetables, full of vitamin C and potassium. They don't recognize it as a topical medicine, an antidote to snakebite, for instance. Nor do

Day Two: And There Was Light . . .

they use it as a beauty product: boiled and mashed with cream and pulverized rosebuds as a wrinkle-fighting mask.

A bite of rutabaga has wildness in it. It's rank, and a little spicy. Like love, it needs some sugar in the cooking to enhance its bittersweet taste.

***

"Zack, Dude! C'mere!" Brian bellowed from the game room.

Who would have guessed that teenaged yelling would be anything like a rutabaga, particularly to a harried businessman, longtime bachelor, and three-times childless husband fighting middle age. Yet the net effect was satisfying-old-fashioned-root-vegetable as he returned to his home in Beverly Hills from another day of not as many deals.

He asked Jelia to whip him up a quick steak for dinner, then allowed himself to be summoned. He liked playing father to Honey's kids.

His two previous marriages had been child-proof by choice, but there came a time as he entered his forties, when Zack began to feel the lack of family, so he'd married the pretty little shiksa who had one. If that sounds too pragmatic, too acquisitive, too cold: Keep Breathing. Remember the rewrite.

In the deal, he also married Honey's dad, whom he knew well before he knew her. He and Red, whom he considered a friend as much as a father-in-law, had been partners in a number of real estate transactions: investments for Zack's clients and himself. If Red came with a conspicuously Christian wife, it was all part of the bargain.

Regarding Honey's children: Corinne, admittedly, was a princess, but Zack was used to the breed. He couldn't help teasing and spoiling her. And the twins, his best audience, his best buddies, with him and them it was special.

Those twins, with their fuzzy upper lips and their two-tone voices, they were going to slay the women in a few more years. They'd be over six feet if they kept growing to match their current shoe size. And handsome once they finished being skinny with zits.

Unlike their real father, they were smart. Zack had rewarded them well for their February report cards: straight A's except for sports. But who cared if they were useless at soccer? Let them know how to add and subtract, because one day they were going to be rich. They'd get most of Red's money, they'd get Roger's, and undoubtedly, plenty of Zack's.

For that, Abraham Newman, Zack's long dead parent, would be rolling in his grave. He'd been president of his synagogue. No way would he understand the handing over of the fruits of Zack's lifetime, seeded by his father, to two young WASPs.

What bothered Zack along these lines was that the boys didn't carry his name. As long as Roger Best was alive, that was legally unlikely. The way things stood, when they wrote FADE OUT: THE END to the script of Zack's life, the name Newman, his branch of it anyway, would die and be buried with him. While he brokered immortality for others – "Film is forever," as Norman Nathanson loved to say – there'd be no trace left of the mover and shaker, the maker and breaker, The Biggie himself.

Unless, of course, he and Honey . . .

"Hey, Dude! Get in here!"

Unless he and Honey should ever decide to . . .

"Zack!!!"

Entering the game room, he found Sean and Brian hunched over the computer and was roundly thanked for his Valentine's present.

Rayanne had bought the twins *Access Four*, a computer program which, according to Sean, contained *Laserbrain*, *Sir Rebrum*, and two other games. They even got *Hankering Plaza* as a bonus.

"Far out," Zack remarked, "I haven't played *Hankering Plaza* since I was a boy."

His comment got a laugh from the twins but not for the reason he expected.

"*Hankering Plaza* isn't a game. It's a store," Sean explained. "You order things and put them on a credit card."

"I wasn't aware they issued credit cards to fourteen year olds," Zack parried, but he was in for another surprise.

Day Two: And There Was Light . . .

"We put it on yours," Brian said. "Like we do with the games, except those we charge on your telephone bill."

"You have to pay for these games?"

"Sure," replied his step-son, regarding him as though he was from another dimension.

Zack never saw his credit card or telephone bills. They were paid by his accountant and written off, as much as possible, as a business expense. But the twins had played nightly games ever since they'd had the computer and the cash was coming out of Zack's pocket. Apparently, these baby bandits had no intention of waiting for their inheritance.

To hide his shock, Zack changed the subject, reminding the twins to finish their homework and call their mother if they hadn't already. He announced his plans to return to the office after dinner to do a little work. Jelia would be leaving, too, but Corie was across the street and Zack would be back by ten.

Sean assured him it would be no problem, asking, without skipping a beat, if he and his brother could buy a couple of things at "*Hankering Plaza*": spend maybe twenty five dollars?

Zack allowed himself to agree to the hold-up. In fact, he rather enjoyed it. As he went in to dinner he took a moment to reassure his father's ghost.

"Don't worry, Pop. The Newman assets will be in capable hands."

***

Despite the opportunity, no charges were added to Zack's American Express account that night. Maybe it was Cupid shooting his little arrows that got Sean and Brian side-tracked because they never did go shopping. Instead, alone in the house, they decided to peruse the centerfold of Zack's latest Playboy magazine.

"She looks like Bianca with no clothes on," said Sean.

"I like the way her boobies have those nipples that look like gumdrops."

"I've got a boner," Brian announced, "My giant penis is engorged with blood."

"Shut up. Now you're getting me horny," said his brother.

"Contest!" suggested Brian.

"Okay, but turn the lights out and lock the door. We're gonna feel stupid if anyone walks in."

"Who's gonna walk in?"

"Anyone could walk in. Maybe Bianca with no clothes on rubbing her pussy. Oo oo, I win."

***

On a Mulholland sideroad, in the back seat of Innocencio Miclantecutli's black Chevrolet lowrider, Jelia Maria Esperanza Emiliana Xicara, better known as Hey Ya, was involved in her own rite.

Innocencio had his fist twined in her long black hair, pinning her down while she arched her back and moved her well-rounded hips against him. She squealed, and sighed, and taunted him in Spanish as he jammed her full of himself. When it was over she covered his tattoos with kisses, whimpering sounds of satisfaction.

She wondered what her husband would have thought to see her acting like *uno puta* with this wild Chicano street boy with the carved face and jungle attitude of his Mixtec forebears. Her husband would, undoubtedly, have taken his belt to her. But then, he was dead from bullets, and she was alive. And she had her reasons for being here.

The Newman's maid took a fetching pose. With one arm stretched lazily across Innocencio's back seat, she stroked the toy dog with the wagging head he kept on the fake fur in the window.

With suggestions in her eyes, and a throaty laugh, she tried for a two candle night.

***

In his overscale office, Zack was similarly employed. Rayanne knew what to do when she got into the bushes. She could turn his

Day Two: And There Was Light . . .

meki into an obelisk, a skyscraper, a monument to what? The "L" word? No. This was just fucking.

But Zack never locked the door. Danger. That was part of it. Fear of getting caught splayed on the sofa, sprawled on the rug, spent and semi-nude nibbling and nuzzling in his executive swivel chair, tasting what was forbidden, yeah, that got the juices flowing. What a difference from the safety and sameness of married sex. It took an Act of Congress to make Honey come.

It hardly ever crossed Zack's mind that his previous marriages had ended because of his inability to be monogamous.

Though once in a while it came to him that he had more, now, to lose.

Now and again he wondered if he wasn't a little too old for this mishigas.

But never, ever, did he feel guilty. To Zack, getting some on the side was an inalienable right.

***

In a cave a world away in Asia, the monk Sah ate his rice gruel while drenching rains beat down steadily outside. Tasting, tasting, swallowing, swallowing, he silently observed, appreciating each scanty mouthful as it passed his lips.

Finishing his feast, he stepped to the mouth of his igneous dwelling, where, with the help of the monsoon, he gratefully washed his bowl: rinsing, rinsing. He bowed to the rain, bowed to his bowl as he placed it on a jutting ledge, then returned to his place on the floor of the cave.

Sitting, sitting, he meditated. Breathing, breathing. He settled into a nice samadhi.

Awaken! Awaken! Awaken! BOK!

Not this again . . . He let the thought go and returned to breathing. But he was breathing doubt. Other men his age had a home, a wife, kids, a backyard garden to putter in, the kind of life his father had lived. They weren't crouched in the middle of triple canopy forest, half naked, half starved, with rain blowing into their cave.

He shivered, trying to regain his concentration, but it wouldn't come.

There had been a girl. The prettiest girl in Southern California. Except for circumstances he might have been married to her now. For a moment he pictured himself with her in his arms in the cramped front passenger seat of his old turquoise and white Nash Metropolitan.

Though only in his mind, he touched her mouth with his tongue, felt her smooth skin under his hand, heard her escalating cries of pleasure.

Sah arose and went out into the weather, walking away from the feast of love.

Breathing, breathing, he reminded himself. Walking, walking. Getting wet, getting wet.

***

For Honey, there was no ingredient of Valentine's Day that could top her heady "my lake" meeting with Dr. Hess.

For a while afterwards, she could hardly say why, she went into his garden and weeded. Racing the waning sunlight, using a tool notched like a snake's tongue, she got rid of unwanted plants. This labor, she'd discovered, unexpectedly gratified her. It was good to tidy up the earth, get down into it, dig up the problem, smooth the soil back down. Doing so, she made space for seeds which were going to be planted tomorrow.

Later, she went to the lounge. She needed to know how the world was doing.

This was more preparation than passtime, so she spent a couple of hours with CNN, took a solo dinner break, then scanned everything in Dr. Hess's magazine rack, from *Time*, through *Fortune*, to *Women's Day*. When, weary eyed, she returned her reading materials to the rack, it had all blurred into nothing. The only thing she could say for sure was that this world, which contained her lake, was anything but a paradise.

As usual, much of the planet's real estate was changing hands, but always with tears and trouble. There was a hole in the heavens and

Day Two: And There Was Light . . .

poison on the ground. There were too many people and not enough trees. Everything we wanted to fix was going to cost money and there wasn't enough to go around.

Whoever was God was going to have their hands full. Whoever was God was going to need more than her four Commandments: Give And Receive Vegetables, Keep Breathing, Do The Friendliest Thing, and Shhhh!

Around nine-thirty the twins called. She thanked them for the chocolates Rayanne had sent, and the card with the heart pierced by an arrow they'd mailed on their own. She reached Zack at the office and thanked him for the pale pink roses. During these phone calls everyone said they loved her but no one asked when she was coming home.

2:5

What is paradise, anyway? Is it a place, so chewed, swallowed, digested by life that it's lost and gone forever?

Or is it a promise? Does our Father have it in his back pocket, holding out on us bad kids 'til we clean up our act (O stale Twinkie, O pie in the sky, O perfidious pattycake)?

Or is it a point of view? A feeling of ease and contentment, a sense of belonging everywhere in the world, a world brimming over with . . .

***

Dr. Augustus Hess had a healing vision of paradise: that it wasn't lost, like a single sock, just temporarily mislaid.

He also thought he knew approximately where and when it had been carelessly set aside, which is why his characteristic cool began to waver as he waited for the hour of Honey's official appointment to go further with her.

And why, when he spotted her in the hospital garden at nine AM, the morning after Saint Valentine's Day, being taught to double-dig a raised bed for vegetables using the French intensive method, he slipped in beside her with his own shovel and bag of manure.

Though his psychologist self warned him not to encroach on her therapy, to let his patient discover things for herself, another side of him, the student, then teacher, of Jung; frequenter of universities; intimate of scholars from other disciplines, was privy to a wave of wisdom which, applied to her God neurosis, might hasten her recovery.

Where to begin was the question. Should he discuss God as a concept: something we invent to help us explain our lives, to see us through the dark times, the hard and sad times, the times when we trust ourselves least?

Or should he describe God as the symbol of a greater truth with which we viscerally connect, whether that symbol is a person, a mountain, an animal, a whole roomful of individuals, or a creature with five heads?

Or should he indicate that God reflects the society in which we live, exemplifies our goals, changing as we change?

He poked in the dirt, trying to find an approach. But why not come straight to the point?

"Did you know God used to be a woman," he said, revealing his secret. "Before He was a man?"

"So I'm not breaking any new ground," Honey answered him lightly, turning over a clod of earth.

Hess had expected excitement or at least interest, but if he was disappointed, he didn't show it. He could offer her a bite of his erudition but she might not like the flavor.

He picked up his shovel and motioned her away from the others to a knoll in the garden where a gnarled old fig tree gave shade – perhaps if he provided a setting . . .

Anthropologists, he told her, were exploring the theory that as our antecedents came out of the trees, as they evolved into ancestors, the males didn't know they played a part in the making of babies. They saw the female get fat, then deliver a child, and thought she, on her own, was responsible for creating their kind.

Day Two: And There Was Light . . .

So they protected her from danger, hunted meat for her and her young, regarding the female with awe.

The earliest objects of formal worship, he claimed, the most primitive statuary, depicted a woman, The Giver of Life: The Great Mother.

Honey was eyeing the tree they were standing under. It was the same tree she had in her backyard. She must remember to ask Hess its name.

"Pay attention," said her doctor, fixing her with those beady eyes of his as he went on with his story.

While the men went off to hunt, he told her, the women gathered grains and fruits and vegetables. It followed they'd be the ones to notice that a seed, dropped on the ground, could grow into something to eat.

"Are you saying women invented agriculture?" asked his doubtful patient, toying with her bag of fertilizer.

"It's scientifically accepted, Demeter," Hess said.

From the look on Honey's face, Hess could see she hadn't the faintest idea what he was getting at. He draped his hand over a low hanging branch of the tree and crossed one foot over the other, revealing a patch of green and yellow sock.

Civilization, he explained, began with the growing of vegetables. Once people could grow their own food, they could stop wandering in the wild and build homes next to their gardens.

"Of course it didn't happen overnight," he said. "It took thousands and thousands of years.

"But if you put together in your mind the credit for the creation of babies and the credit for the taming of vegetables, you can see why Woman was worshipped as the metaphor for Life in all its abundance."

By the time humans lived in villages, he went on to say, they probably knew it took two to tango, but by then The Great Mother was long entrenched as the bringer of plenty, so instead of dancing around a tree in Her honor, temples were built and She was given a name.

Around the pre-historic Mediterranean, up and down the fertile crescent, Her name was Neith, Innana, Nana, Astarte, Ashtoreth, Rhea.

He didn't give Honey time to say he'd mentioned her mother's name because he went right on with his tale.

In the remains of goddess temples which had been found, he said, were tablets with early writing which paleologists – people who studied the oldest sign languages – had decoded. They were all about crops and harvests and real estate.

"Real estate?" Honey remarked. "My dad's in that business. He's done very well."

"Listen," said Hess, "women, not men, ran these temples. You were the priestesses.

"And the head priestess was queen.

"You represented The Goddess on Earth.

"You took care of Her real estate.

"You made the rules which protected the land and supported them with religious observances.

"You were the trustees of its bounty.

"You shared out the seed and the harvest.

"Not only that, you passed the trust from mother to daughter.

"And your daughters were fathered by various men. A woman could make love to whomever she chose. And did. As a ritual of fertility. In the temples."

"Hmmmm," said Honey, hugging her hoe. She still didn't see exactly what this had to do with her.

But one day, Hess told her, invaders arrived: men with better weapons and superior transportation. They conquered The Goddess's garden and took it for themselves. They took over the temples and stopped passing the plenty from mother to daughter. They handed it from father to son.

That's when things changed. A female lost her right to inherit anything, she couldn't be a priestess any more and she couldn't have children with what The Bible calls "her passionate lovers." The father of her child had to be her husband or else that child was illegitimate.

"Do you know what 'illegitimate' means?" asked the psychologist. "It means outside the law. And who made the law? Who drew up the rules of this brand new game? God!" said Hess, answering all his own questions.

"And guess who their God was?" he asked, leaving one for Honey.

"A He?" she said – this was getting good. "A He with thunderbolts?"

"Correct," Hess replied. "These conquerors didn't just show up in Goddess territory and say, 'Hi there. We want it all. And you have to give up your custom of sharing, give up your name, suppress your sensual nature, accept our puny picture of the family and who belongs in it, tell your daughters they're nothing compared to your sons, wear long hot clothing to cover your beautiful body (don't you dare show your breasts!), stay with your husband who will have economic control over you.' They couldn't just ride in and grab all the goodies without expecting an endless fight. So they said, 'This isn't our will. It's God's. And if you don't do things His way some very bad things are going to happen.'"

"Wow," said Honey.

And then, as conquerors do, Hess related, they made a lot of bad things happen, destroying as much as they could of Goddess culture, smashing statues, destroying records, changing the meaning of the holy days and celebrations, outlawing worship as it had been known and converting the temples to suit themselves.

By the time books were finally written about the way things had been, The Great Mother got barely a mention, and Woman was pictured as a brainless bad-girl, preoccupied with sex, who ruined everything for all of us because she was tempted by a snake.

"Now, see how you like this," said Hess. "The snake is one of the earliest icons of the female religion."

2:6

This might be as good a time as any to look into the when of Eden, and to notice that humans have been on earth a lot longer than we usually admit.

ON THE SEVENTH DAY SHE RESTED

According to science, it all started with apelike creatures: anthropologists date their appearance to about eighty-five million years ago.

Four to five million years ago, they evolved into apelike creatures who could walk on two legs.

Beings who could use fire and complex tools and produce and pass on a culture – one way to define a human ancestor – lived fifty to a hundred thousand years ago.

Modern humans, who knew how to grow their own food, have been around for ten to twelve thousand years.

Humans who lived in cities, knew how to smelt metals, and recorded their experiences have been here for a mere three thousand.

That last three, that raindrop, that spitball, in the lake of our existence is what we refer to as "history." And somewhere in those other umpty-ump years, in the "pre" part, the She part, lies that utopian time which we may never know enough about no matter how deeply we dig for it, but which all humans carry in our collective unconscious, accompanied by longing.

***

Corinne had never spent time in the kitchen cooking, but it was pleasant, she was discovering, washing and chopping vegetables under the watchful eye of her maternal grandmother, Missy Johnson, who was making dinner at the Newman house on Jelia's day off.

Corie's nana, like their housekeeper, knew how to make delicious things to eat, and do all the other things that mothers used to do.

If only she would quit sighing, and saying, right in the middle of splitting and seeding an acorn squash something depressing like, "My poor l'il Honey. It about breaks my heart."

And making racist remarks about Jelia. It wasn't her fault that the dishwasher and the trash compactor and the In-Sink-Erator and the food processor and the electric can opener and the microwave flamed out.

Corie was glad for the reprieve when, with a slam of the kitchen door, the tromping of size twelve sneakers, and the usual hysterical

Day Two: And There Was Light . . .

laughter over private matters, the twins came home from school. Missy waylaid them, inflicting grandmotherly hugs, enquiring, as they jettisoned their books on the kitchen counter, what they'd learned that day.

Sean was eager to tell. They'd been studying China where you were only allowed to have one child. After that they made you have an abortion.

"My Lord! What sort of school . . ." Missy interrupted.

If your child died, Brian picked up the story, you weren't allowed to have any more. But if you had twins you could keep them both.

"So twins are like gold," he enthused. "And boy twins . . ." he did a little dance step, "need I say more, Ladies?"

He put his arm through Sean's and they treated Missy and Corinne to a grandiose bow as they departed the kitchen for the game room.

In spite of herself, Missy beamed with pride, but only temporarily. Her happiness gave way to another deep inhalation, another breathy sigh, and Corinne's time-out was over.

"It's just not right that your mother isn't here," Missy moped, forgetting to prep her squash. Corie handed her a knife in hopes of distracting her, but Missy could slice and moan.

"It's all my fault, this confusion of hers," she insisted on saying. "The girl had no religious training. I was raised Methodist myself, but Red, his religion is real estate. Not that they had a Methodist church in Paradise, only a Baptist one, but I can't help thinking if only I'd taken her dear little hand and walked her over to Sunday School . . .

"Now Gene, your daddy, your real daddy I'm talking about now, his family were Lutherans. I'm not fond of Lutherans, but I've always thought, if things had been . . . different . . . at least there would have been some Christian influence.

"But then we got Roger, with his cockeyed ideas. Imagine a man who thinks sitting in a room with a lot of other people and not going to the bathroom is going to change his life! And will you ever forget the time he had us all eating clay?"

The sound of a loud car exhaust popping and crackling in the driveway gave Corie an excuse to escape to the door.

ON THE SEVENTH DAY SHE RESTED

Jelia was being returned early to the house by a male person of Hispanic and possibly indigenous-American heritage in a black Chevy lowrider. He was definitely the most attractive disadvantaged guy Corinne had ever seen: all legs, no behind, she noted, as he sprawled out of the automobile in his black leather pants, with an unbuttoned black leather vest over his bare torso; not tall but well proportioned; the arms, hard, brown, with veins that stood out on the undersides of them; muscular shoulders, knotted biceps, the tracery of tattoos; and the face, with those heavily lashed eyes, that beatific smile. Corie decided that if this was Innocencio he was perfectly named.

In the glow of sunset, he waited lazily for Jelia to come to him for a kiss, bent over her, pressed her to him, then swallowed her mouth with his own. It was almost embarrassing to watch. Nobody Corie knew kissed like that.

Innocencio released the Newman's maid, turning his knowing gaze on Corinne. He laughed, baring animal teeth and blew her a kiss for herself.

Corinne, though she disappeared, blushing, from the doorway, caught it, kept it, and lived on it from that moment.

In the background, her grandmother maundered on:

"And now we have Zack, who's a big 'ol darlin', but he's – well, he's Jewish!"

***

By the way, there was no acorn squash in Eden.

Squash evolved in Central America where it's been eaten for about nine thousand years.

They still don't have acorn squash in China.

But they do have a Great Mother.

***

With the usual blaring of music from his tape player wreaking auditory havoc, Lowell scraped shavings of freebase onto a fine mesh

Day Two: And There Was Light . . .

screen and made a torch out of a Q-tip as Honey sat on his bed reporting that day's incredible news: how we used to have a Heavenly Mom who gave us vegetables and babies, not a Heavenly Dad with an arsenal of thunderbolts.

How, for tens of thousands of years there was, what had Dr. Hess called it? gynocracy? in the fertile crescent. It existed everywhere Eden could be, and all around the Mediterranean. According to him, women were in the driver's seat of civilization.

Lowell lit his Q-tip, heated the square of screen and took a long drag of the smoke that began curling off it toward his lips as she rattled on about goddesses and goddess worshippers, with their shared lands, their children-who-were-never-illegitimate, and their habits of making love.

"But then," she said, "just so men could own everything, the world was put under contract, including the marriage contract with its straight-jacket taboos."

Lowell leaned back in his chair and surrendered to the drugs he'd inhaled.

"Aren't you listening? I'm trying to tell you how life in general and sex in particular got so complicated," said Honey.

"Sex can give you a disease," he replied, foggily. "Sex can make your mother blow her brains out with a pearl handled pistol because your father's giving it to everyone but her.

"Besides," he added, "drugs beat sex, like a rock beats scissors and scissors beat paper."

"I thought you came here to give up drugs," she said, although sympathetically.

"Get over yourself," shot back Lowell. "This God trip of yours is fine but let's not get pushy, okay?"

He prepared another scraping of freebase and began heating it with his torch. Honey watched helplessly as he inhaled the dangerous substance. He closed his eyes. A mild expression came over his face lending him a momentary resemblance to Gene Green.

He pushed the paraphernalia in her direction.

"Forgetfulness," he offered.

But Honey didn't want to forget. She'd just started to remember.

She patted him on top of the head and wandered back to her own room, eagerly anticipating her next meeting with Dr. Augustus Hess.

2:7

Looking at early gardening around the fertile crescent, it's remarkable how many vegetables took care of feminine needs.

Asparagus was known as a diuretic weight-reducing aid in Libya when Amazons worshipped the goddess Neith.

In pre-dynastic Egypt, in the days of the goddess Au Set, cabbage prevented constipation during pregnancy.

In Palestine/Lebanon/Syria, as Canaan, under the goddess Ashtoreth, shallots drunk in women's milk were used to heal the womb after miscarriage.

Radish promoted menstruation, parsnip aided conception, garlic brought away the afterbirth.

But here's an odd thing: each of these vegetables was also known as a remedy for snakebite.

Though whether they were eaten or worn . . .

Okay, okay, okay. Let's get on with the rewrite.

***

Like a cobra in a cave, a python up a tree, a moccasin on the water, or, some said later, a garden variety snake-in-the-grass, Dr. Hess was at home with the hypothesis that human beings create gods in their own image, not the other way around. By observing their gods, he said, you could tell what people were up to.

At his next-morning meeting with Honey, he related what happened after The Great Mother of the Mediterranean married the Johnny-come-lately who'd invaded her turf, the lightening-bolt wielding storm god/war god, who demanded a capital "G".

Day Two: And There Was Light . . .

"You didn't say The Goddess got married," said Honey, "only that people did."

"Put it this way," said Hess. "He married Her wherever She was too powerful to be summarily pushed aside. In some places where they ruled together, She was the dominant deity. In some places the whole family got into the act. But eventually, He was able to replace Her in every country of Her reign."

By saying "country," he was getting ahead of himself. There was too much to tell, but he backed up through the Iron Age and tried to fill Honey in.

When The Goddess was in charge, he explained, there was no such thing as a country. There were settlements which grew into temple/foodbank/cities, some of which were elaborate, feeding Her people and giving them surpluses to exchange, which they used to establish friendships with their neighbors based on trade.

Her Mate, however, insisted He owned the land that produced the plenty. He marked it off and laid claim to everything on it, including Her.

Once a hunter, he became a herdsman, Her Husband, whose idea of marriage was how many cows He could put to the bull. As His herds increased and His heirs increased, he needed more real estate.

He went to war to broaden His borders (the concept of countries arrived). But the enemies he made kept coming back to make war on Him. His endless fighting brought famine, poverty and disease to Her once-prosperous people. Then, too, Hess admitted, there was this big flood which may have made Her lose face.

Though Her worshippers found it hard to forget Her, they began to depend on Him. They needed more protection than She could give them in an increasingly hostile world. In time, to keep Him happy, they said He was the only God for them, but when times were good, or very, very bad, they'd still sneak out to dance around a tree.

In the west, Hess expounded, we inherited various versions of the God with the I-Me-Mine philosophy, which tended to pit even His own followers against each other. And though a man known as His Son tried to turn things around by preaching "less is more," the capture and control of real estate continued to motivate every war ever fought under any banner, holy or unholy, for the rest of human history, beginning, as Dr. Hess reminded, with the battle of the sexes.

"Great," said Honey, "and, as usual, women are still getting creamed."

"Not any more," the doctor told her, calmly digging himself down into his box of sand. "You've got the big ammunition, or perhaps I should say, the antidote."

***

Vegetable query: In the case of the parsnip, its seeds were the antidote to snake bite.

But were cabbage, radish, and garlic preventatives? Or . . . okay, okay, okay.

***

"We have the remedy?" said Honey happily.

"Birth control," said Hess.

"Oh, for Pete's sake, you sound like my daughter."

Hess twined himself forward on his desk and pinned her with his unwavering black eyes.

"It's only the most important human development since we got up on two legs," he said. "Merely the next step in evolution."

Now that women could effectively choose whether and when to have children, he told her, they were finding the time to resume their former leadership role in economic and political life.

Statistics showed that they already controlled at least half the wealth of the United States. And they had fifty-three percent of the vote.

They were re-learning how to trade, how to influence, how to vote, not just with a ballot, or their time and energy, but with their dollars.

American women, all women, were coming back into their own. They'd have a strong voice in decisions that affected life on Earth, the great hope for the future being that they, because they were still the ones who "gave life", would encourage an older, more reverent atti-

Day Two: And There Was Light...

tude towards it; because interdependence was something they innately understood, it was expected they'd also return to an older definition of family; and an older definition of wealth, which in the days of The Great Mother, had more to do with sharing.

"Where do they get these ideas?" said Honey. "We can't even pass the ERA or whatever-it's-called."

"Who cares if you pass the Equal Rights Amendment?" Hess said testily, his composure finally deserting him. "You *HAVE* equal rights. Take them!" He was halfway across his desk by now.

"You, Demeter, are standing outside some imaginary door, banging on it and whining 'Let me in,' when you're already in. You're *BACK IN*!" he said flatly before sliding back into his chair and the cooling comfort of sand.

"But now that you are, don't forget your rules of conduct," he added, noticing that he'd unintentionally tipped a splotch of sand onto the carpet.

Hess disappeared from view as he slipped beneath his desk to tidy up.

"Give And Receive Vegetables; Keep Breathing; Do The Friendliest Thing," said his disembodied voice. "And, Shhhh! Now there's a good one. Strong doesn't mean strident. Even when you have to say 'No'.

"There *IS* enough for everyone," he said, peering around one leg of his desk. "There's plenty to go around. At least, that's how we saw things in paradise."

***

Something needs clarifying: What's the connection between early females and snakebite medicine?

The snake in the Garden of Eden doesn't bite the lady, it feeds her. It feeds her an apple, or was it a fig?

Or was it information?

***

ON THE SEVENTH DAY SHE RESTED

That afternoon, Zack came for his scheduled visit, requesting a meeting with the doctor first so he could check on the latest nonsense his wife had been spouting about Eden and ancient religions. Was her mental health deteriorating?

On the contrary, Hess assured him. His wife was doing beautifully. She was much calmer, less lost, beginning to get a real sense of herself, especially since her God fantasy had been brought into focus.

"You mean she knows she's not God," said Zack, relieved.

"Not exactly. In the Sufi sense, I think she knows she is. Do you understand Mr. Newman?"

"Me? Sure. I'm very close with Sufis. Some of my best friends are Sufis."

"The adepts of every religion tell us *all* is God and God is *all*," Hess explained. "It's when we think we're the only one who is that we run into trouble."

"Uh huh," said Zack. He was not smiling.

"Though I have to say," the doctor added, "her Commandments are worthy of the divinity she's named for, The Great Mother of classical Greece, Goddess of Agriculture, Giver of Laws, Demeter."

"I'll be taking my wife home now," said Zack.

"I'd like to spend more time with her," said the psychologist.

"I'm sure you would at a grand a day. I may not know a Sufi from a bicycle seat, but I know a thief when I see one."

With that, Zack yanked Honey out of Dr. Hess's hospital. Or so he told himself. But the truth of the matter was that leaving there was his wife's decision.

With her husband and her doctor at an impasse, she came up with a compromise. It was time to go home. But not yet time to discontinue her relationship with her mentor.

She opted to become an outpatient and pay for her own therapy by getting a job. That way she'd also have dollars of her own to vote with.

She packed, said a fond goodbye to Lowell, took a satisfied look at her contribution to Dr. Hess's garden, then left the former beach club which, for her, had been an adult education center, the oars for her

Day Two: And There Was Light . . .

boat, the basket for her rutabagas, her ticket to a trip beyond what's written.

On the drive back to Beverly Hills, Zack couldn't stop apologizing for leaving his wife in a place like that. A "snake pit" he called it.

He vowed to make it up to her. If she wanted a job, he could get her one in a minute.

Her first thought was of real estate, the family business, but Zack said she'd be setting herself up for failure. Real estate was flat because of the recession.

Besides he had something in mind.

"Will I be All Powerful?" she kidded him.

"Can we forget that crap?" He drove silently for a few moments, overcoming his dread.

"How'd you like to be a secretary?" he said.

DAY THREE: And Behold, There Were Bucks To
                Be Made Out Of Everything . . .

3:1

Observe the effect of a rewrite on one woman, Honey a.k.a. Demeter Newman as she returns to home and family, and simultaneously prepares to go out into the world. Her step is lighter. She smiles more. Her relationship to her past has been altered indelibly by words.

Her relationship to her future has been altered too, with a new word added: possibility.

If she hasn't answered every question for herself, or even some we might be asking, like "What's the scoop on the snake?" let's give her time.

And if she isn't exactly being taken seriously yet, what's a few more days in the context of many, too many, millennia?

***

When the monk Sah first knocked at the gate of a monastery, asking to enter as a trainee, he was kept outside waiting for three days and nights to test his aspiration, subjected to hunger and thirst, apprehension, loneliness, and the opinionated stares and comments of curious passers by.

A similar ritual awaited Honey at the meeting Zack arranged for her with Calvin Still, publisher of *The Los Angeles Sun*, though she came to her job interview looking more like a goddess, or at least a queen, than an aspirant to anything.

Day Three: And There Were Bucks To Be Made . . .

Perhaps it was inappropriate of her to show up in an expensive pink linen Halston day dress with matching coat. Perhaps she should have changed her mauve snakeskin sandals for a more practical workaday shoe. Possibly even her wedding ring, a solid band of D flawless emerald cut diamonds from Fred Joaillier was too much for the office and screamed, "Regular inhabitant of Rodeo Drive! Rich man's wife! Woman taking job away from someone who needs it in a city with 10% unemployment!"

Whatever it was about Honey, she did attract attention as she sat, for what seemed like an eternity, in the publisher's reception area with a filled-in application in her hand. Actually, just her being there was enough to make *Sun* regulars give her the once-over. How many job-hunters were interviewed by Mr. Still, sole owner of the city's most prestigious newspaper?

She fidgeted self-consciously in his outer office for close to an hour and a half, enduring the half-heard "tsks" and titters of his busy staff as they came and went, and the unabashed eyeballing of his tall-and-tan-and-young-and-lovely executive assistant.

As the reception area emptied except for Honey, she smiled nervously at tall-and-tan and prayed that the drop of perspiration presently slipping between her breasts would evaporate before it left a stain above her carefully chosen Hermes belt. This thought itself evaporated as she finally heard "Mrs. Newman" announced. She was shown into the publisher's office.

Wainscoted paneling, a wall of books, Chinese carpets caught her eye, and a real pegged tongue-in-groove oak floor, not the kind your buddy with a router can lay in a day, the kind they made by hand before the turn of the 20th Century. Still's well-worn wing chairs had probably belonged to his family before they were antique, since his was the fourth generation to publish this newspaper in downtown Los Angeles, in this building, built by his great grandfather Enoch Calvin, which the Stills had captured by marriage in 1879.

Calvin Still was short, balding, and lacked a neck. He looked like a .44 caliber bullet in a suit and exhibited a corresponding charm. Without ever perusing her application, he brusquely outlined the position for which she was being considered, general factotum to the newspaper's advice columnist Arlene Morrigan, known to millions through syndication as Miss Arlene.

If Miss Arlene approved of her, she would be sorting mail, filing, answering the phone. There would be some typing. Here the publisher paused as if to inquire whether Honey had such a skill. She assured him she could bang out 43 words a minute and went on to warble that she began every morning with a peek at Miss Arlene's column, so she was completely familiar with . . .

Still cut her off. He was five minutes late for a meeting. His assistant would show her where to go.

He shook her hand. Honey couldn't remember what he said next but his manner indicated that he was doing this as a favor to Zack and he hoped she wouldn't embarrass him.

He pressed a buzzer. The door to his office opened and was filled with tall-etc. Still's eyes glowed in appreciation of her assets.

Honey was ushered out, almost a working girl.

Keep Breathing, she reminded herself as she walked the halls of this hub of information, *The Sun*, toward Miss Arlene's office, passing the Metro, International, Sports, Business, and Editorial departments where hundreds of fingers typed out their versions of the news.

Wouldn't it be something to be part of this place with the universe at its fingertips? If only as a secretary. Secretaries had fingertips, too. She hoped Miss Arlene wouldn't hate her on sight: take one look at her and say, "Next."

She asked for the Ladies Room so she could recomb her hair and apply fresh lipstick before meeting the household name who would either approve of her or point the way to the street.

But there was no time, as she was told, and it turned out there was no need, because it wasn't Miss Arlene, but her dog, Bones, an elderly dachshund, who held the key to her livelihood. That he didn't bite Honey as she entered Miss Arlene's office went a long way toward ensuring her employment.

Miss Arlene looked shorter without her trademark top-knot, also greyer – make that whiter. She was twenty-five years older than the

Day Three: And There Were Bucks To Be Made...

picture at the top of her column. Her trademark smile was missing, too. She greeted Honey without a tooth in her head.

"New choppers," she gummed, by way of saying "hello," pointing to an upper and a lower plate, set amidst a mass of letters and an overflowing ashtray on her desk. "Can't get used to 'em. For fifteen thousand bucks you'd think they'd fit."

Honey nodded politely, Doing The Friendliest Thing. Bones, the Personnel Director, had by now sniffed her thoroughly. There had been no bark, no growl; one mighty sneeze – was she wearing too much Shalimar? It looked as though she might just be acceptable to him.

Whether he would be acceptable to Honey was another matter. From the stains on the carpet and a long brown dog log lying under her prospective employer's desk, she could see he wasn't exactly office-broken.

Shhhh! she commanded herself, her eyes glancing back to Miss Arlene's. It was hardly a time to start complaining.

"I hope I can do a good job for you," she fluttered. "I haven't really worked in the last sixteen years."

"Calvin says you raised three kids," said Miss Arlene. "That's work isn't it?"

"I guess so," said Honey, "But I did have help."

"I'm hiring you to help me," said the old woman. "It doesn't mean I don't write my column."

Miss Arlene aimed blue veined hands at her aged Smith Corona typewriter and began to hunt and peck. It took a moment for Honey to understand that the interview had been a success.

As her first official act, she took a tissue from her purse and removed the stale brown item under Arlene's desk. Never a fan of feces, she nonetheless floated gratefully in the direction of Arlene's private washroom, the door of which was standing ajar, with the thought occurring: God disposes of dog do.

Hearing Honey's stifled laughter as the toilet flushed, Arlene exchanged a look with her canine companion which said, "What can you expect for minimum wage?"

"By the way," she remarked as Honey emerged from the john, "There's one new wrinkle around here. The secretaries all use word processors."

"Me, too," lied her brand new assistant, taking a flying leap into the rewrite.

***

Zack took his wife and her kids out for steaks to celebrate the new job. But they didn't stay long. Although Honey could have rhapsodized endlessly about *The Los Angeles Sun* and its denizens – the lovable Mr. Still, the helpful tall-and-tan, the benevolent Miss Arlene and her adorable pooch – nobody ordered dessert. Zack had to go back to the office and Corie and the twins had homework.

So did Honey. She'd need the computer, she told the boys when they got home, in a tone which she hoped would mask her ebbing confidence.

To her surprise, they not only relinquished the game room and their their favorite machine, but set it up for word processing, sharing with her the details of the commands she'd need to know.

"A typewriter was less complicated," she complained.

"Tell that to the guy who invented writing with a stick on a wet clay tablet," Sean replied.

"Or maybe the girl," said Honey.

"Excuse me?"

"You know, the stuff I've been telling you about the early temples with the priestesses . . ."

"Yeah, right," said Brian skeptically. "Anyway, Mom, it's the Age of Information. You have to be computer literate." And they left her alone.

Honey wiped damp palms on her designer jeans and prepared to copy an upcoming Arlene Morrigan column.

>Dear Miss Arlene:
>My fiancee eats her vegetables with a spoon.

Day Three: And There Were Bucks To Be Made . . .

    How can I tell her I'm
       – Put Off In Portland

Honey poised her fingers over the computer keyboard but first took another moment to admire her new boss. Here was a lady who was doing something meaningful. With her motherly advice she helped people make important decisions about their lives. Arbiter of taste, friendly adviser, and referee, Miss Arlene was also known as a wag.

To her reader she'd replied:

    Dear Put Off:
    Suggest she buy my book on etiquette, *The*
    Knife and Fork, or spoon with somebody else.

What a woman. Witty. Wise. Worldly yet warm. Wholesome yet not wishy-washy. Alright, enough procrastination.

    Der Missarl

Wrong. Try again.

    DearMiss Arlene:
    My fi annCe ea tsher v

Honey pushed the various computer keys which were supposed to help her edit her mistakes but she only made things worse.

    Dear Miss Arlene:
    My Ggfi annCe eats GGG er ve gtles
    Wit hasp j.s. How   OL+

This being back in was not as easy as it looked, but she started over, setting margins, tabs, and line spacing as she would have on a typewriter and it worked.

    Dear Miss Arlene:
    My fiancee eats her

ON THE SEVENTH DAY SHE RESTED

"Mother, I've decided, since you won't do anything about it, I'm going to pay for driving lessons for Hey Ya," Corinne interrupted from the hall.

"It worked!" said Honey.

"Did you hear me, Mother?"

vegetab4es

"Darn!"

"The only thing is," said Corie, "I've spent my allowance so I need you to borrow the first fifty dollars from Zack."

"If you'll wait a week 'til I get my first check," said a preoccupied Honey, "I'll give you the money."

GGGGveeteables

"Can't you get it from Zack? I need it in the morning, okay?"

FFFgggGETAB4ES>>gg

"Okay?" Corinne insisted.

VVVVeggggeTABL

"Mother!!!"

In turning to give her daughter the attention she demanded Honey's elbow brushed the keyboard by mistake.

FATAL ERROR

read the computer screen.

DELETE FILE

"Damn!" Honey eyed the monitor with its now blank screen. "Dr. Hess never said there'd be a computer in my lake!"

Honey's love-child eyed her mother. Zack should never have brought her home, she thought. She's still nuttier than a fruit cake.

Day Three: And There Were Bucks To Be Made...

***

Brian's, Sean's and Corinne's mom went to bed early. It had taken two more painful hours at the computer, with hands-on help from the twins, for her to learn the rudiments of word processing. And she had a job to go to in the morning.

A job to go to in the morning!!!

As she slid between the Portheault sheets and closed her eyes, the lack of Zack's back never crossed her mind. When she sat back up a moment later, it was not to question what work her husband might be doing at ten-thirty at night. It was the painting of Adam and Eve at the foot of her bed which entered her consciousness as she started to doze.

She got up, wrestled it off the wall, and hauled it into a closet.

Then she went back to bed and slept a deep, refreshing sleep.

3:2

Eve, whose name means "life", emerged from Adam. This information, as Dr. Hess inferred, is part of a relatively recent Eastern Mediterranean myth about the mother of us all.

In older stories She emerges from water. Or She comes out of the earth. In some, She is the water. In some, She is the earth. She doesn't make the water and She doesn't make the earth, although in some She does make humans out of a combination of the two.

The trouble with these older legends is that they're muddy. They raise the mind-bending question: Which came first? The chicken or the egg? And they don't answer it. They don't try. They leave us with a circular gesture about the interconnectedness of life, a way of looking at things which may have seemed reasonable tens of thousands of years ago but which lately hasn't been box-office.

But the real flaw in these Earth Goddess/Water Goddess stories is that they don't say enough about what else our Mother was making with Her mudpies: irrigation systems for Her gardens; pottery for the cooking and storing of Her vegetables; bricks to pile up into ovens, houses, temples, granaries; pitch-sealed boats on which to load the surpluses of Her thriving culture, which she traded with Her neighbors for other things you can find in the mud: tin, copper, gold, and precious jewels (Yes, Honey, God can go shopping and wear jewelery).

It's easy to misunderstand a legend.

But, once in a while, the legend personally presses the stick into the wet clay tablet.

***

Unlike Zack, Miss Arlene didn't believe in working late. One night about a week and a half into Honey's tenure, she was leaving the office at 4:00 PM with her dachshund under her arm. She wouldn't have spotted her assistant behind the overflowing mailbags if it hadn't been for the muffled crying that alerted Bones, requiring him to bark.

A tear-stained Honey looked as though she'd been peeling bags of onions instead of opening bags of mail. Miss Arlene enquired as to the trouble, but she couldn't make much sense of what was said, coming as it did through a Kleenex clenched to an already rosy nose.

She did make out the words "recession," "people having a hard time," "sorry for them," through the blowing and sniffling. She leaned in and snatched out of Honey's hand the page of correspondence which appeared to be the cause of her excess of empathy.

> Dear Miss Arlene:
> Last year the factory closed and I can't find a job. The bank is foreclosing on my house. My wife ran away with a tombstone salesman, my mother is dying of cancer, my son is in jail for smoking pot on a bus, and my dog got run over by a truck. Sometimes I go to the bridge outside of town and stare at the dark swirling waters . . .

Said Arlene, "You like it?"

"Like it?" cried Honey. "This man could be dead by now!"

Day Three: And There Were Bucks To Be Made . . .

"Calm down," said her boss. "I wrote it. I needed a grabber for a week from Thursday."

"But that's dishonest," blurted Honey, instantly sorry to have said such a thing to a woman whose moral standards were renowned.

Miss Arlene, not at all insulted, put her dog down and made herself comfortable on a mailbag. Speaking as though to a five-year-old, she asked Honey what she thought was the object of her advice column.

"To help people?" said the five-year-old.

"It's a way to make money," Arlene replied.

Her assistant, Arlene had observed, was pathetically naïve. You couldn't blame her for it. All she'd ever been was a mother. It was time somebody brought her up to speed, shoved her into the world of business whether she wanted to go or not. Arlene decided to continue kindergarten class.

"Think of my column as a carrot," she said, pointing out how it was listed on the front page of *The Sun* between Horoscope and Crossword. It was a sales incentive, she explained, so it had to be entertaining and appeal to all kinds of people. The broader the audience she attracted, the more newspapers Calvin Still would sell.

She quoted *The Sun*'s numbers: the price of advertising was based on circulation and went up or down accordingly. Up was the desired direction.

"But you do help the people who write in," said Honey, eyeing the mountains of mail.

"It's not the ones who write in we're concerned about," lectured Miss Arlene. "It's the ones who read the column. If they keep buying *The Sun*, they see products advertised. They buy 'em. So the advertiser keeps buying space. Which keeps Calvin Still in the black and able to pay my outrageous salary . . . and you your pittance."

She named other newspapers which also carried her advice and asked Honey to guess at her syndication deal: Calvin Still got a piece.

Adding the advice pamphlets she sold at three dollars each, and the five hard-cover *Best of Miss Arlene* anthologies which Still had published, and their paperback sales, and the foreign rights, the money to be made was substantial.

ON THE SEVENTH DAY SHE RESTED

To keep her goldmine rolling, she had to turn out a varied and topical product seven days a week. If she didn't have the elements, she admitted, she wrote what she needed and mailed a copy to herself in case anyone should happen to ask.

"But you do help people," insisted Honey.

"I'm trying to help you right now to understand, that like everyone else, I'm in business to make rectangular green dollars."

"Dollars you can vote with?" Honey ventured.

"Dollars I can spend!" Arlene aimed a smack at Bones who was about to lift a leg on a mailbag.

"Of course this isn't the way to make *big* money," she said in the tones of a tipster. "It's real estate. Real estate," she repeated, scooping up her hound and sweeping out of the office, leaving her secretary open-mouthed.

***

The carrot, that invader vegetable, wasn't always thought of as a sales incentive. Brought to the fertile crescent by its Northern conquerors, you might not have recognized the carrot when it came. It was purple and phallic, food for armies to travel on.

Onions, those other invaders, fed the workers (some say slaves) who built pyramids on real estate which came to be known as The Valley of the Kings.

***

Is this what it's like to be back in? Honey wondered.

She was also wondering how to file the letter.

Should it go under Factory Failure? Marital Failure? Sick Mother? Dead Dog? Arlene's filing system needed revamping so you could get your hands on things.

She was considering how to begin such a project when the phone rang in the inner office, Miss Arlene's private line.

Day Three: And There Were Bucks To Be Made . . .

She hurried, efficiently, to answer it, but before she could test her newly acquired telephone manner, she heard the heavy breathing: rasping, insistent, ugly.

Honey hung up. Wrong number, she thought. Or a random dialer. She started to leave but the phone rang again.

She thought to ignore it, but realized that this could be a different, an important caller.

"Yes?"

"Don't hang up on me, Arlene," said a creepy male voice. "I want to tie you up and gag you and slap you senseless."

Honey did hang up, in a hurry. The person had called her boss by name.

Again the phone rang. And rang. She was afraid to pick up, afraid of what she might hear next. But then, her employer, as a celebrity, was an obvious target for perverts. Do The Friendliest Thing, Honey commanded herself, deciding to lift the receiver, handle the situation, and never mention it to the dear old lady.

She paraphrased Dr. Hess:

"You, sir, are the warped product of eons of an overly aggressive religious/economic/political system."

"Huh?"

He didn't understand her logic, so she quoted Aretha: "All we're asking is for a little respect."

"What?"

He still didn't follow, so she parroted Lowell:

"Just . . . get over yourself," she said, placing the receiver back in its cradle and going back to opening the mail, Arlene's legend still intact.

At least for the time being.

***

It was almost officially spring before Miss Arlene's secretary again set foot on Rodeo Drive. These occupied-with-the-office days, no speculations about God or godliness assailed her, and Rodeo was neither the street of dreams nor a street of strangers, just an avenue from

ON THE SEVENTH DAY SHE RESTED

Wilshire to Santa Monica, the way to LaVie 'n Rose, where she waited for her hairdresser to arrive and open shop.

Her appointment was for 7:30 in the morning but LaVie was late, so she amused herself by looking in adjacent store windows crammed with the best of everything, remembering her earlier anxieties, marveling that it had taken intensive care at Dr. Hess's hospital, tapering to her current bi-weekly sessions with him, to make her see that the reason there was nothing to buy was because things were not what she needed.

Other shoppers must have had other needs, too, judging from the SALE signs which now bleated 80% OFF, begged WHOLESALE TO THE PUBLIC, whimpered GOING OUT OF BUSINESS, coldly stated FINAL LIQUIDATION, making Honey realize that one way of voting with your dollars was not to spend them.

She glanced at her own reflection. She did need a haircut. This was to be expected, she thought proudly, when trying to juggle home and career.

Well, maybe you couldn't call it a career yet. For a career you were paid an outrageous salary, not an accurate label for her take home pay, even considering a recent small raise.

As the sunlight glinted off her diamond wedding band, her thoughts glinted similarly from the weather, still no rain, to Zack and her children.

An unexpected aspect of her newly busy existence was that the less time she had for her family, the more they seemed to want it. Whereas in the past she'd felt like a bump on the log of their lives, these days Brian and Sean wished she were there when they came home from school, wanted to share with her their expertise at the computer. Corinne, cranky as ever, was only satisfied if it was her mother she was being cranky to.

Honey had always understood the chip on her daughter's shoulder, but that didn't mean she wasn't hurt by it. Since returning from Dr. Hess's she'd tried to find gentle ways to bring up the subject of illegitimacy, to dissipate the curse of it, as it had been dissipated, miraculously, for her. But the mention of matriarchal societies and the

Day Three: And There Were Bucks To Be Made . . .

way women ran things worked no miracles on Corie. She continued to feel irrevocably sidelined, left out of the way life is supposed to be.

Zack, too, was feeling left out. Last night, in the kitchen, she was trying to tell him about her raise, granted because Miss Arlene was happy with her work, when he interrupted, or rather exploded, right in the middle of her good news. He'd been trying to make himself a snack and the toaster-oven was broken, the electric knife didn't work. Where the hell was Hey Ya? With her damned driving lessons she hadn't been home since Purim! He'd whacked his bread down on the counter and gone out of the room, sulking.

Honey cut his tomato with an ordinary knife, toasted the bread with a fork over the gas flame of the kitchen stove as she once toasted bread over a campfire back in Paradise. She delivered the sandwich to the den. He had liked it. He'd apologized. He'd hugged her.

Later, in the privacy of their bedroom, he'd initiated some closer personal contact. This had been going on sporadically, recently, but there was something not quite smooth about it. From his side there was a hint of possessiveness, and from hers an over-eager motivation to throw off the lost years and behave more like her uninhibited female forebears. Coming together last night they'd frightened one another and backed off into safe, sane, married sex. There were no gymnastics, no animal cries, but there was comfort. After it was over, he'd finally congratulated her on her ten dollar a week raise. Then he just had to add: "Don't spend it all in one place."

She laughed, remembering this exchange. She was grateful for him and for her children. No matter their moods it was good to go home to them after a day at *The Sun*. Miss Arlene, though much more successful, went home with Bones to an empty apartment.

Alright, half an hour of waiting for LaVie was too much. She had to get to work. Lack of friendliness was about to set in when her hairdresser rushed around the corner, puffing apologies.

Honey was ushered into the beauty parlor, the décor of which featured some article from every decade of the 20th Century.

LaVie's chairs were Bauhaus, her sofa Beidermeyer. Her sinks were from the twenties, her lighting from the thirties, her music from the forties, her mirrors from the fifties. Her posters, mostly of gurus, were from the sixties and seventies, but LaVie was trapped in today.

"Slept late. Not sick. Just bummed," she blinked with eyes ringed in two-tone liner, her mouth a purple lipstick slash, her shocked face framed by voluminous red hair gelled to a frenzy. "I've been like this for weeks.

"Remember Garth? My boyfriend?" she said, handing Honey a wrap to change into.

"We went to this Wizard of Oz bash? I went as Dorothy? I had the ruby slippers."

Honey emerged from the changing room and was pointed to the sink.

"So anyway, the party cooks and Garth is real cowardly – he went as the Lion – but now it's over? And everyone's leaving? And it's time to go home to Kansas?" she seated her client and leaned closer, her souvenir of Florida earrings dangling as she wetted down Honey's hair.

"And I'm waiting and waiting and waiting for Garth, and clicking my red plastic shoes?

"When somebody tells me he's in the bedroom with the Wicked Witch of The West. And the Witch is, like, another guy? I mean, I went home to Kansas and stayed there!"

LaVie got busy with the shampoo.

"Oh, it's not what you're thinking. I got tested right away. They can tell you in five days if you've been exposed to . . . whatever. But it isn't that. It's just, why me? Why Garth? I almost married him.

"Life!" she sighed. "How's yours?" lobbing the ruby slippers into Honey's court.

Honey allowed that things had been interesting.

"So I heard," said the hairdresser massaging lather into the Newman locks.

"I'm working now," said Honey. "I got a job at *The Sun*."

"Not that," said LaVie. "Tell about the farm."

Honey wracked her brain for the meaning of this sentence.

Day Three: And There Were Bucks To Be Made...

"The funny farm," clarified LaVie. "I heard you were out at Dr. Hess's place in Malibu for a month. Lowell told me. You know, Whatchamacallit's son? That schitzed-out little druggie? He said you were God. That's what I want to hear about."

Honey kept her face impassive. She didn't want to go into it.

But her hairdresser did.

"Lowell says you're going to be great," Lavie insisted. "He told me your Commandment about the Vegetables? And the Breathing one? And the one about Doing The Neatest Thing? And Shhhh! They sound kind of deep, so I know he's right."

"Look," said Honey, simply, "I was having a nervous breakdown. I guess I wanted some control over my life."

"That's what everyone wants," said LaVie, wrapping Honey's wet hair in a towel and moving her to another chair, "including me."

She combed the tangles out, and got her scissors ready.

"Which is why I've decided to become your first d'votie."

"C'mon, LaVie."

"I mean it. In the last five years I've been with Radananda? I was a Sikh for a week. I met Garth at McMurphy Baba's ashram up in Ojai? I've got a closet full of turbans, robes, and prayer beads and you know what? With Garth in the bedroom with the Wicked Witch, it all seemed nil, dumb and void.

"It's getting too rough out there," she said. "I need a new creed."

She paused to examine Honey's hair from a number of angles.

"I think we'll change the style a little. I don't see God with bangs, do you?"

"I like my bangs," said Honey firmly.

"Okay, Most High. Speak and I will serve."

She knelt, flailing scissors, as she bowed her forehead to the black and white tiled floor.

"LaVie, get over yourself!" laughed Honey, using her new favorite phrase, hoping to communicate the unsuitability of her hairdresser's actions.

"Get Over Yourself," LaVie savored the words.

"Savage Commandment," she said, getting up from the floor. "Semi-Buddhist. I love it already. Do I have to get an outfit?"

3:3

Spring days are days of heavy labor in a garden: spading, weeding, seeding, feeding fill the list of things to do. But the vernal equinox found Honey digging in at *The Los Angeles Sun*. Her encounter with her hairdresser put aside, half forgotten, she was content to be laboring for Miss Arlene, a boss in a million.

Miss A. had been all for it when she suggested a complete reworking of the filing system, making correspondence more accessible under major topics of interest – letters about Sex, Health, and Money filled the most file drawers so far. She didn't mind at all that Honey ate lunch while filing and sometimes changed her appointment with her psychologist in order to file after five.

Which was already paying off. Just by looking at the bulk of letters under any topic, Honey could tell what aspect of what issue people were most concerned about.

Under Sex, for example, it was abortion, which some people said was being overused as a method of birth control, and which others said was not available enough to the very young and the very poor. Some people said it was a crime even though it was legal. Others said it was the right of every woman and girl.

Miss Arlene, however, said the topic was a no-no, a not-for-her-column. Whatever side she took she'd make somebody mad. She'd lose readers.

Under Health it was AIDS, but Arlene wasn't jumping on that roller-coaster, either. She said it was preventable, therefore not a plague, though terrifying to insurance companies who were doing their best to avoid paying for the costly hospitalization of its victims. By her calculations it had infected a mere .00003 percent of the American population, even though Calvin Still, with his provocative headlines, might have the public believe otherwise.

Day Three: And There Were Bucks To Be Made . . .

Worse, it was a political hotcake, with the religious right using fear of it to smash the sexual revolution, and the liberal left using fear of it to push the right into accepting birth control in the form of condoms.

Miss Arlene had decided to let them duke it out and then pick a side to be on. Meanwhile she'd stick with less controversial diseases like ordinary, everyday, cancer. One in three Americans was stalked by that contemporary saber-toothed tiger. It rightfully scared the daylights out of everyone. She planned to do more on it soon.

Prevailing sentiments in the letters in each file worked as an informal poll. This was the component of Honey's filing system most useful to her employer.

Take the subject of smoking in public places, which Arlene planned to use in kicking off her cancer columns. Though she personally went through three packs of Camels a day, Miss Arlene would align with the clean air types because, as letters from readers indicated, that was the way the wind was blowing.

Yet she intended to keep her smoking readers sanguine by pointing out that although most people with lung cancer were smokers, only seven percent of smokers got lung cancer. If a genetic key, some chromosomal similarity could be found, which made the seven percent susceptible, it was possible that the winds would shift. Then she'd scrap her pamphlet *How Second Hand Smoke Affects Your Lungs* and switch to *Your Rights As A Smoker*.

As Honey had by now discovered, Miss Arlene, whose business was opinion, had her opinion formed by business. She didn't necessarily always Do The Friendliest Thing. But this disappointment only slightly lessened the thrill of being an insider.

In addition to her filing project, Honey had been given a new challenge: to do research for the column, interviewing experts who could be quoted so her boss didn't have to stick her neck out. Arlene prepared a list of people and subjects. Under cancer was a name Honey knew, a name she had never read, or said, or thought, without putting a spin on it; a name which had had a direct and dramatic impact on her life. Of course, by now you've guessed that the name was Margo Best.

ON THE SEVENTH DAY SHE RESTED

***

Cucumber, chicory and rue were the abortifacients of choice in the pre-historic Mediterranean, used if and when other vegetables didn't live up to their billing: when dill didn't work to weaken the powers of generation; when lettuce, with its slightly sedative properties, didn't reduce the urge to merge.

Cancer, or carcinoma, was known in Pliny The Elder's Rome. He recommended an already-age-old vegetable cure. It was root of wild lupin pounded together with . . .

But perhaps we should concentrate on more modern matters of life and death and dinner.

***

Here's something different: Honey making the long trip from the city out to Broad Beach on an early April evening to visit her ex-husband's wife.

But the day had been full of surprises: Margo's unstinting accommodation when she called her at her laboratory – the first substantive conversation she and Margo had ever had – which led to an invitation to dinner at Margo and Roger's home. What really surprised Honey was hearing herself say "yes."

She had never set foot in what used to be her own home since Roger's second wife had occupied it. It wasn't that Margo never invited her. She'd always refused to go. She could never forget the moment during the divorce when her lawyer told her there was no community property. Roger had placed all his assets in trust for the twins. When she signed the papers, she hadn't understood that if she and Roger split up, he'd keep the house and everything else.

Honey jammed her foot down on the gas pedal of Zack's castoff Mercedes, much as she used to over-rev her mental Mack truck, and was doing close to eighty on Coast Route One. She almost didn't notice she was passing Dr. Hess's hospital. His beach club sign whizzed

Day Three: And There Were Bucks To Be Made . . .

past her windshield and she had to brake to have a look at the property stretched calmly along the ocean under a rising crescent moon.

Property. Assets. In her youth, girls, even the daughters of real estate tycoons, weren't taught much about such things. Nor did they teach each other. They talked more about frivolous subjects like love.

Thankfully, girls were smarter now. Women were smarter now. She was smarter, thanks to Dr. Hess. And Miss Arlene was a good teacher. Honey hadn't missed the point where her instructors' philosophies merged: that wealth, the capture and control of it made the world go around.

But while Arlene stopped there, Dr. Hess went further at their bi-weekly meetings. He emphasized that the acquisition of wealth ought not to become the whole goal of women just because they were back in a position to complete for it. If history and pre-history meant anything, greed was not the route to paradise but the high-road to hell.

As he said, getting richer could be viewed in more ways than one. There was real gold in the golden rule.

The way for women to change the world, he thought, was to keep reminding it of the values which humanized humans: sharing, loyalty, selflessness, qualities often considered feminine. These qualities, held as ideals, could turn the next century into a renaissance instead of a rehash. But they needed restating. Here he paid her a compliment: "Your Commandments are right on the button."

Honey turned off the highway down the beach road she'd driven so often and pulled her car into Roger's parking space. "Sharing." "Loyalty." "Selflessness." Those three words weren't in his dictionary.

Reaching for her tape recorder, she headed for the familiar cedar-shake cottage on the dunes.

Tonight, Margo had said, Roger was going to see his channeler. In Honey's day he'd been sleeping under a pyramid and raising his endorphins with sex. But at least it would be easier not having to deal with him and his parameters. And the way he always had one hand on Margo's behind.

ON THE SEVENTH DAY SHE RESTED

Keep Breathing, she reminded herself. She'd come here to work, not to inflame her animosity.

The porch light bathed two baskets of orange impatiens in a warm glow. Margo had painted the front door turquoise and bricked the steps. It all said "Homey, comfy, beachy, happy." Two windsurfing boards leaned casually near the door insisting "healthy, fit, coordinated, happy." Two pairs of foot-massaging sandals sat toe to toe on the top step singing "inseparable, sensual, intimate, happy."

"Shhhh!" Honey commanded the entryway and herself.

Margo had heard the car pull up and opened the front door before Honey could ring the bell.

"The daiquiris are made," she said. "I put in three shots of lime juice. We deserve it."

She showed the former occupant of the house into the living room which looked prettier than Honey had ever seen it.

Margo was growing orchids in the bay window.

She was a competent watercolorist. Her beach scenes decorated the room.

A Caribbean supper of duck and yam salad flaunted itself on her deeply shining sideboard. Was she expecting a photographer from *Bon Appetit*?

Honey compared her own anything-but-green thumb, her lack of any particular talent, her inability to put together more than a B.L.T., and felt ashamed. No wonder Roger ran off with this absolutely terrific girl.

Margo small-talked amiably until all the ice was broken, asked how Honey liked her new job, said how fond she was of the twins, and, of course, Corinne; enquired whether she was giving an Easter, or rather a Passover dinner this year.

While her attention was always on her visitor, her eye caught things that needed doing. She picked a dead leaf off the schefflera near her hibiscus-yellow sofa, tidied some magazines in a basket near the sideboard on her way to the promised libation which she offered her guest.

Eventually, Honey raised the subject she had come to discuss.

Day Three: And There Were Bucks To Be Made...

"Cancer research?" said Margo, bringing extra cocktail napkins in case Honey should need one. "Basically, it's about making money."

***

Yams, science says, originated in India on the east side of the Bay of Bengal, then were carried into Africa, Europe, and to the farthest Pacific islands.

There are also two yams of African origin, and one which evolved on the Atlantic side of Central America.

Can a vegetable "originate" in three places? This is a question which needs looking into.

Yams, to their credit, contain an estrogen precursor. Perhaps they were the pre-historic hormone replacement pill.

***

Jelia put food in the stomachs of the twins and Corinna, all the while hiding her disapproval. Neither Senor Zack nor Senora Honey would be eating at home because both were working late. Senor, he was the breadwinner. His absence was as it should be. But she couldn't fathom why Mrs. was spending so much time away from her children.

After loading the dishwasher – that was now fixed: she wasn't an idiot – she finished dying the colored eggs which would be hidden at the Newman family's upcoming Easter-Seder, along with the matzo.

By now she was used to their strange celebrations, but where, in either tradition, did the bunny come in?

It must have something to do with spring, she decided, making sure not to place all her eggs in one basket.

Si. Spring. Season of renewal.

But since when did a rabbit lay eggs?

Never mind. If she just put the eggs away and completed the Newman ironing, she'd be ready for her driving lesson.

There might also be time to call about an ad she'd seen in the Spanish language newspaper about part-time help that was needed at a fast food stand in East L. A. If she could moonlight on her Monday off, she'd be able to get the money sooner, the out of reach money that she needed to pay El Coyote to smuggle her own little ones from Guatemala into the United States.

As she bent to complete her chores, she dreamed of a holiday table surrounded by her dear Ruphina, her darling Asuncion, her charming Srafin, and her mother who was caring for them now: her sainted mother who raised so many children of her own, providing for Jelia and her brothers and sisters by selling vegetables in the street, as their father became more and more alcoholic with the birth of each baby, his pride destroyed because he couldn't make enough money to feed and house them all. Although her mother had begged the village priest, she'd given birth to fifteen children before he finally said she wouldn't burn in hell for all eternity if she tied her tubes.

***

Getting back to those multiple yams, did they spring up individually in various Gardens of Eden, or did they have a common ancestor?

The latter is the accepted answer. But how did those sneaky yams get themselves around the world? Yams can't walk. They can't fly. And they make no seed for an animal to carry.

It looks like Eve was more than a farmer. She was quite a traveller, too.

***

A post-midnight moon was high in the sky and Honey was just leaving Broad Beach. It would take her close to an hour to get home.

The breeze off the Pacific was heavy with the smell of the ocean, a reminder of rain, still lacking in Los Angeles. She rolled down the car windows to let in the sea air and tried to sort out what Margo had told her.

Day Three: And There Were Bucks To Be Made . . .

Every year in the U.S., she'd said, hundreds of billions of dollars were being spent on cancer. Millions went into research, but more millions went to the hospitals, pathology labs, nursing homes, doctors, drug and insurance companies, who provided goods and services to the cancer consumer. Although Honey was sure Miss Arlene would never print it, Margo said cancer was one of the biggest businesses in the country.

Margo's piece of the pie was a sizable grant from a pharmaceutical house to the university where she worked. The funding had a time limit, and within the next ten months, if she didn't prove her experiments valid scientifically, the money would run out, her research would stop and might be completely discarded.

The research involved administering doses of a newly discovered hormone to terminal cancer volunteers in a effort to increase their white blood cell counts, and, as Margo put it, shift their immune systems into overdrive. Her work held promise for AIDS victims as well, but so far results had been spotty. Some patients responded immediately, others died. Margo said it was like doing a jigsaw puzzle with half the pieces missing. Some of these pieces were being worked on by other scientists, but Honey was surprised to hear her say there was an expected lack of cooperation between them. It was built in.

"Why?"

"Because, whoever breaks through is going to make the bread. They'll own the patents on the drugs."

"What if it doesn't take drugs?"

"That'd be a shock to The Man, wouldn't it?" Margo had said, serving Honey her second cup of coffee, tidying the sideboard, tidying the coffee table, tidying everything in sight before she finally sat down.

"There are so many factors in disease that the health industry isn't sure how to incorporate into its thinking," she said, sinking into the sofa. "Genetic predisposition: that's the hot one right now." She slipped her shoes off and put her feet up. "Did you know that we humans share DNA with everything else on the planet? It goes way beyond our being related to chimpanzees. We're related to plants!

We're related to billion year old simple celled organisms floating around in the water.

"In the future it may be possible to replace our defective genes with genes from some living thing which never gets the disease we're trying to eliminate." She failed to stifle a yawn.

"Of course, right now they're just starting to figure out the chromosomal similarities."

"And then there's psychological makeup," she added, rubbing her eyes. "Some people cure themselves, y'know. They just decide to, with diet, religion, even. Some people live because their families refuse to get along without them. Others die when you know you've cured them.

"I don't know," she leaned back and closed her eyes. "What's a carcinogen? What is its antidote? Every day I wonder whether I'm barking up the wrong tree.

"Maybe I'm just selling snake oil. Maybe I've wasted the last ten years of my life. At least," she added faintly, in the instant before she fell asleep, "that's what Roger says."

Honey could never have explained her next move. In it were traces of mother and daughter, two members of the same high wire act, a couple of Amazon queens. She leaned over, took Margo's sleeping face in her hands and kissed her on the forehead. Then she erased everything on her tape recorder and went home.

***

Chromosomal similarity question: yams again. If yams from India, Africa, and Central America have a common ancestor, would it be fair to say that they had one mother and a bunch of different dads?

***

At one-fifteen AM, Zack was sliding his white Rolls Royce Corniche into his home driveway, gingerly aiming his automatic opener at the garage door.

Day Three: And There Were Bucks To Be Made . . .

After Rayanne left the office, he'd fallen asleep. When he finally awakened to find it was after midnight, he'd jumped into his clothes and hurried home like a teenager expecting to get a geshrei from his parents. Now here he was trying to sneak into the house. He hoped the noisy automatic door to the four car garage wouldn't wake Honey.

With a sound like two freight trains dancing a gavotte the metal door rolled up into its tracks and came to a stop with a bang. Zack was too busy wincing at first to notice Honey's car wasn't there. Once he spied the empty space he experienced a wave of relief. There would be no questions. But then it came to him that there were, perhaps, a few questions he should be asking, like: Where the fuck is my wife?

In the kitchen he read the note, "Gone to Roger's," with a twinge of, what? Jealousy?

"Putz," he castigated himself. No problem there. He helped himself to a banana out of the fruit bowl.

Still, maybe he should call and see if she left Broad Beach.

He checked this impulse and headed upstairs. You didn't go bothering people in the middle of the night. What if they were in bed?

He was halfway up the sweeping staircase with the banana half peeled and sliding into his mouth when this thought turned on him.

Put it out of your mind, he told himself. Honey and Roger? It's disgusting.

She must have been to bed with him, though.

She lived with him for nine and a half years.

They had twin boys to show for it.

Maybe he should pick up a phone.

Forget it, he thought. She hates Roger. She loves you.

He finished his banana in the bedroom, left the peel on the Duke's campaign chest, changed into his pajamas, but a new question arose: Then how come you don't have kids together?

Zack should have figured out how hard it would have been for Honey to conceive with the birth control he'd been using: Rayanne. But he chose to think of it another way.

She didn't want any more children. She had enough children already.

And now she had her little job.

He climbed into the four-poster but a new thought nagged him. What if she never went to Roger's to begin with? What if she . . .

Not a chance, he decided. Honey wouldn't fool around. She didn't have that strong a sex drive.

Confidently, he adjusted his pillow, closed his eyes and got ready for sleep.

Well, she didn't used to, but . . .

Wakeful again, he reached over and turned on the stereo. An old rock 'n roll tape was already on there, hadn't been rewound.

"Sock it to me, sock it to me, sock it to me, sock it to me . . ."

Zack extinguished the music, got up and found himself a magazine, then climbed back into bed. Was he waiting up for Honey? No. He just wasn't tired yet.

Except he was. Soon the words blurred on the page and his head drooped forward. Hey, he tried to keep up with the rewrite, but glottal sounds began to emanate from his windpipe, then built to a crescendo until the bedroom rocked to the sound of his snoring by the light of the pale morning moon.

3:4

The moon, the moon as the female principle, The Mother as The Moon, is another early Mediterranean myth, a myth still shared by people around the globe. In it She's the oracle in the sky who advises when to plant and harvest, when the tides will rise and fall, when women will conceive their babies, and when refresh their wombs.

But there are scholars who say that myth is a demotion from a time when She was The Sun (it's hard, even for an agricultural goddess, to grow vegetables in the dark).

To pre-Arabs, pre-Australians, and pre-Indians in pre-India, she was the one who rolled around heaven all day.

It was She who warmed the frozen north in lands where She shone until midnight.

Day Three: And There Were Bucks To Be Made . . .

She was The Sun in Anatolia, pre-Turkey, in 17000 BCE, and She's still The Sun in Japan, today, with thousands of shrines in Her honor and Her image on the national flag.

***

Honey was in her office by 8:30 the next morning. She wanted to sort and file a stack of incoming letters before Miss Arlene's nine o'clock meeting with Calvin Still. She wanted everything, her organized desk, her neatly secretarial appearance, and her soon-to-be-empty file basket to impress her boss and the publisher.

She opened one gleaming white drawer in the bank of files which covered one wall of her office, slotting letters which she deemed of interest into hanging folders where they'd stay until Miss Arlene had a use for them.

Her filing system was becoming a work of art. By now she'd classified and sub-classified Arlene's backlog of mail under specific topics.

MONEY filled five drawers.

> Main heading: MONEY
> Drawer One: Not Having Any
> Drawer Two: Having Some But Not Enough
> Drawer Three: Having Enough But From The Wrong Source
> Drawer Four: Having It Just Right But Worried It Will Stop
> Drawer: Having Too Much

The readers' dream was to find themselves in Drawer Five like Bianca on *Inheritance*, or Norman Nathanson himself, the series' super-rich producer.

At one time the amount to strive for was a million dollars, but these days a million was a drop in the bucket if you wanted to be taken seriously. Even in a recession people wanted it all. They wanted what Zack called "the fuck you money." Zack wanted the fuck you money, which some people might have thought he already had, but which he didn't think he had because he couldn't say "fuck you" to Norman Nathanson. Still, Norman Nathanson couldn't say "fuck you" to the Queen of England.

But how much was more than you needed?

As Honey had observed, the more money you had, the more you spent, until you found yourself working around the clock, like poor Zack, to pay off the bigger mortgage and the flashier car. And the more time you spent making money, the less time you had to take care of the too-many things you owned, so you had to make more money to pay the people you had to hire to do everything for you because you were too busy making money: help like Jelia who could barely keep up these days with half the appliances broken, and the appliance repairman who never seemed to come, and the gardener, the one Zack hired, who'd quit when a neighbor offered him more money.

Which reminded her, neither she nor Rayanne had been able to find a qualified replacement and Zack was having a fit. She'd rushed around last weekend herself, pulling out dead flowers, which made things look a little tidier but now she had these gaping beds of dirt.

The exposed black earth made her think with pleasure of spring days in her old home town, of double-digging at Dr. Hess's, and of long-lost springtimes when civilization began with cultivation of the land. Land which, when women were in charge, they supposedly shared.

But if the tablets they'd found in those goddess temples talked about real estate . . .

For a moment she pictured Eve hammering a "For Sale" sign on the Garden of Eden.

She chuckled. It was ludicrous. Though if Eve was anything like Miss Arlene . . .

"Filing," she admonished herself and went back to it. She'd think about gardens later.

Another five drawer topic was SEX, which broke down, surprisingly, just like MONEY once she weeded out the no-nos: letters about abortion, which she ditched, and letters from people who were Scared Of Dying From It which she placed in their proper file under Health, sub-heading AIDS, which her boss was still avoiding like the plague.

Main Heading: SEX

Drawer One: Not Getting Any

Day Three: And There Were Bucks To Be Made . . .

  Drawer Two: Getting Some But Not Enough
  Drawer Three: Getting A Lot But From The Wrong Person
  Drawer Four: Getting It just Right But Worried It Will Stop
  Drawer Five: Getting Too Much

 Again, readers were programmed from cradle to grave to long for Drawer Five, but if they got there they didn't much like it. Honey had been in that drawer with Roger, a man ruled by his senses. She knew it was no nirvana.

 She'd been in Drawer Four with Gene Green and that, to quote the country song, was nothing but a heartache.

 Lately, with Zack, she'd jumped from Drawer One into Drawer Two . . .

 Sex. No one was ever satisfied. She wondered if they'd been any happier when women were on top.

 Her third major topic was HEALTH.

 Main Heading HEALTH filled seven drawers but here her subheads were less cut and dried, the subject was so vast and so weighted.

 From what Margo said, she ought to make a file for Health As A Percentage Of Gross National Product, but Miss Arlene was never going to find that angle useful. She'd never question the health industry in print.

 For the same reason Healing Alternatives would turn out to be a dead letter file even though more and more readers were writing to enquire about old remedies, treatments from other cultures, home care, preventive medicine, including eating more vegetables. What they seemed to want was a kinder approach to illness.

 They still wanted to be cured, though. And fast. North Americans didn't approve of sickness or death, didn't accept it for themselves or others.

 Even so, they didn't want their next of kin kept on life support when there was no hope of recovery – Honey was unsure whether to file those letters under HEALTH or under MONEY.

 Strangely, the subject which filled the smallest number of drawers was LOVE. This was because so many letters about love could more accurately be filed under SEX.

More could be filed under MONEY. Who had the assets, how they got them, and what they were likely to do with them complicated every relationship: another "yes" for Dr. Hess.

Did anyone even know what LOVE was anymore? Should she start a drawer for Doing The Friendliest Thing? Should she set up files for Sharing, Loyalty, and Selflessness? Or were they doomed to be empty?

She was engrossed in these filing issues when her hairdresser walked into her office.

"You have given me no sign," said LaVie.

"I beg your pardon?" replied Honey.

"I've been waiting for The Call."

"I'm sorry. I haven't had time to make a hair appointment."

"I'm not talking hair, here. I'm talking about my divine mission. What is it?"

LaVie shook out her own cloud of red hair and pushed up the sleeves of the 1930's flower print dress she was wearing with a pair of tall black cowboy boots, a costume she'd rounded out with an armful of Mickey Mouse watches.

Honey checked her own watch. In approximately five minutes her boss and her boss's boss would be arriving for their meeting. Perhaps, she suggested to LaVie, they could talk another time.

"Thy Will Be Done," said the hairdresser. "But I have amazing stuff to tell you. I can wait 'til you're free." Remembering not to bow, she put her hands together in a worshipful position and knelt in front of Honey's desk.

With one eye on the door, Honey hurried to the younger woman and helped her to her feet, deciding it might be better if they talked now.

"First of all," LaVie began, "I want you to know I'm not going into this thing lightly. I don't just, zap, become a d'votie anymore, not since Lama Labow screwed me out of my last forty dollars.

"So I went to the library? And looked up if God could be a chick?

"And know what I discovered? Girls were God *all over the world*! Gaia, Isis, Amaterasu, Al-Uzza, Shing Moo, Fir Dea, Harmonia, Ma

Day Three: And There Were Bucks To Be Made...

Mata, Unakuagsak, Nu Qua," she paused to catch up with herself, then whispered conspiratorially, "Demeter!"

Old habits die hard and Lavie went down into a deep bow from which she showed no sign of coming up.

"*Please* don't do that," said Honey fervently.

"Oh, yeah, sorry." The girl arose. "So anyway, My Goddess, where do we go from here?"

Quietly, Honey explained that she wanted LaVie to redirect her energies. She, herself, was concentrating on being Miss Arlene's secretary. She'd only had the job a short while and it might not look good if it got around that she had other pretensions.

"You don't trust me to spread the word," pouted LaVie.

"Please understand," said a frustrated Honey.

"I understand. I must make myself worthy. I must Give And Receive Vegetables. I must Keep Breathing, Shut Up, Be Friendly, and Get Over Myself." She headed for the door. "Don't worry. When you're ready, I'll be ready."

For a moment it seemed as through she'd bow again, but she thought better of it, adding: "I already took a bag of sweet potatoes over to Garth and his boyfriend. But they wouldn't let me in."

Honey could hear the sound of Miss Arlene and Calvin Still's laughter in the hall as they walked toward the office.

"So I left them on the doorstep. I guess it's a start." With a reverent last look and a wave of her many Mickeys, she left the office, brushing by Mr. Still and the advice columnist as they came in.

Honey glanced at them sheepishly, half-expecting questions, but the publisher and the aging oracle didn't even acknowledge her. Absorbed in their business discussion, they walked into Arlene's office and closed the door.

***

A sweet potato, we need to note, is different from a yam. And different from a potato. It's a root, not a tuber, discovered by Columbus on his second trip to the New World, a world which was actually not that new since people had been living there and probably eating sweet potatoes for what? ten thousand years? before he came.

The storming Spanish introduced the vegetable into Northern Mexico, and the storming English introduced it into North America. But if you wanted to introduce yourself to the mother of a sweet potato, you'd go shake hands with a morning glory.

***

Heel down, arch down, toes down, sweating, sweating. In his own world, the monk, Sah, put one foot in front of the other under a tropical sun. He had no questions left about sex or health or money but he still had one burning desire. For months he'd felt he was close to his goal, if only he could reach out and grab it.

Right here, right now, for a moment, he could almost taste it – oneness – feel it, be it, empty/full, when suddenly every living thing in the steaming rainforest seemed to be shouting at him, "Awaken! Awaken! Awaken! BOK!"

He stopped walking, blinded by tears, utterly discouraged, and lowered his head in defeat.

"Okay," he choked, breaking his twenty year silence. "Okay, I give up."

A drop of water fell from his eye, catching the sunlight in an exquisite way, as though a diamond had dropped into his path. Then, quite simply, it disappeared into the mud. Near his big toe, splashed by his tear, an anonymous green sprout quivered.

At once, Sah was taken with a fit of the giggles as silly as those which frequently visited themselves on Brian and Sean. And every rock, bird, bug and branch, extinct pterodactyls, unborn babies, everything in the cosmic continuum laughed with him.

He returned to his cave, packed up his bowl and blanket and toddled down the mountain. Entering the gates of the monastery, his brother monks observed the grace he exuded with every step, the light which radiated from him.

His teacher, too, saw a man who'd gotten it all.

Day Three: And There Were Bucks To Be Made . . .

"What now?" he asked, once they were alone.
Said Sah, "I think I'll go for a walk."

3:5

In some Mediterranean legends The Great Mother *is* it all. She's the face of the universe, the head of heaven and earth, the source, the circle, the whole shebang, the beginning and the end. She's the active, the positive, the energy of day, and the passive, the negative, the restful night: the darkness from which everything, animal, vegetable, mineral, even an idea is born, and to which it will inevitably return, only to be born again.

Now some people equate darkness with evil. Some people equate darkness with sin. But we've come too far for that argument. It's wearing very thin.

***

When Honey got back from her coffee break, Miss Arlene remained closeted with Calvin Still. The mail had arrived so she got to it.

> Dear Arlene:
> The pictures came out nice.
> I like the ones of you with the midget wrestlers.

This was the one aspect of her job that Honey hated. Miss Arlene, as she'd suspected, was often the target of cranks but this letter was the cruelest she'd ever seen.

> I want $50,000.00 by Wed. Apr. 11 or these go to *The National Probe.*

The letter was unsigned. Honey decided to destroy it as she did with all mail from pranksters and perverts. But the envelope wouldn't crumple. There was something inside it.

ON THE SEVENTH DAY SHE RESTED

She shook the contents onto her desk and gawked at three photographs of her boss, with her withered breasts bared, in a red lace garter belt, net stockings not hiding her bony legs, spike heels, and a satin half-mask, united, variously, with the obliging gentlemen. It was unmistakably her, with no teeth and her dog Bones napping in the background.

It would be a lie to say that Arlene's assistant didn't have at least one judgmental moment. It would be stretching the truth to say that she didn't have two or three. But an irresistible further glance at the photographs convinced Honey that her aged employer, engaged in her rituals, was more to be pitied than despised.

Honey had no idea how she got through the rest of the day, which happened to be Wednesday, April the eleventh. The threat to her boss was real and immediate but Honey couldn't get a moment alone with her.

After Calvin Still came the United Association of Undertakers, lobbying Miss Arlene to use her column to push embalming and traditional burial instead of other methods of disposing of the dead. Honey took distracted notes as they outlined the benefits to the family of a full, and expensive, funeral.

In exchange for their views in print, with perhaps a mention of the advantages of pre-arrangement, where the cemeterians could have the money in advance, in particular the money for the scrap of land where the loved-one was going to be be buried, they promised to provide Miss Arlene with the grandest funeral L. A. had ever seen, including top-of-the-line coffin, deluxe limousines, choice burial site, an elaborate monument, and flowers in perpetuity. All would be free of charge whenever the need should arise, which, they were sure, would not be for a long, long, time.

Miss Arlene accepted their offer because, as she put it, a funeral gave everyone a chance to say goodbye. It was a healthy outlet for grief and she had always believed in it.

This was a load and Honey knew it. Office gossip was still buzzing about the way Arlene had cremated her husband Sidney, scattered his ashes at sea, and bragged that it had saved her thousands. There had

Day Three: And There Were Bucks To Be Made...

been no funeral, no plot, no monument to the man she'd lived with for forty-one years.

But Miss Arlene's assistant had more pressing matters on her mind. Her concern mounted as her employer took the undertakers' gift certificate of death and went off with them to lunch.

When Arlene returned there was no chance to take her aside. Waiting was a delegation from City Hall with plans for a "Miss Arlene Day."

A frazzled Honey served coffee, half hearing, as the city's representatives outlined their proposals. Arlene Morrigan was to be given the key to the city. There would be special television coverage. As part of the celebration, the delegates thought it would be fun to fly in certain people who'd written unforgettable letters, like that fellow who went bankrupt, whose wife ran off, his dog died and his son was in jail. He was suicidal when he wrote to Miss Arlene. She'd undoubtedly saved his life.

Honey started to pay attention. How was her boss going to get out of this one?

"Unfortunately," said Arlene, frowning, "we didn't get to him in time."

"He died?" said a saddened member of the delegation as she nodded mournfully.

Huh, thought Honey, I wonder if he had a prepaid funeral.

As the City Hall people left, Miss Arlene's lawyers arrived. She had several real estate deals closing. With the recession causing land values to bottom out, she was snapping up as much property as she could.

She also snapped at her secretary when asked discreetly but urgently if Honey could see her privately. What she wanted "Right now!" was for Honey to order hamburgers for everyone, then type up contracts.

Honey complied, forcing herself to gulp down her own burger while concentrating on the complicated legal documents which recorded the change of ownership of land: contracts defining boundaries and buildings, conveniences, contingencies, mineral rights, taxes, insurance, and dollar value.

Nowhere, she noticed, did they define trusteeship of the acreage. Caretaking was not a part of the contracts, nor was there any mention of vegetables. Or babies. The babies which came with the vegetables which came with the land when The Great Mother was Queen.

***

Lying on her bedroom floor, propped up by the ridiculous pink gingham pillows which matched her dopey pink gingham duvet (Honey's decorators had just assumed she'd have a frilly, girly lack of taste), Corinne sampled television channels which were also an insult to her intelligence: first the eight o'clock movie, another peurile film about teens trying to get lucky, then MTV which was about everybody trying to get lucky, then an ecological program on insects, but before she knew it even the spiders and the moths and the praying mantises were trying to get lucky.

She settled for an in-depth discussion of world hunger which detailed promising new methods of growing food in underdeveloped countries where famine raged.

"Birth control," she said to the TV set, reiterating a favorite theme, positive that it was lack of family planning which got these starving women and their starving children in a bind in the first place.

Was Corie using birth control? No need. She wasn't seeing anyone at the moment. Well, the truth was she never had seen anyone.

She went out with friends, but most of the boys she knew were so ignorant. They wouldn't know a social issue if it landed in their soup. They were just like her multiple parent figures, only interested in money. The parking lot at school looked like an exotic car dealership. At least Corinne had the moral conscience to drive an old Volkswagen, which she'd paid for with her own money. Hadn't she saved every birthday and Christmas check Red and Missy had given her? And hadn't she contributed some of that money to the Food Project at Ralph's Market, helping to feed the hungry?

Which brought her back to her point. With birth control and a practical approach to abortion there wouldn't be any hungry, and nothing,

Day Three: And There Were Bucks To Be Made...

not wild horses or the throaty rumbling of dual exhausts in the driveway could sway her from her strongly held conviction. The crackling of glasspacks on a black Chevy lowrider with tinted windows and custom chrome only underscored her disgust with reactionaries who refused to recognize the simple truth. The revving of the V8 engine and the shrill sound of the air horn as it played *La Cucaracha* could only – *HIM!*

Corinne raced to the window.

It was him. The actual Innocencio. He was getting out of the car. He was coming to the kitchen door. And her only pair of Guess jeans was in the wash!

With the back door buzzer ringing insistently, Corie scurried to improve her appearance, smoothing the wrinkles out of her Camp Beverly Hills teeshirt and straightening her baggy khaki army pants. She ran her fingers through her hair, wet her lips, pinched her cheeks and ran down the stairs, taking them two at a time in her purple high-top sneakers.

In the kitchen, she stopped herself to get a grip, deciding to let the buzzer ring two more times before answering.

"Good evening, Innocencio," she finally said, opening the door to him. "How are you this evening?"

Right away she felt foolish for saying "evening" twice.

"Isn't it a nice evening?" she commented, then wished she could drop into a hole. Innocencio was staring at her. No wonder.

"So what are you up to this evening?" she said, humiliating herself completely.

Innocencio was up to lounging in the doorway with one foot on the opposite wall.

"How come you dress like a dude?" he said.

Corie knew that disadvantaged males frequently overcompensated by displaying bad manners and an attitude. She decided to forgive his cheap shot about her clothing. She knew he couldn't help it.

"I suppose you're looking for Hey Ya," she answered. "Unfortunately, she's out this evening (*Oh, no!*) having a driving lesson."

"Pffff!" said Innocencio, removing his foot from the wall. "She could have gone cruisin' on Hollywood Boulevard." He made it sound like a once in a lifetime thing. "Tell her she loses." He walked away.

"She'll be back in half an hour," called Corinne, trying to hold him a little longer.

Innocencio didn't answer. He slid into his waiting Chevy and burned rubber as he backed out of the driveway, blinding her in the glare of his headlights.

She had turned, reluctantly, to go inside when she heard the screech of brakes and saw the custom lowrider ease its way back up towards the house, its dual exhausts burbling, as one tinted automatic window lowered, allowing Innocencio's finger to emerge. He pointed it at her.

"You can come," he said.

"Me?" said Corinne.

"But first you put on a fuckin' dress."

A less socially conscious girl might have ransacked her closet for the one dress she owned, ignoring the program on world hunger going on in the background, but Corie stopped ransacking to tape it for future viewing.

As to Innocencio's later suggestion that they skip Hollywood Boulevard and head for Mulholland Drive: who cared where you taught a disadvantaged person English? What did it matter where you helped him to improve himself?

***

It was half past ten by the time Honey finished typing Miss Arlene's real estate contracts. It was close to eleven by the time the lawyers left. The extra three minutes her employer then spent in the washroom seemed excessive as Honey waited to corner her.

With shaking hand, she gave her boss the blackmail threat and the photographs. Not knowing what else to do, she turned to go.

Perhaps the columnist misunderstood the set of her shoulders because she began to beg.

Day Three: And There Were Bucks To Be Made...

"Don't leave me like the others," she said (was that a tear she was brushing away?) "You're throwing away a career." (No, just smoke from her cigarette). "I want you to start working on the column," she appealed.

That stopped Honey in her tracks.

"I was just leaving the room," she said. "I didn't want to embarrass you."

Arlene took new stock of the situation. Still, she felt some explanation was necessary for her too-well-documented sexual behavior.

First she took out her teeth. It had been a long day.

She rationalized that it hadn't been easy being stuck with Sidney for forty-one years – without teeth it came out "ftuck wif Fidney". A divorce would have ruined her career.

Before pleading further, Arlene decided to put her teeth back in in case she wasn't being properly understood.

Honey did understand. Sort of. When women ran the world it was natural to express one's sexuality. But after so many years of repression under an unreasonable set of rules . . .

"Aw, hell," the old girl interrupted, "the truth is I wanted it all. Now I'm afraid. You've got to help me."

If there ever had been one, this was a chance for Honey to demonstrate, to embody, every one of her Commandments.

She surveyed the sunken eyes, the puckered mouth, the wrinkly neck, the frail body of the elderly woman who'd been so good to her.

"Anything . . ." she said.

"Great. Give me your wedding ring. It'll shut blackmail-face up 'til the banks open in the morning."

Honey knew a bad idea when she heard one.

"Please, Honey. *Please*. I'll have it back to you by noon tomorrow at the latest." Rounding her desk, Arlene wrenched the sparkling diamond band off Honey's hand, saying: "I've got to stall her. She'll send this stuff to *The Probe*."

"She?" said Honey. "This horrible person is a she?"

"What can I tell you," Miss Arlene shrugged as she reached for her handbag. "The girl runs a lucrative catering business, if you know what I mean. She got three grand out of me for one night of whoopee." She dropped the ring into her open purse. "Though I don't recall requesting pictures."

Honey found herself thinking of babies again: having babies, diapering babies, tucking babies into bed, nursing babies, kissing babies, hugging babies – her babies.

She hardly heard Miss Arlene exclaim on her way out of the office, "I do look pretty good in this shot with Barry."

She wanted to call Dr. Hess to ask for an emergency meeting, some guidance through these suddenly choppy waters, but it was much too late to disturb him.

"Give And Receive Vegetables; Keep Breathing; Do The Friendliest Thing; Shhhh!" she recited her litany. "Get Over Yourself," she commanded. But it wasn't enough.

3:6

One thing all legends about The Great Mother have in common, they're about reproduction. Fertility, after all, is what she was worshipped for.

A clue to the ancient age of her liberal attitude toward sex is right there in the story of the vegetables: the oldest cultivated edibles were also known as aphrodisiacs – throw away that rhino horn, boys! have a bite of this asparagus.

But wait, let's not swarm all over the word "aphrodisiac" with our modern conditioning. It needs to be approached from a pre-historic point of view. Where there's plenty of food, there can be plenty of life. For a supply of both, see The Goddess.

***

Miss Arlene's enervated assistant made the thirty minute trip home to Beverly Hills from *The Los Angeles Sun*, each mile of freeway another blessed mile away from life and death as a business.

Day Three: And There Were Bucks To Be Made...

Writing was a business to her employer, not an opportunity for communication.

Land was a business, not a garden to be shared.

Sex was a business, albeit with a twist. Traditionally it wasn't the woman who paid.

Or was it?

These days, everybody paid. Even with AIDS skulking, not to mention herpes, the new syphilis, and venereal warts, Los Angeles obstinately remained a carnal marketplace. The movie industry competed with the cable industry which competed with the music industry to see who could break which sexual taboo and make bucks out of it. Hardcore films, once relegated to XXX theaters were now available for your living room. Housewives were encouraged to spend their rectangular green dollars on lickable love creams and unconditional underwear. Not at some seamy smut shop – at the mall!

It was even big business on the telephone: dial 900 for "Women's Sinful Secrets." The next thing you knew they'd be putting sex on a computer.

As for Dr. Hess's evolutionary answer, birth control, Honey questioned whether it was a boon or a bribe. While it offered women new confidence and an atmosphere of abandon they hadn't enjoyed since God was a young girl, it tended to trivialize the most mystical of human activities by preventing the payoff: the birth of the innocents, those small packages of love and beauty, copies of yourself and your passionate lover, on whom you lavished your affection and protection while you watched them grow.

Maybe Zack and I should . . . she thought for a moment. But she already had three times the children they allowed you in China.

Though you couldn't call her children children any more. They were old enough to be interested in . . .

"Oh, boy," she said with alarm as she pulled her car into the garage and parked it next to Zack's.

For the first time in her marriage Honey hoped to hear the familiar sounds of snoring as she padded up the stairs of her darkened home, looked in on her dreaming teenagers, then opened the door to the master bedroom, a place where she longed to be after a very disconcerting day.

Tonight she'd be quite happy to curl up next to her sleeping husband and forget about . . .

"Hiya, Kid."

He was awake, wearing a nice silk robe he hadn't had on since their trip to Hawaii three years ago. He smelled of his best cologne. He had soothing music playing on the stereo.

She took a long hot shower to wash off the grime of L.A. She powdered down and prettied up and got into the waiting four-poster.

As she sank into Zack's arms and his caresses began to relax her a little, her eye caught a glimpse of something at the end of their bed.

"Who put that painting back up?" she asked, mid-kiss.

"I did," said Zack. "It cost me thirty-six thousand dollars. The least we can do is look at it."

Long after her husband drifted off to sleep, Honey lay awake and stared at the painting, Zack's snoring a dull thunder underlining its dispossessing message:

SEX = SIN

GIMME ALL THE VEGETABLES!

P.S. NO REAL ESTATE FOR YOU, BABE!

Women would never go back to that. And men shouldn't either. It wasn't healthy.

But, without a storm god and his thunderbolts, without the lumpish Adam and the hussy Eve, without finger-pointing and fear of eternal damnation, would human beings check their appetites, moderate their desires, re-examine having it all?

With the whole planet gearing up for the 21st Century doing business as usual, would we counsel each other to be gentler, more giving, more loyal, more kind: remind ourselves to be motherly?

In what her son Sean had referred to as the Age Of Information it ought to be easy to get the word out, though not through Miss Arlene, an Amazon without an ethic in her armory.

Day Three: And There Were Bucks To Be Made . . .

Then who was going to inspire the people who were making her file drawers bulge? People with complex questions. And seekers like LaVie.

Who was going to make this competitive, commercialized, and still warlike, world-with-women-back-in, the world her kids deserved to live in?

"Your Commandments are right on the button," Dr. Hess's words rang in her ears.

Honey buried her face in her pillow and covered her head with another.

But then, she hadn't yet heard from a monk named Sah. He could have told her all she had to do was put one foot in front of the other.

𝔇𝔄𝔜 𝔉𝔒𝔘ℜ: And There Was Power . . .

4:1

"History depends on who writes it," so said Richard Nixon according to history, though some historians say it was said by Aldous Huxley. And then there are the ancient Greeks who say it was said by an ancient Greek.

Voltaire declared: "History is a trick we play on the dead." That's also according to history. But let's not go around in circles.

Our founding mothers would undoubtedly echo these sentiments. Their stories, too, have depended on people with pens.

Picture a scribe in Sumer around 2000 BCE. He hasn't had lunch. He's translating ideograms from a stack of fragile snakeskins into the newer cuneiform-on-clay which, he's been told, can last a hundred years. He has five more snakeskins to copy before he can down a stuffed pita. He's working on the story of an ancestral monarch, the fabulous Queen Puabi of Ur, ruler of that temple/city before it was swallowed by the Sumerians. As queen, she's stand-in for The Goddess at Ur, by divine right and direct descent from a queen who invented bread.

Bread . . . His stomach growls. He feels a little faint. He writes: "Daughter of a king, with painted eyes." In a hundred years who's going to care?

Ouch! Say our mothers, and ouch! again to Eve's biographers, who penned her story – and their agenda – a thousand years later in the Iron Age.

Day Four: And There Was Power . . .

Ouch! as well to the folks who named the Iron Age, and all the prehistoric periods leading up to it. They named each one for rock and metal, reminding us of advances in tools and weapons, but not the life-giving, population expanding, achievements of the gatherers and growers of food.

The Neolithic or New Stone Age, which began ten thousand years ago, opened with a booming, blossoming, fruiting and vegetabling agriculture already well established. But the words "Stone Age" present a meaner ideogram. The ghosts of our ancestresses yearn for those days to be re-named for the time when they tamed the edibles.

They wish we could remember when potatoes were the size of peas and who puzzled over them and gained the know-how to nurture them into a crop. They want us to know who found the best seeds for grinding and baking into bread. And who learned to gather and winnow and boil and eventually plant rice. And who developed corn into a staple food, and manioc, and taro, and beans.

They want us to know who rocked the many cradles of civilization, and Who, so gracefully, guided the hands that rocked the cradles.

In setting down a more informational account of original events, let's, at the very least, accomplish this.

***

"You've met her," said Lavie, painting bleach on the roots of her customer, Mrs. Whistler's, hair. "One time when you were getting a wash and set, She was having Her bangs trimmed."

Dab, dab, dab, she parted hanks of Mrs. Whistler's platinum blonde shading to coffee-colored tresses and carefully covered the brown.

"We're so lucky!" the hairdresser exclaimed. "She's re-emerging on the planet at a time when we desperately need a goddess. The rules we've been playing by are making things worse not better. Have some celery."

"Yes, well, I suppose there are many women who want more of a say in religious affairs," Mrs. Whistler reflected, nibbling genteely at the vegetable. "My sister says it's okay for a woman to be a priest,"

ON THE SEVENTH DAY SHE RESTED

she added, with a thoughtful tilting of her head, which caused LaVie to smear bleach on her left ear and then have to hurriedly wipe it off. "But then my sister has always been the radical member of the family. She never would wear a hat to church."

"Mrs. Whistler," said Lavie, "When Honey, I mean Demeter Newman comes to power not only will a woman be a priest, a woman will be . . ."

"But now no one has to wear a hat," interrupted her client. "Not even on Easter. I have five hats moldering in the closet. Maybe I should wear one next Sunday. What were we talking about? Oh, yes, your friend Honey. Tell me, does she give recipes for these vegetables of hers?"

***

How about we change the name of the Old Stone Age from Paleolithic to PaleoROOTic?

Can't you suddenly see those early girls out in the hills and meadows with their digging sticks?

Back at the cave after dinner someone drops a half eaten raw yam onto the garbage heap and a new plant grows. It's marvelous. Convenient. Next time they do it on purpose. Then they decide to move the okra closer to home.

***

Twelve o'clock noon on Thursday, April 12th, was zero hour at *The Los Angeles Sun*, the moment when a certain advice columnist was to give back to its owner one extremely valuable diamond symbol of marriage. But noon came and went without Arlene Morrigan.

Honey busied herself around the office with filing and tidying and answering the phone. She sampled lunch; drank too much coffee. Still no sign of her employer.

Nervous wandering. Into Arlene's office. Monday's column was waiting to be proofed on her boss's desk.

Day Four: And There Was Power . . .

She took a look at it.

> Dear Miss Arlene:
> My fiancee eats her vegetables with a spoon.
> How can I tell her I'm
> – Put Off In Portland
>
> Dear Put Off:
> Suggest she buy my book on etiquette . . .

Honey wrinkled her nose. That old thing was finally getting printed. It seemed formula to her now. Flog a pamphlet, go for the gag. She found herself noodling another answer next to Miss Arlene's:

> Dear Put Off:
> Do The Friendliest Thing.
> Shhhh!
> Get Over Yourself.
> Pick one.

With her mind thus occupied, the butterfies in her stomach took a break. For moment she almost forgot about rings and things. But Miss Arlene's door-slamming entrance and the look on her face were enough to return all butterflies to their posts.

Something was wrong. Couldn't Arlene get the money?

Yes. But it wasn't going to be enough.

"She has other pictures," Arlene said with disgust as she sat down at her desk. "Me with the ministers, me in rubber, me with that tranny Miss Toronto. Fifty thousand is only the beginning."

"But did she – she did give you back my . . ."

"Nope. She's keeping it until she gets another fifty."

"Do you have another fifty?"

"It's tied up in real estate." Arlene fingered the paperwork on her desk. "What's this nonsense?"

"Well . . . yesterday you said you wanted me to start working on the column, so I . . ."

"I lied," said Miss Arlene, cutting Honey's mess off her proof page into her wastebasket. "Relax, I'll get your ring back next time I see our friend."

"How?" asked Honey, her voice gravelly. "What are you going to do?"

"I'm going to kill her," replied Miss A. matter-of-factly.

Arlene's words took on jackhammer timbre in Honey's brain and the butterflies in her stomach responded accordingly. She had to get out of the room. She was afraid she was going to throw up.

Bones sensed her fear and acted in accordance with the instincts of dogs, especially small dogs, in such a situation. He nipped her on the ankle.

***

And let's change the name of the Mesolithic, the Middle Stone Age, to the MesoSEEDic. Does that say seed collection followed by seed selection?

The Neolithic era needs a better description, too. How about the Neo-plant-and-pick-the-plenty-in-the-global-Garden-of-Eden? Or is that too big a mouthful?

***

"Busymind" the Buddhists call it, the tendency, unique among the animals, that human beings have, to try to alter reality by mentally running away from it.

A monk, walking, walking, breathing, breathing, might train himself to forego this tendency, but for a former housewife with knowledge of an impending murder to which she could be connected through a diamond wedding ring inscribed "Zack Loves Honey", things were a little different.

On Good Friday her busymind played the game of "If Only."

If only I hadn't opened the mail.

Day Four: And There Was Power . . .

If only I hadn't let Arlene take my ring.
If only I hadn't taken a job in the first place.
If only I'd kept shopping on Rodeo Drive.

She tried Rodeo, too, but all it provided was a Missoni sweater for Zack which he didn't like, didn't want, and which she couldn't take back because she bought it at a bankruptcy sale.

By Saturday, the beginning of Passover, her busybrain had changed the game to "What If?"

This was more like it. In this mindgame you took action. But what if the result wasn't what you wanted?

ACTION	RESULT
I call the police.	Panderer releases shots of Miss Arlene.
I go to Zack or my dad and help Arlene raise more money.	Blackmailer ups the price again.
I get a gang together. We burst in on "caterer" and demand my ring.	She laughs at gang made up of Zack, Mom, Daddy, Corie and the twins.

And so it went, whether she was hiring a new gardener sight unseen from a flyer left in her mailbox, or carrying out her holiday obligations at her family's Easter/Passover: as she hid the colored eggs, the chocolate bunnies, and the matzo and the money, which her twins still loved to hunt; as she welcomed Margo to her table and worked at being civil to Roger; as she passed the hot cross buns to her parents, the ham to her children, and the brisket and the bitter herbs to Zack . . .

I go to horrible person and ask her to Do The Friendliest . . .	Oh, *please!*

***

ON THE SEVENTH DAY SHE RESTED

"She's dead," said Calvin Still, anxiously pacing his office after the holiday weekend.

"The blackmailer?" said Honey. It came out as a squeak.

"Who?" said Still, "I'm trying to tell you Miss Arlene is at that typewriter in the sky."

Honey sagged on the publisher's down-filled sofa. This was a scenario not posed by her whirling grey matter.

"As I'm sure you've guessed, Mrs. Newman, there's a scandal here and I'm going to need your help to hush it up," said Still. "You're to tell no one, not even Zack, because if one word of what I'm about to say should be leaked to the American public, millions of people who thought of Arlene as family would be irreparably harmed."

If Honey had stopped to think about it, she'd have realized he meant his bank account would be irreparably harmed, but she nodded her loyal assent.

"Miss Arlene died sometime Sunday after a struggle with a twenty-eight year old girl, allegedly a procuress," Still said, his newsman's restraint showing. "The girl died of a blow to the head inflicted with an oversized dildo."

"And Miss Arlene?" said Honey, wincing.

"Suffocated," stated the publisher succinctly, "her head in a potty chair."

4:2

Since history depends on who writes it, it's always subject to change. And change, we're told, will be rapid and rampant in the Information Age.

It's already happened. Think of poor Edison, the hero who turned the appliances on for the world, now he's viewed as an architect of planetary pollution.

And then there's Stalin, who used to have statues and cities named after him but who subsequently got de-Stalinized.

Day Four: And There Was Power . . .

And how about Columbus, discoverer of America? Now they tell us he wasn't the first European to come here. They tell us he came by mistake (he thought he'd landed in India). They tell us, if he'd only stayed home the "new world" might still be a paradise, and no native American would be misnamed to cover up his error.

Yes, change will come like seeds on the wind in the Age of Information.

But it never does happen overnight.

***

It wasn't the grandest funeral L. A. had ever seen. There were no limousines, no crowds attending. A eulogy would have to wait since no one was to know Miss Arlene was dead.

Luckily for Calvin Still, the police had been planning a raid on Miss Arlene's nemesis for some time. When they burst in to her sordid studio, they were the first to discover the bodies. Since Still had friends on the police force, as a newspaper publisher must, it was him they called before so much as a fingerprint had been taken, and a deal was cut in which Miss Arlene's body was quietly removed. Certain photographs when they were found were handed over to him so that no evidence remained of his famous columnist's indiscretions.

It was unspoken but understood that in return he, too, would Do The Friendliest Thing, using his powerful paper and the television station he owned to positively influence public opinion about those who had been so helpful to him

Miss Arlene was said to be on holiday in Australia as *The Los Angeles Sun* sensationally covered the police raid and the dildo death, making headlines out of selected juicy details; selling lots and lots of papers.

So everyone was pleased. Except Honey. Through careful enquiry she learned that no wedding ring had been found at the scene of the crime. But where the thing might be or what trouble it might bring her

ON THE SEVENTH DAY SHE RESTED

was not the cause of her tears. They were for the departed Arlene Morrigan, pure and simple, and they fell faster than the rain which had finally come to L. A.

In a soggy corner of an out-of-the-way graveyard, Honey, Bones, and Calvin Still committed Miss Arlene to muddy eternity. A fake death certificate had cost the publisher a bundle and he was anxious to get the proceedings over with.

"Let's go," he said, pulling Honey away from the dripping hole in the ground. She barely had time to throw the white camellias she'd brought onto Miss Arlene's cheap plywood casket to wish her a sad farewell.

Bones, wet and whining, had been trying to hurl himself into the grave.

"You'll have to take the dog while Arlene is on vacation," said Still.

"Fine," sniffled Honey, her heart going out to the poor orphaned mutt.

Back at the newspaper Still was all business, personally going through the dead woman's office with a fine-toothed comb. While on actual vacation she always left a backlog of material to fill her space. Now, on eternal leave, she'd left him short.

"Who's going to write the column?" Honey asked.

"I'll have to," declared the publisher, "until we can say the old bag died decently and I can hire another writer. Although where I'm going to find the time . . ."

"Perhaps I can help," Honey offered.

Still's first inclination was to scoff, but he stopped himself and considered her suggestion from another angle. She did have knowledge of Arlene's vacation plans.

He accepted off-handedly – better not to let her know she was being taken seriously.

"As long as you can keep up with your secretarial duties," he said.

***

So Honey did it all, answered the phone, filed the mail, fielded the questions, soothed the dog. Canceling all appointments with Dr. Hess to clear more time, she secretly worked with Calvin Still on Arlene's column, her fingers flying at her word processor as she obeyed his commandment, Shhhh!

The only way she knew that the rest of April had vanished and most of May was that her thirty-ninth birthday came and went with a small celebration at home, a quick bite of cake, and more work.

One other way she might have noticed the passing weeks was the regular deposit of checks to her bank account. But she mustn't have been thinking of rectangular green dollars because the amount of the checks did not increase.

The pressure of keeping Arlene "down under" sapped her energy.

And Calvin Still was hardly an ally.

He was tough and demanding, pushing more of the column on her, then insisting on rewrite after rewrite.

In Arlene's style. Now it was Honey who had to flog the pamphlet, go for the gag; find the grabber then steer it safely down the middle of the road until she came to the commercial.

One evening after another impossible day, another distracted dinner with the kids, Honey was, once again at it in the living room at home.

Not missing Zack who was still at the office; not hearing the rumble of dual exhausts as they came and went from the driveway; only disrupting her concentration to hug the twins goodnight, she sifted letters, trying to find an interesting mix for an upcoming "Ask Miss Arlene" column.

> Dear Miss Arlene:
> My husband's been wearing white cotton boxer shorts as long as I've known him. He just bought red bikini underpants and hid them in his drawer. Do you think he's having an affair?

Yes, thought Honey. She could think of nothing more clever to reply.

And, unfortunately, Arlene didn't have a three dollar pamphlet on the subject of red bikini underwear.

> Dear Miss Arlene:
> My daughter is dating a boy who's a bad influence on her. But in this day and age I'd feel old fashioned forbidding her to see him. What do you think?

Miss A. did have a pamphlet to cover this one entitled "*If You're Living Under My Roof*" but, as Honey had no trouble remembering, similar use of raw power had been useless when she was a girl and was probably just as ineffective now.

She read letter after letter, keenly aware of her responsibility, wanting to Do The Friendliest Thing, yet stymied by Calvin Still's needs – If You're Writing Under My Roof . . .

Some letters were meatier than others.

> Dear Miss Arlene:
> When I was fifteen I got pregnant. My parents threw me out of the house. I had my girl in a home for unwed mothers and gave her for adoption. She was never supposed to know who I was. But now there's a law that says a mother can look for their kid and the other way around and I listed myself and she did, too, and we're going to meet soon, which is real exciting but also it makes me mad. Because these days its okay to have a baby and no husband. Movie stars do it on purpose and nobody bats an eye. I'm not crying over spilt milk or nothing because "Jennifer" was taken in by a nice family and raised right. She's been to college and all but I still can't shake the feeling I got screwed. Ha ha, that's funny. Oh, why am I writing this letter? You wouldn't understand.
>   – BW Never Mind Where From

Day Four: And There Was Power . . .

For what it was worth, Honey understood completely. But how would her dead predecessor have answered? A slick comment wouldn't comfort the woman.

What BW needed was a slice of a much older, or much newer, a more alive way of thinking. Reluctantly, Honey put the letter aside.

It was only ten PM but it felt like midnight.

"Doesn't it, Bonesy?" she said to Arlene's canine who was asleep on the sofa next to her and who didn't respond.

"Who're you talking to?" Zack appeared in the doorway.

"Just the dog," she answered, hiding her work, disturbing Bones who started to growl.

"I hate that fucking animal," said Zack.

The dachshund had not endeared himself to the rest of the family either, having pee'd on Corinne's rug, chewed through the cord of the twin's answering machine, dug up half the garden, and laid more doglogs in more locations that Jelia could keep up with.

"Arlene goes on vacation, my house becomes a dog toilet," he kvetched. "I want him out of here first thing in the morning."

"Okay, Zack."

"I mean it."

"Yes, Zack," she said wearily as he left the room.

Then suddenly he was back and staring at her left hand.

"Where's your wedding ring?" he said.

"Uh, uh, getting fixed," she improvised. "It's at the jeweler's. One stone was loose."

She tried to remember what it had been like to be in charge of her life, to be rowing happily on a sunny lake that she owned, but the picture that came was of somebody sinking, chained to a plywood coffin which spiraled downward and downward.

4:3

If cats had written history, one historian has said, history would be mostly about cats.

If dogs had done it, we can extrapolate, there'd be plenty of growling and woofing.

Since history, at least on paper, was written from scratch by priests, bought and paid for by conquerors who became kings . . .

Is that another story? No, it's not.

But if snakes had written history, they'd have had to write about goddesses.

And if goddesses had written history, they'd have had to write about snakes.

***

Although it wasn't a requirement of her new religion, LaVie just had to have an outfit. She was used to wearing a uniform which defined her as a devotee.

Research on goddess cultures provided a range of fashion choices. But what was the ultimate goddess-worshipper look?

Furs were favored by northern matriarchs, pre-Scandinavian, pre-Siberian, and pre-Inuit women. Hand dyed woven yak wool garments were the mode pre-Tibet, pre-Peru. Quill embroidered deerskins were pre-North American. All these styles she logically rejected as too warm for Beverly Hills.

She also passed on the breast-baring draperies of temperate and tropical climes. She liked the statement made by these costumes but she knew they would get her arrested.

She finally settled on a lightweight crimson kidsuede top and pantaloons tied with red ribbons, worn with red snakeskin boots, her new ruby slippers, which she copied from a Greek description of Amazon dress. Though she wasn't a horsewoman, loose pants were comfortable. Plus she looked great in red.

Regarding the serpentine face and body tattoos which went along with the costume, she decided on an update, a simple tomato inscribed on her left hand.

LaVie borrowed the milk and honey in her diet from Canaanite priestesses of old. She fasted often like Abyssinian queens and, for exercise, took up archery to emulate her Assyrian Amazon heroines, though she drew the line at cutting off her right breast to facilitate accuracy with an arrow.

When, occasionally, she questioned the aggressive tendencies of these powerful warrior women, remembering that they were defending their gardens made it possible to rationalize their behavior. She respected the fact that instead of sending their sons to war, they shouldered their arrows and axes and went into battle themselves.

With each new hint of matrifocal ways to quicken her pulse Lavie wanted to know more. After work, most days, she'd head for a library. As Honey was doing her homework, LaVie was up to her scarlet elbows in information about The Great Mother.

She loved looking at pictures of artifacts from "Paleo, um, paleolith, um, back when the veggies were still wild. There was this statue of The Goddess they found in Austria, twenty-seven thousand years old, short, fat, nude and pregnant, with Her huge breasts ready to feed Her children. Compared to the length of time She'd been around, every other deity was an upstart.

In Neo-whatever India She was also a heavyweight, decorated with snakes.

In China, up through the Bronze Age, She had the body of a snake and a human face. It was said She smelted the stones of the five colors, so She was a working Mother.

In Sumer-before-it-was-Sumer She was snake headed, but in Egypt snake body again, until later when she just wore golden snakes as bracelets or as a crown on her head.

The reason for the snakes, LaVie discovered, was that when they shed their skins it made people think of rebirth, renewal. LaVie was ready for that.

But it also reinforced the notion that She had babies by herself – when the snake splits open, out comes a brand new snake. So the snake was a symbol of virgin birth – parthenogenesis. "As in that temple to Athena? The Parthenon?" she exulted to her client Mrs. Whistler.

ON THE SEVENTH DAY SHE RESTED

Priestesses of the female religion knew a lot about snakes. They kept jars full of them, basements full of them. Which, LaVie guessed, was probably why they grew so many anti-snakebite vegetables. It's impressive to hang out with poisonous serpents but you don't want to die from it.

"And the oracles used to drink venom? From which they'd been, y'know, immunized? To make themselves have visions?" LaVie reported to Mrs. W., after one of her research trips, "So the snake also stood for, like, supernatural wisdom."

By 5000 BCE The Goddess looked like a movie star. She'd lost at least a hundred pounds from Her early days and now stood lithe and lean, with Her skin aglow, Her youthful breasts bared, and Her arms held out to everyone. Around the Mediterranean as winter segued to spring and spring to summer and summer to autumn, Her priestesses would gather the women and girls to honor her.

"Then they'd have a big feast, pick out some good looking guys and make love, because to them sex wasn't this bad thing that was responsible for the fall of man, man. I mean, sooner or later they learned the secret, sex is why we're here.

"One thing I don't quite get, yet," LaVie admitted, "the queens started taking their brothers or sons as lovers, then sacrificed them at the end of the year, along with anybody else they didn't much care for. But anyway . . ."

Recently she'd discovered how God being female would affect people's everyday lives. That a girl lived at her mother's house and guys just came over to visit. Her brothers and uncles helped raise her kids because nobody'd heard of a husband. That daughters weren't exactly heirs to the land, just heirs to the care of it. That there weren't any heirs at all until land became personal property.

But women eventually owned, dealt in, and bequeathed land. This had been possible for LaVie to discern, since many of the earliest written laws were written to take it away from them.

"And you know that temple to The Goddess Artemis in Turkey? The one that was bigger than The Parthenon? One of the seven wonders of the ancient world?" she told Mrs. Whistler, her voice hushed with awe. "It was an international bank."

She also relayed word that in a women's world there were advantages to being mature.

"You didn't run around trying to stay young and attractive to men. They had to run around staying young and attractive to you. Wear skimpy clothes? Jewelery? Make up?"

That in a matriarchy the young man, if he was pretty was often reserved for an older woman, a producer of wealth.

And that the matriarch didn't worry about her teenaged daughter or grand-daughter being "um, deflowered," she found someone experienced to do the job, a handsome stranger who could bring new blood into the family.

"Sounds like last night's episode of *Inheritance*," Mrs. Whistler mused. "Bianca's a banker. She's fifty if she's a day and she's already dumped one younger fellow for that baby of a poolman in the tight pink satin jogging shorts."

"And she's trying to push her twenty year old son on Congresswoman Mendez, the one who's trying to rescue the tree frogs."

"And she's turning a blind eye while Jodie sleeps with . . ."

"Come to think of it," Mrs. Whistler reflected, "it sounds like my own family."

"Alright!" LaVie replied with satisfaction as she handed her an artichoke.

***

The full moon of May lit the avenue leading to the Newman residence like an extra streetlight. There were lights on in the house, too. Through the living room window Corinne could see her mother poring over a pile of letters so she asked Innocencio to drop her off away from the house. She didn't want Honey to see them together.

Or Jelia. Since Jelia had gotten her driver's license, Corinne had offered her the use of the Volkswagen on her Monday off and two nights a week. Her kindness making Corie the one who was available

ON THE SEVENTH DAY SHE RESTED

when Innocencio cruised by looking for company. Actually, she hadn't intended things to go this far. But they had. Corinne was finally seeing someone, and that someone was Jelia's boyfriend.

"Boyfriend," what a childish term, she thought, looking over at Innocencio as he brooded behind the wheel, slouched in his black bucket seat. This was a man, this heart stoppingly handsome, meta-macho, diamond in the rough. And this man was her passionate lover.

She'd been skittish that first night on Mulholland when he kissed her with one hand drifting under her dress. But his tongue felt good in her mouth as his hand moved, deftly, higher. He used his lips, his fingertips, his satin body, in ways she couldn't have imagined, and she forgot to tell him to stop.

Lately, she was the one who steered him to Mulholland Drive. Just thinking about it made her want him again.

It was late though and she had a test tomorrow on "Integrating The Immigrant Into The Existing Population."

Reluctantly, she took her leave.

"*Te quero, mi amor,*" she whispered, kissing his fingers as she slipped the four dollars into his hand – because Innocencio was disadvantaged, Corinne insisted on paying for the gas. "That's 'I love you' when you say it in English."

"I know what it is, bitch," said Innocencio, barely giving her time to get out of the car before he floored it and roared off in a shower of sparks as his black custom tailpipes hit the pavement.

***

Jelia was getting some much needed rest when the sound of Innocencio's glasspacks woke her. Now, listening to Corinne humming in the shower, she crossed herself and thanked the Santa Madre for making things work out the way they had. As long as Innocencio was giving it to Corinne, Corinne would be giving her car to Jelia which meant she could drive to East L.A. instead of taking the expensive bus, to work at the taco stand, netting an extra $72.60 per week, bringing her mother and children closer. She gave thanks, also, that Corinne was paying for the gas.

With help from heaven there was nothing that could not be accomplished. There were those, however, too foolish to ask for it. The daughter of the household, for example, who had such half-cooked ideas. Jelia's sharp eye had noticed the round dispenser of birth control pills in Corie's bathroom cabinet but she put no faith in such things.

Corinne helps me, she thought to herself, I will help her.

Getting out of bed she lit a pure white votive candle and placed it on the window sill next to her statue of the Virgin Mary where it flared and flickered and glowed in the dark.

4:4

The name of the Bronze Age will need changing, too. Any ideas?

How about The Age of Additional Edibility? Vegetable Variety? Vegetables To Spare?

Nah, it's not quite right. But if we call it what it was, The Age of Trade, will that say Queen of Sheba crossing deserts with her camel trains, and Queen Hatshepsut building ships?

Will it say, "Have asparagus, have salsify, have cabbage, have shallots, have lentils, need rice, will travel?"

***

The next morning found Honey still trying to keep her head above water.

Quietly, she'd tried to find a kennel for Bones, but he must have read her mind because, while she was taking him for his morning constitutional, he ran away from her and disappeared.

Next she had an argument with Calvin Still over the status of Miss Arlene Day. The organizers were pressing for answers to a million

ON THE SEVENTH DAY SHE RESTED

questions. It had reached the stage where they demanded to speak to Miss Arlene via long distance.

"Just tell them there are no phones where she is."

"But it isn't fair. They're making all these plans, Mr. Still. I think we should cancel."

"No. It's good for the paper."

"But there *IS* no Miss Arlene. There isn't going to *BE* any Miss Arlene."

"They don't know that."

So she stalled City Hall and tried to trace the dog, while second drafting a week's worth of columns which she delivered to the publisher's office at four-thirty in the afternoon.

Still was still not satisfied. His red pencil slashed this and circled that, sending Honey back to her desk.

She slogged her way into another rewrite, trying to please him. Far from her mind was her missing wedding ring, which is why she was caught unprepared when Lowell walked into her office at six o'clock and dropped it on her desk.

"This yours?" he grinned. "It says 'Zack Loves Honey'."

Honey reached for her ring but Lowell got to it first.

He put it on his little finger which, like the rest of Lowell was paler and thinner than ever.

"This girl pimp traded it to me for coke," he announced, leaning closer to impart the news.

That loud thumping of Honey's heart, could he hear it?

She started to lie that the ring had been stolen.

"She got it from Miss Arlene who got it from you," Lowell said.

Without an invitation, he made himself comfortable on a corner of Honey's desk.

"Looks like shrinkage worked for both of us," he said. "I'm a major success story. Pharmaceutical salesman. I got a Maserati downstairs – my father thinks it's rented. And diamonds!" He flashed the ring.

"And I hear you're doing great as God. I ran into LaVie. She says her new religion has changed her life. Looks like her old boyfriend Garth and his lover Vince are interested, too."

Day Four: And There Was Power . . .

"Lowell, I . . ." Honey tried to get a word in but couldn't . . .

"She told them when you take over you'll change things back so you girls control all the property and money, like the old days. She said she isn't mad at Garth for not marrying her since there isn't going to be any marriage anymore.

"She said his family won't hate that he's gay because he won't be an heir and he won't have to father any heirs. It'll all be up to his sister."

"Lowell . . ." Honey tried again, but he went on.

"She told him the pressure's off and he and Vince loved it, though Garth said he'd been counting on some dough when his father dies to help him in his tool and die business. LaVie told him not to worry, he'll get it from his mom. So you've got two more converts for sure and maybe this Mrs. Whistler who likes the idea of the old battle-axes getting the young guys. Well, I gotta split," Lowell got up and started for the door.

"Uh, about my ring?" Whose tinny, tiny voice was that?

"Shit. I've been speeding four days straight. I nearly forgot why I came here," Lowell said. "I guess you know the young lady I got your ring from was murdered. I'm not saying it proves anything, but it could cause a lot of people to ask a lot of questions. It could be ugly in the wrong hands.

"Which is why I'm gonna Do The Friendliest Thing and keep it.

"And you can keep something for me." He opened his jacket and brought out a package wrapped in birthday paper. It was bean-baggish, soft looking.

"It's a present for my step-mother," he leered so she'd know it really wasn't. "I'll come back in a while and we'll trade."

"But Lowell . . ." she tried to plead.

"This is gonna work great," he said, "God's holding my stash. Amen to that! Hallelujah!" he added as he drifted out of her office.

And the day wasn't over yet.

Bones hadn't been found. She'd have to go and look for him herself. With appropriate anxiety, she shoved Lowell's package into her desk drawer, put aside her work, and left the office.

ON THE SEVENTH DAY SHE RESTED

She drove to Miss Arlene's apartment building first, searched the hallway outside Arlene's door, and the underground garage where her long white Cadillac was still parked. She combed the surrounding grounds but there was no sign of Bones.

With trepidation, she scouted the vicinity of the double murder and was grateful to see no dog.

It was getting late. The dusky light was making it harder to see. She'd all but decided to give up when she thought of the cemetery.

As she parked her car on the dimly lit street and walked through the gate of the burial grounds, memories of the dingy day they'd buried Miss Arlene flooded back to her.

It was hard to find the location of the grave in the growing dark. To her left she heard scratching noises coming from a mound of earth. A new pit being dug for some poor unfortunate?

But then she heard the barking. Bones.

It was him alright, three feet down in a hole he'd made on the site of the late great columnist's grave. Earth flying in all directions, he was trying to dig up Miss Arlene.

Appalled, Honey scooped up the protesting animal, pushed back as much dirt as she could and got out of there in a hurry.

That night she told Zack everything.

Well, almost everything.

She didn't want to distract him with the story of her purloined wedding ring and the drugs in her drawer.

Or –

She didn't want to upset him with the story of her wedding ring and the drugs in her drawer.

Or –

She was too gutless to tell him about the ring and the drugs. Anyway, she didn't.

Nor did she say a word about the religion forming around her.

***

To what shall we change the name of The Iron Age?

Day Four: And There Was Power . . .

The Age of Wheat? That might work, but . . .

The Advent of Agribusiness? That's more like it, but . . .

It may be too soon to rename The Iron Age, which the Greeks put down as "the worst age of the world, characterized by wickedness, selfishness and corruption."

Perhaps we'd better wait to rename it until after we stop living in it.

4:5

Of all the imagined reactions Zack might have had to Honey's edited version of the story of Miss Arlene's demise, laughter was the last, the least, it wasn't on her list.

She couldn't believe it when Zack failed, completely, to appreciate the gravity of her situation. The thought of Arlene's death by potty chair had him in convulsions in their fern-filled den, demanding to hear again the part about the pictures of the iniquitous advice columnist and her choice of sexual partners. He was already wondering if Fox would buy it as a film or whether it had potential as a television mini-series. It sounded like an NBC show, he thought, possible counter-programming for Norman Nathanson's ratings blockbuster *Inheritance*, but then rejected the idea because the midwest was probably not ready for prime-time fancy dress orgies. Though they ate up incest, wife-beating, sex slaves and elder abuse, along with their daily dose of gratuitous gunplay.

Honey brought him back to reality, reminding him that Arlene's death was a secret and that she was up to her ears in the cover-up. It was stupidity, she admitted, that got her involved in the first place.

But again Zack surprised her.

"You're in fat city," he said. "Don't you see?"

She didn't see.

Zack expressed his amazement that he should have to explain the bottom line of business, use of power, to his wife. She'd had a successful father and two successful husbands. Hadn't she picked up anything along the way? Didn't she realize she had Calvin by the

ON THE SEVENTH DAY SHE RESTED

kishkes? She had information which could destroy him. She could walk into his office tomorrow morning and ask for anything she wanted.

"But that's no different than that woman and Miss Arlene," said Honey.

"Correct," said Zack, "except in some circles it's known as making a deal." His eyes glittered. "Where the blackmailer went wrong was to ask for more than Arlene could give. A good deal leaves everybody happy."

"Like Mr. Still and the police?" said Honey.

"Right," said Zack. "Like Norman Nathanson buying Starfilms out of bankruptcy so he could own *Inheritance*."

"Like Bianca okaying Congresswoman Mendez's marriage to her son in exchange for her swing vote on CFCs?"

Now she had it. Genes would surface eventually.

"So what are you going to ask for? What do you want?" asked Zack.

"Well, I'd like to keep Bones. He has no place else to go."

"Let's start again," said her husband, "from the beginning."

***

If history is subject to rewrite, you can bet most myths have been through more than two drafts and a polish. Which is why historians don't take myth and legend seriously: how many philosophical, scientific, economic and political shifts has it suffered through?

Like a rumor it's been told and retold, copied and recopied, edited, translated and interpreted to the point where it would be impossible to know who put what in, who left what out, and why.

For example it would probably be fruitless now to enquire how Eve ended up under a tree, albeit with snake, having her first birthday party at which legend tell us they served ribs.

Well, that's not exactly what legend tells us, but let's say it again: there is no story that can't be altered with just one stroke of a pen.

Day Four: And There Was Power . . .

***

In one clean shot Calvin Still announced Honey's new position at *The Los Angeles Sun* to the reading public. He wrote it as an aside to the kind of news that sells papers.

MISS ARLENE LOST AT SEA

read his headline, followed by an account of the passing of a legend in a boating incident off Wollongong, Australia.

He went on to describe the freak accident which ended the accomplishments of a household name. He listed all her books and most of her pamphlets in case anybody should want to buy one. He expressed his corporate admiration and grief. That done, this squib:

> Miss Arlene's column will be taken over by
> her longtime associate Mrs. Isaac Newman.

And there was hardly a murmur. Few questions were asked though there were bags of sympathy notes. And a few congratulatory calls to Honey. Mostly salesmen. No one of any importance except for scientist Margo Best.

Things couldn't have worked out better.

As a neophyte, Zack Newman's wife was the cheapest possible replacement for Arlene Morrigan.

She knew the ropes and, by now, she could do the work, but, most importantly, there'd be no strangers poking around the office.

He turned his attention to Honey's maiden column.

But what the hell was this?

> Dear Demeter:
> When I was fifteen I got pregnant. My parents threw
> me out of the house. I had my girl in a home for unwed
> mothers and gave her for adoption. She was never
> supposed to know who I was. But now there's a law
> that says a mother can look for their kid and the other

ON THE SEVENTH DAY SHE RESTED

way around and I listed myself and she did, too, and we're going to meet soon, which is real exciting but also it makes me mad. Because these days its okay to have a baby and no husband. Movie stars do it on purpose and nobody bats an eye. I'm not crying over spilt milk or nothing because "Jennifer" was taken in by a nice family and raised right. She's been to college and all but I still can't shake the feeling that I got screwed. Ha ha, that's funny. Oh, why am I writing this letter? You wouldn't understand.
— BW Never Mind Where From

Dear BW:
Tell your daughter we were out for quite a few innings but now we're back in. Hand her a rutabaga. Give her a hug. Re your actions when you were fifteen, you did the friendliest thing.

Calvin frowned, the woman's guilt, that was a grabber, but the rutabaga sentence – was Honey trying to write a gardening column? And the name she wanted to use. Demeter? He'd talk her out of that. And what was this shit about being back in?

He summoned his new columnist to his office and demanded changes. He wanted her to lose the rutabaga reference and put in something more to the point.

"Without the rutabaga there is no point," said Honey. "And, as you may recall, Paragraph 12B of my contract gives me creative control of the column."

"Ooookay," said Calvin. "I just hope we make some money."

"I hope we help people," she replied, letting him know she'd be taking the rest of the afternoon off.

"Fine," said the publisher a little sharply. He decided not to bring up the name she was using.

"Has anyone ever told you," he said, changing his tone, "you have the best legs on the planet."

Day Four: And There Was Power . . .

Sex beats power, Calvin knew, like paper beats a rock and a rock beats scissors.

4:6

The sunny summer day was nothing new for Southern California, but a taste of victory had added its exclamation points. Demeter Honey Newman, wife, mother, longtime possessor of great legs, and soon to be published columnist, zipped through traffic, slipped her car into the garage, tripped into the house, changed clothes and headed for the backyard, planning to relax a little, put her feet up before Zack and the kids came home.

But she was shocked to see the state the garden was in.

Their latest gardener was doing a terrible job. The grass was yellowing from Bones and lack of water and the big tree with its spreading limbs looked desolate. It was dropping leaves and unformed fruits all over the lawn. The long bed behind the gazebo, once ablaze with flowers, was still barren except for weeds.

At first, bending over the bed of dirt, she merely plucked at a couple of dandelions, but her now familiar work mode took over and soon a pile of them had been pulled.

By the time her family arrived, including her parents whom she'd forgotten she'd invited for dinner, she'd watered and fed the tree, cleared the flower bed and was double digging it according to the method she'd learned at Dr. Hess's.

It would be nice to say that she, namesake of The Earthmother, came up with the idea of planting vegetables. But it was actually Jelia, arriving home from grocery shopping, complaining about the price of tomatoes which caused Honey's mother to comment that she used to grow them for free, which prompted the twins to say they'd never seen a tomato growing and Zack to admit he hadn't either, which made Missy state it was high time that happened, and nothing would do but that they all troop out to the garden center to buy seeds and starter plants.

ON THE SEVENTH DAY SHE RESTED

Carrot seeds were decided upon because Missy said you could start them anytime in Southern California. Tomatoes and bush beans were purchased as plants, though she thought June was late for putting them in.

Honey wanted peas and butter lettuce but Missy said their growing season had come and gone. It was the right time for yams, though, and lima beans, and zucchini and eggplant and collards and kale.

"We have to have rutabagas," Honey insisted.

"Okay," said her mother, "it's your garden."

They returned to the house and all hands planted while Jelia charred steaks for dinner under the fig tree, the broken gas barbecue being no problem because Jelia built a fire in the grate.

They talked about the days when there was no such thing as a gas barbecue, or a swimming pool in the backyard: how Honey's father, Red, had a catfish pond in his; how Missy had a cow in hers and a beehive.

Jelia brought out dessert and the twins, eating, watched the spot where the weeds used to be as though vegetables were going to spring up any moment.

Corie took Bones into her lap and petted him, the real surprise being that he let her.

Honey held hands with her husband, marvelling that even the promise of produce could bring such ease to her household.

And energy to her, an Amazon energy which flowed across the Ages from the Paleorootic to the present.

She answered the call to arms. When the others had left or gone to bed, she led Zack upstairs. In the master bedroom she said, "Lie back, let me do everything."

And he did. And she did, arousing him sweetly and completely.

She was getting pretty worked up herself as her lips and hands moved daintily over him, when he, admiring her nakedness, became aware of the nakedness of the third finger of her left hand, and asked, "Didn't you get your ring back from the jeweller's, yet?"

"Mmmm, ask me later, okay? said Honey, fully involved in her silky ministrations.

Day Four: And There Was Power . . .

Zack was concerned, "I'm gonna call Fred and ask him what's the fucking hold-up."

She didn't answer, just kept moving and moaning and hoping the subject would go away.

"I'm gonna call him in the morning," Zack insisted.

"That's okay, I'll call," she said, her mood dissolved.

She got out of bed, put a robe on and went back down to the garden, tempted to tell Zack that, like Gene Green, her ring was missing in action, but she'd just begun to look like a winner in her husband's eyes. Why make another confession and watch the smidgeon of respect she'd earned slip back into indifference?

But no, it wouldn't wash. She'd have to get over herself.

"Zack, I have something to tell you," she said as she came back into the bedroom. But he had fallen asleep as was more than evident from the strangled sounds which reverberated around the room and echoed from the painting of Adam and the luckless Eve, leaving a certain place.

***

The next morning, Demeter Honey Newman called her decorators: "You know that paradise painting? Have I got a deal for you!"

Next she called her current gardener and offered to loan him the money to go back to trucking school.

Then she called Lowell – she knew LaVie had given her the right number from the wall of sound in the background. She told him she wanted her ring back. Promptly. Or she'd send the package he left to his father.

"You know who my father is?" said Lowell, apprehensively.

"Everyone knows who your father is," Honey said.

She also knew that the drugs in her drawer were not a great deal for anyone. To trade them back to Lowell wouldn't be Doing The Friendliest Thing. So she dumped the cocaine in the toilet, refilled the plastic bag with salt, re-wrapped it in its festive paper and had it ready and waiting for him when he showed up.

ON THE SEVENTH DAY SHE RESTED

After Lowell delivered her wedding band, she called Zack to tell him she'd picked it up from the jeweller's. She suggested they rendezvous that night and take up where they'd left off. But Zack declined her offer. He was going to be working late again he said.

***

As we renew Eve's reputation via vegetables it might be possible to revive some others, too.

Columbus: He sailed to the new world in search of sweet potatoes.

Stalin: He named his army for the beet.

Edison: Inventor of the growlight.

Nixon: If he'd only known, he'd have taken acorn squash to China.

4:7

Margo Best messengered her approval of Honey's debut "Ask Demeter" columns with a basket of swiss chard, okra, and sorrel. Was it unintentional? – her message spelled S.O.S.

Readers of *The Sun* reacted too, with diverse opinions, mostly about premarital sex. It seemed that Honey's heartfelt correspondence with BW was stirring up an entertaining and, for Calvin Still, lucrative controversy, though Honey was beginning to be sorry she'd raised the subject of sex at all, a somewhat slippery topic for a person who was back in Drawer One.

Rather than helping her readers, it was getting them all worked up judging from the quantities of mail she was receiving and printing.

The issue of teenaged mothers without husbands was more upsetting to her audience than the subject of contraception. It made them angrier, even, than abortion. People were madder at the girls who had the babies than the ones who didn't. As in her own case, they were maddest at those who kept and raised their kids instead of giving them away.

Day Four: And There Was Power . . .

Politically it had reached the stage where teenaged girls were considered a threat to church and state. Young single mothers and their children were being blamed for all the ills of society – crime, drugs, violence. This was a personal issue for Honey but she didn't have any rutabagas to hand out at the moment. She didn't have a solution to their problems, though she thought the best place to look for one would be in the two words "real estate."

Deciding she needed a break from the subject, she called LaVie for a hair appointment. But if she thought she could escape her column she was mistaken. It took LaVie three hours to do a wash and set, she so distracted herself applying her latest goddess research to the topic Honey had put up for discussion.

"This Greek dude, Strabo, from a thousand years before Christianity, says the unmarried mother was worshipped!" LaVie told Honey. "And not just in his neighborhood either.

"And guess what, a virgin wasn't a virgin-virgin, she just hadn't had a baby yet. And every woman served The Goddess in the temple by, y'know, making love? To them it was full-on holy. So was the resulting pregnancy.

"And this fornicator/harlot/whore name they came up with later? World's oldest profession and all that? My guess is people left donations, like they do in church today, but it wasn't as though we, like, charged for it. I mean, the highest thing you could do was go and watch the queen mate with her relatives!

"I'm telling you, it's the wave of the future. Relationships don't work. Why bother? This way we can just grab a guy? Go to the temple? Have babies if we want to? And get on with it."

Home was another hotbed of opinion.

Walking to the house from the garage after work, Honey was forced to hear Corinne's . . .

"Give me a break," she was saying, her assertive voice carrying from the kitchen, "this BW should have had an abortion."

And Brian's . . .

"Back then? She couldn't get one. It was illegal."

"Women have always gotten them and they always will," Corinne argued. "Then she wouldn't have put her kid through all this worrying about what her real parents were like."

And Sean's . . .

"Wouldn't you like to meet your dad some day? If he isn't dead I mean."

"I have enough fathers, thank you," Corinne replied acidly, before further presenting her theories.

"In the future," she insisted, "with birth control and abortions, there won't be any mistakes. A woman will get an education, have a decent job, and a husband who's going to stick around for more than five minutes before she goes ahead and has kids."

"In the future," Brian contradicted, "women won't be having babies. People will just get cloned. That's how Sean and I are going to have our kids. We're going to bypass women entirely. Just keep them for love slaves."

There was one person in Honey's household without a vehement opinion about her column.

Zack's only comment, that night, when she really wanted to talk about it, was that he couldn't connect with the content.

Which led her to believe that Zack was sulking again. And she was getting fed up with it.

4:8

Regarding history – to sum up what's written down, it ain't necessarily so.

And, conversely, because something wasn't written doesn't mean it didn't happen.

Fifty percent of women in Northern India can't read or write. They'll be left out of our version of the Age of Information. But that doesn't mean they don't exist, or that they don't paint their faces and the faces of snakes with red dye once a year, and bow to the snakes and venerate them, and ask for fertility and abundance.

Day Four: And There Was Power . . .

And if no one knows much about the secret rites performed at the temple in Eleusis, that glorious, snake filled, Greek temple to Demeter and her daughter, it doesn't mean the mysteries were never celebrated.

***

As it turned out, there was a Miss Arlene Day after all. The publisher of *The Los Angeles Sun* capitalized on that lady's passing by turning June 21st, the day of the summer solstice, into an occasion for "Remembering Miss Arlene."

In arranging for Honey to accept a posthumous key to the city for her former boss and appear in her stead on local talk shows, he found a way to introduce Arlene's replacement to a wider audience for free.

With the morning's ceremonies at City Hall completed, and several Arlene-honoring interviews under her belt, (thank goodness they didn't have to hear the real story), Honey began to feel like a pro: relaxed, enjoying it, her frame of mind enhanced by her publisher's daylong attentions.

To everyone, he introduced her as "the beautiful and talented Mrs. Newman." Whenever she showed a trace of the jitters he'd lean his bullet body close to hers and whisper something to make her laugh, like, "When are we going to do it?"

Honey'd been good to look at all her life. He wasn't the first man to make a pass at her. And yet, she had to admit his remarks were making her feel noticed in a way she hadn't been for years.

By mid-afternoon, as they entered the makeup room of the television station which Calvin happened to own, she saw him looking at his watch and realized she was monopolizing his very valuable time. She told him she was confident she could handle the rest of the day alone. Why wait around as they re-combed her hair and touched up her lipstick? Why wait another hour or more for her interview?

He left but not before murmuring one more proposition in her ear.

A few sips of white wine offered by his helpful staff added to her it's-my-lake-again mood. When it came her turn to appear, she strolled easily onto the set, greeted her host warmly, and took her seat like a celebrity.

Nor was she ruffled when he departed from the pre-arranged set of questions, asking not about Miss Arlene but about herself.

"Tell me, Demeter, if I may call you Demeter, how it happened that you took over the Miss Arlene column."

"It's a long story," said our heroine, smiling her heartbreaking smile. "I guess you could say it all started 'cause I wanted to be God."

DAY FIVE: Yea, Verily, And There Was Glory . . .

5:1

Wheat, wheat, and more wheat. Wheat's the one that got The Goddess, Eve, and the rest of us, into trouble.

Wheat can feed a lot of people and a lot of cattle, too. It can be stored in a temple/granary for a long time. It can be cultivated on a large scale – think waving fields of grain.

But wheat means fences.
Wheat means city/states.
Wheat means countries.
Wheat means war.

As to its origin, so far no one's been able to say definitively, though this is a donkey we need to pin a tail on.

Science can say who played a part in wheat's sophistication: pre-Ethiopian Abyssinians selected the seeds for durum wheat, but it makes pasta, not bread. Wheat for bread is probably a Neo-Plant-And-Pick-The-Plenty development.

More than one site can be cited where the baking of bread began. Northern India, and Mesopotamia – now Iraq – are two of the earliest spots. Large stores of grain have also been found in Turkey in Anatolian digs.

Remember Anatolia, where The Sun Goddess reigned in 17000 BCE?

Remember Northern India where they still venerate the snake?

Remember Queen Puabi who lived in Ur, pre-Sumer, pre-pre-Mesopotamia, pre-pre-pre-Iraq?

ON THE SEVENTH DAY SHE RESTED

Looks like wheat has "woman" written all over it.
Remember the Amazons?
How big were their gardens?
Remember Demeter, Goddess of Plenty, holding a sheaf of grain?

***

TO: Calvin Still
FROM: Demeter Newman
MEMO: What do you want me to do with all this money?

Honey had to put this question in a memo because her publisher wasn't speaking to her and wouldn't take her calls. In one televised moment she'd gone from being his star player and would-be romance to non-person. There was talk amongst the office staff that he was thinking of replacing her, which must have been cause for amusement judging from the smirks she was getting around there.

Things were even worse at home. Her kids, beginning their summer holidays, scattered when she walked in the door: they had urgent business in the computer room, needed to hurry to the mall. Her maid, too, scurried at the sight of her.

Zack was more forthright.

"You blew it," he barked upon her return from the now infamous Miss Arlene Day. "Did you have to tell your f'cockta Commandments, too?"

And then, when LaVie camped out in a pup tent on Honey's front lawn and started preaching The Message to every passerby, shouting "Hail, Queen of the Universe," every time Honey stuck her head out the door, calling Zack and the kids The Holy Family, and Jelia The Hallowed Housekeeper . . .

Honey told her hairdresser to cease and desist, but it seemed her landlord had done the same when LaVie tried to give him vegetables instead of the rent. It didn't make him any friendlier when she explained she'd closed her beauty shop to become a Demerite priestess and confessed that she'd spent the last of her savings on six cages of snakes.

Day Five: And There Was Glory...

Result: LaVie was broke with no place to live.

Zack didn't see this as his problem, but his wife felt somehow responsible. She'd moved the young woman and her serpents off the street and into the backyard, housing them in the pool cabana – "Temporarily, Zack, temporarily" – making nobody happy, least of all LaVie who wanted high visibility so she could reach the faithful.

"There aren't any faithful," Honey insisted.

"Yeah, well, there never will be the way things are going," LaVie had complained.

Honey Kept Breathing, barely, wishing she could turn the clock back two short weeks, and that before she opened her big mouth on TV to say what she'd said, someone had slapped a wide piece of duct tape over it.

She paper-clipped the checks and the cash, which had been arriving daily, totalling eleven thousand dollars, to her memo and personally took them to Calvin Still's office, hoping to get a glimpse of him, but, as usual she was informed by tall/tan/young that Still was out, even though she could see his phone button lit up and hear him talking behind his office door.

Dejected, dispirited, her prevailing condition lately, she left the memo and the money with the secretary and went back to her office, unaware that one-half hour from this low point in her history (or shall we call it her pre-history?), Calvin Still would once again pick up the pen.

Well, it wasn't exactly a pen. It was a telephone receiver.

"Get me Zack Newman," he said.

5:2

Give Us This Day Our Daily Bread – that human plea is central to the story of what happened in paradise.

Botanists who study the remains of grains can tell, based on the shape of an ear of wheat, whether it was gathered from the wild in

ON THE SEVENTH DAY SHE RESTED

baskets or planted and harvested using sharpened tools; an iron plow, an iron sickle, an iron scythe.

What a segue: wheat led us from the Garden of Eden into the Iron Age.

***

It was with understandable misgiving that Honey, entering her home that evening after work, heard laughter in the den: chuckles from her husband, mingled with the guffaws of Calvin Still, which came in short bursts, like gunfire.

It took some nerve for her to open the pair of tall oak doors which separated the den from the foyer to find out what was going on.

Not unfounded was her bewilderment when both men stood up to welcome her, ushered her into the room and seated her, ceremoniously, on the wobbly Chippendale settee which Honey had gotten from her decorators in trade for the painting which formerly graced her bedroom wall.

"We're finally going to have it all," Zack said gleefully, beaming at her, beaming at Calvin.

"That's 'all' as in custom made His and Hers and His Italian yachts," said Calvin, beaming at her, beaming at Zack. "Like Norman Nathanson's," he added.

"Cal has the recession-proof formula for the fuck you money," Zack announced, reclosing the doors to the foyer, and sitting next to Still on the mint-green watered silk sofa, as Still brandished Honey's memo and the wad of checks and cash that went with it.

Honey's confusion grew. Did they think they were going to go shopping for yachts with eleven thousand dollars which didn't belong to them?

The money had been arriving since her impetuous afternoon on television, in small amounts, sometimes with a note attached, sometimes anonymously. Of all the checks, only two were made out in her name.

Day Five: And There Was Glory . . .

Honey wanted something to drink and started to get up, but Zack jumped to attention. He buzzed around, bartending, deciding to open a bottle of champagne he'd been saving for a special occasion.

"To my brilliant wife, and, I hope, new client," he toasted, handing Honey her glass and Calvin his. "I'm proud of you, Kid. You were way ahead of us on this one."

"To the incredible Demeter," toasted Calvin, clinking glasses with Zack, "soon to be known as . . ." he leafed through the sheaf of checks, held a few up for Honey to see, and pointed to the name of the payee. They were made out to GOD.

The doorbell rang. Bones began to bark neurotically. Her impulse was to go and answer it, but Zack squeezed in next to her on the settee. He was pitching.

"You gotta go for it," he enthused. "Look at this ten dollar bill, it's got 'Save Me' written on it! Look at LaVie in our pool cabana! They're desperate out there for something to believe in."

Said his wife quietly, "That's the way I was feeling. In some ways, I still am." Bones yapped his disagreeable yap in the background.

"Here's something to believe in," Zack said. "You're going to be famous."

"Make that immortal," said Calvin Still, unable to resist a rewrite.

"Guys . . ." said Honey, shaking her head. The doorbell was ringing again. Why didn't somebody answer it?

"Okay," said Zack reasonably, "maybe we won't bill you as God. How about God's Little Girl?"

***

Corinne, watching the six o'clock news in her room, heard the doorbell and the dog go off again.

Why didn't that dumb beaner answer the door, she wondered, catching herself immediately, mindfully revising her racial slur to dumb person from Central America. She couldn't revise the "dumb" part because it was true. In the several months since Innocencio had been seeing Corinne, Jelia hadn't figured things out. Didn't she wonder why he never came by any more, at least not when Jelia was home?

The bell rang again. She tore herself away from the TV set – refugees were still starving all over the place – and ran downstairs to the front door, opening it to find a stranger there.

He looked like something of a refugee himself: tall, robed, very thin, bald. His eyes were haunting.

"Yes," said Corie, surprised to see those eyes light up at the sight of her.

"Honey?" said the stranger incredulously.

"That's my mother. I'm her daughter, Corinne."

***

In the den, Calvin and Zack were still selling.

"Zack'll do the promotion. I'll take the lead with the press."

"But we gotta be tasteful. No billboards on Sunset. No ads in the trades."

Corinne interrupted.

"Mother, there's someone to see you. He says his name is Sah or something."

"She's busy," said Zack. "Tell him to wait." Then, "Who the hell is Sah? And what's with that dog?" he grumbled as Corie left the room.

Honey didn't know and didn't care. She simply wanted to get these two off the track they were on. She arose and told them decisively to count her out of their plans.

She suggested, as she headed for the door, that they give the cash to Missy for one of her charities, rip up the checks, and that was the last she wanted to hear about it.

She said, "My wanting to be God was never intended as a business venture. In case you're interested, that's what started most of the problems in this world in the first place."

"This isn't going to go away," cautioned Calvin, riffling the checks as she opened the doors to the foyer.

Day Five: And There Was Glory . . .

"It is if we ignore it," said Honey forcefully, leaving them, stepping into the hall, forgetting for a moment that someone was waiting to see her.

She almost walked right by him. So quietly was Sah sitting in her vestibule, stroking the now oddly silent Bones, that he might have been a part of it, but he coughed, being allergic to dog hair, and the catch in his throat caught her attention.

"Gene," she said. Despite the shaved head, the added years, the loss of weight and those strange grey robes he wore, she knew him immediately. "Gene Green," she stated it, as if to make his presence a certainty.

The questions of twenty years were waiting to be asked, but at such a moment, only the tritest came to mind. "What are you doing here?" she said, as Zack and Calvin followed her out into the hall.

"Sitting," Sah replied, sincerely. "Coughing."

Honey didn't know whether it was the shock of seeing her long-ago lover after all this time or the pressure being put on her by the other two, but she sat right down in the two story entry hall and gave them her impression of Niagara Falls.

And no amount of patting, or soft words, or glasses of water, or tissues offered by any of the men could make her stop.

***

Gene Green, or Sah, viewed life as a pebble dropped in a still pond. If the pebble was a good one, ripples of good would spread, touching those he knew, eventually touching everyone and everything in the universe. But what Sah dropped on Honey and her family was more like a shock grenade. Waves of reaction shook the household and threatened to engulf the gentle monk at the same time.

After Honey, it was his turn to cry. The news that Corie was his daughter, too, produced that effect on the man who had spent two decades trying to conquer his emotions. All the rigors of Sah's training had not prepared him for this one curve of karma, the beautiful, teen-aged Honey look-alike, who's birth and babyhood he'd missed.

ON THE SEVENTH DAY SHE RESTED

Images arose of himself crouched in a dripping cave while a little blonde child ran, laughing, to Honey, thousands of miles away. Regret overwhelmed him.

And love. As Corinne came out of the kitchen eating an apple, he held out his hand to her, introducing himself by his American name. He wanted to touch his child, this extension of himself that he hadn't known existed.

But that only made it her turn to cry. Her tears were of disappointment. The bald headed geek in the robe couldn't be her own true dad, the dad she'd secretly dreamed of all these years, who would be a combination of Robert Redford and Robert De Niro with a little Robert Palmer thrown in. She bolted to her room, shoving her way past Brian and Sean who were on their way downstairs to find out what the fuss was about.

Honey ran after her, wanting to hold her daughter in her arms as she had when Corie was small and hurt, but the girl was having none of it. She pushed her mother away, and, with her, Gene Green or whatever he called himself, and everyone else in her whole non-family, demanding to be left alone.

When Honey, red-eyed, came back downstairs, Sah was the new focus of attention in the den. He'd already explained the series of coincidences by which he happened to see a newspaper article about her during his first days back in Los Angeles, learning her new last name. He'd told how he tracked her down – the garage attendant in The Newman Company's building was a budding Buddhist and had given out Zack's address to the holy man.

As Honey entered the room, he was responding to Zack's questions about his longtime absence, his unused English coming slowly. She could hardly find a place to sit. She was the one who most needed to hear all this and they'd started without her.

"We were pinned near Lao Bao. We didn't know if the Viet Cong had moved out or if they were waiting to hit us with everything they had," Sah was saying. "Our relief didn't show. Our wounded were screaming."

"Like in Apocalypse Now?" said Brian.

Day Five: And There Was Glory . . .

"It's a movie," Sean explained because of Sah's uncomprehending look.

"I haven't seen a movie in many years," said Sah, scratching Bones behind the ears.

"You're kidding. We've got it on cassette. We've got lots of war movies. We could show them to you."

"Boys," said Honey, "maybe later, okay?" It was the first time any of them had noticed she was there. "I'd kind of like to hear what Gene has to say."

Indeed, but as he talked about his war, she could see there was something different about his eyes. They were lit now with a piercing sweetness but there was something missing. And then it was Honey's turn to lump up again because there really was a middle aged monk named Sah sitting in her fern filled den, not her cars-on-the-brain, Mr. Mulholland, "Ain't No Mountain High Enough," Eugene B. Green.

"By moonlight," he was saying, "I saw ants making a nest, long lines of them, coming and going. When the load got too heavy for one ant, another ant picked it up.

"They were cooperating, building something, taking care of each other, but we humans, all we did was," his face clouded and he stared at nothing, "kill."

"Kill," he repeated, and the word took on new meaning for all of them.

"I decided I should stop," he said. "So I left."

"How?" asked Calvin Still, his newspaperman's ears pointing straight up.

"By putting one foot in front of the other," answered Sah. "I followed the river, hiding by day, until I crossed into Laos. After that I could sometimes use the road to get to Thailand. There I entered a monastery. After three years I was sent to Sri Lanka to deepen my practice in a cave in the forest, where I've lived, alone, ever since."

There followed an astonished silence which was only broken when Honey finally spoke.

"You could have written," she said.

ON THE SEVENTH DAY SHE RESTED

***

"Give Us This Day Our Daily Bread" means a crumb to some, and to others, all the rectangular green dollars they can lay their Iron Age hands on. But it's a goal of the rewrite to disassociate the word "grim" from the word "reaper."

Therefore, at some point in our research, we'll have to ask again: How big *were* those Amazon wheatfields? Under what circumstances did the women fight? Did they only kill in self-defense, or were they the aggressors? Did they decide to keep their daughters home and send their sons to war?

***

Though only a few weeks had passed since they'd planted them, the tomato vines behind the Newman house had already doubled in size. The green bean bushes were burgeoning too, the rutabagas were sprouting nicely and the baby black/green collards were crisp with dew, but Honey skirted the backyard entirely that next morning, wanting only to evade it. She took the street and the alley from the house to the garage and hurried to work, skipping breakfast, skipping out.

Skipping out on Gene, now housed at the twins enthusiastic suggestion in the pool cabana, two doors down from LaVie. As they begged Honey, he had nowhere else to stay and he'd travelled half way around the world to see her.

Skipping out on Zack. Though he was being non-judgemental, even unselfish, in allowing Gene to stay, it was one more shift in family behavior that required her response.

Skipping out on Corie, who in no way shared her mother's hope that she could know her father. She, despite Honey's, Zack's, and the twins' attempts to communicate, was refusing to speak to any of them.

Honey ran from her vegetables, her lovers, her babies, heading to her office for time alone and a chance to Get Over her emotionally exhausted Self.

Day Five: And There Was Glory . . .

But privacy was short-lived. No sooner had she closed the door to Miss Arlene's old workplace and collapsed onto the couch, than the ubiquitous Calvin Still came knocking, carrying release forms and a hefty check for the rights to Gene Green's story which he wanted Honey to obtain for him.

He asked where the monk was now.

"In our pool cabana," Honey said, remaining prone on the sofa. "Temporarily," she emphasized. "Temporarily."

"M.I.A. FOUND IN BEVERLY HILLS," Calvin envisioned a headline, proferring his paperwork. But she was unwilling to look at it.

He went out to the anteroom and made her a cup of coffee. He added the nondairy creamer and stirred in the packet of sugar. He handed her the mug, sat next to her on the sofa, and patted her knee.

Honey removed his hand, his attempt at intimacy unwelcome. And untimely, as she mentioned, coming from a man who'd ostracised her for the last two weeks.

"Don't take it personally," he said, working hard to reingratiate himself. "It was only business."

"Business!" she sputtered, sitting up, withdrawing from him. "Now you want to plaster my private life all over the paper. Corie's an illegitimate child. You think she wants that discussed at every dinner table?" She toyed with her coffee mug. "Or my mother – she's never really forgiven me."

"We could say you and Gene were married," the publisher tried.

"Calvin!" Honey warned. It was the first time she'd used his given name.

"Alright," he said, "if it means that much to you I won't print one word of the best story I've heard in all my years as a publisher." He made it a promise.

"And this money-making God idea of yours?"

"Forgotten. Solemn promise on that, too."

He went further. He suggested she take the day off. Take the week off. He would handle the column while she sorted out her life.

"Go ahead," he said. "Don't worry about a thing."

ON THE SEVENTH DAY SHE RESTED

He waited while his meal-ticket finished her coffee, saw her to her car, then sauntered upstairs to his office.

True to his promise he never did print one word of the Gene Green story. He just called the publisher of *The National Probe* and told him where to find LaVie.

5:5

Another top priority of a rewrite of the story of the Garden of Eden is to redefine the family, to restate who belongs in it.

Vegetables are dying to pass along the aboriginal answer. They reveal that turnips are related to brussels sprouts. And that Chinese bok choy is a turnip. And that each of them is also related to cauliflower and broccoli and horseradish and kohlrabi, and daikon and collards and kale.

They nudge – and it's a sharp poke to the ribs – that a rutabaga is a cross between a turnip and a cabbage.

A rutabaga is a love child.

***

At first Corie gave Zack a flat "no" when he suggested the family share Honey's week off and go up to the grandparents' cottage at Big Bear Lake. But when she realized she'd be stuck in the city with school out and Innocencio out of town, alone in the house, except for Jelia and the two weirdos in the backyard, she changed her mind, managing to retain a shred of her dignity by driving her own car to the mountains.

Red and Missy's cottage, with its deck overlooking the water, and its piney interior, reminded her of carefree summers of childhood. Easy breezes, warm sun, and her old room in the loft of the A-frame began to work their magic. When Zack took her waterskiing she almost began to enjoy herself.

Day Five: And There Was Glory . . .

From the moment she arrived, it seemed to Corie that Zack was paying more attention to her than usual, increasing in direct proportion to the awe in which the twins held her biological father. Sean and Brian couldn't stop talking about Sah. To them he was a combination of Rambo and Obiwan Kenobi. For the first time she saw Zack looking a little hurt when they called him "Dude" instead of "Dad."

Maybe that was why he'd suggested leaving Jelia and even the dog in the city and just the five of them coming up to the lake, as though he didn't want outsiders around, wanted to consolidate his borrowed family, re-establish himself as the head of it.

Corinne thought he was stretching it when he said it might be fun to divide the chores, like they did when he was a boy and nobody had money, but then he made doing the dishes into a game with the washer racing the dryers and it was sort of okay. Her mother looked pretty standing at the sink, laughing at Zack with his hands in soapy water.

Maybe there was even something to admire about her mother. Corie found out that Honey had spent the whole summer of her first pregnancy up here at the lake, often alone. Was she in some kind of exile? It began to impress her how hard it must have been, having a baby in your teens with no husband to make it acceptable. Going through Corie's birth on her own must have been rough. All of it must have been.

"Why you no thank her for you precious life?" Jelia had said. She'd feel pretty silly blurting something like that, but she did manage, "Hey Mom, how about a game of checkers?"

There was still the matter of Sah to deal with. Zack suggested a family meeting and at this pow-wow, held informally on the deck, after a sightly burnt breakfast made by the twins, Corie discovered there was plenty to admire about Zack.

With characteristic pragmatism, her step-father reduced the situation to its bottom line which was that two homeless people were living in their pool cabana. Whether or not members of the group felt moral or emotional obligations to either of them, they were going to need help re-establishing themselves as contributors to society.

ON THE SEVENTH DAY SHE RESTED

One of them, LaVie, had a skill with which she could earn a living. But the other, having been out of the workforce for twenty years was going to need job training. Both would need a more permanent place to live. Zack offered to assist with money and connections.

It wasn't lost on Corie that, at the "emotional obligations" part of his presentation, Zack cast a sidelong glance at his wife: not a worried glance, exactly, but it was the first time she'd ever seen Zack vulnerable.

Neither did she miss the softness with which her mother returned his glance, such tenderness that he had to look away. Without words her mother had said there was no choice to make between Zack and her past. Silently, her mother had said, "I love you."

For the short term, Zack thought, hotel accommodations could be provided for their backyard guests, something inexpensive, but clean, not necessarily close to Beverly Hills.

"And nobody needs to know he's my, my . . ." Corie found herself gagging on the word.

"No," her mother said, quietly. "Nobody needs to know."

Corie's relief was apparent. For two more days she forgot the embarrassment of her birth, her lack of what she still thought of as a traditional family. She joined in every activity and let herself have fun, but all that crashed and burned the day *The National Probe* came out.

Corie saw the article at the local supermarket when she drove into town to buy milk.

On the front page, sharing space with the news that Elvis, John F. Kennedy and Adolf Hitler had been spotted together in St. Louis, was a long range shot of her mother in a bathing suit in a row boat at Big Bear Lake. Inserted was a photo of the bald, berobed, Gene Green, above the headline: HOLY MAN FATHERS GODDESS'S CHILD.

The article was full of the gospel according to LaVie, whom it identified as priestess of a new California religion which deified the advice columnist of *The Los Angeles Sun*.

LaVie was quoted as saying that Sah, the monk who used to be a Marine, had "actualized Demeter as The Great Mother." She also

Day Five: And There Was Glory . . .

stressed the importance to a matriarchal religion that the child born was a girl.

The article went on to outline Corie's mother's Commandments, but Corie didn't bother to read them, though she bought a copy of *The Probe*.

She fled the supermarket with the offending newspaper, called Honey from a payphone, lied about a forgotten dental appointment, got into her car, and lead-footed it back to the city.

***

Unaware of Corinne's changed mood, the others remained at the cottage, going for walks in the woods, discovering woodpeckers and wildflowers and watercress growing at the edge of a stream which fed the lake. They swam and boated and read and relaxed. They went to bed healthy/tired.

And Zack discovered that it didn't take an Act of Congress to make Honey come. All it took was an act of kindness.

***

Guess what? Watercress is another member of the turnip family. Isn't that wild?

5:6

Well insulated from July in Los Angeles by rectangular green dollars, Norman Nathanson browsed through a week's worth of *The National Probe* in his air conditioned, chauffered stretch limousine, on his way to the office. Story ideas for his TV series *Inheritance* could be sparked by newspapers or popular fiction, and *The Probe*, which fell into both categories, was a potential source.

An article about Zack Newman's wife caught his amused eye, but it was too unbelievable even for his audience.

ON THE SEVENTH DAY SHE RESTED

Norman Nathanson laughed out loud and discarded the article, wondering what outrageous lies *The Probe* would come up with next.

Despite Norman Nathanson's low rating, in a tiny town in Alabama, a woman shelling Crowder peas onto *The National Probe* saw Demeter's Commandment about the vegetables and was prompted to take some of her home-grown produce to her mother-in-law to whom she hadn't spoken in a year and a half. The mother-in-law, upset at being caught with her hair in curlers, made ungrateful remarks about the quality and size of the offering. But later she came over with a pot of home-made Hoppin' John. The pipe of peas had been smoked.

During a domestic argument in Ishpeming, Michigan, a woman's eye fell on the Commandment "Shhhh!" She stopped herself from shrilling, "I want a divorce," in time to hear her husband say, "I'm sorry. It's just that I can't stand the way you eat taco chips in bed."

In New Orleans, Louisiana, a man about to swat a mosquito with *The National Probe*, saw the words "Do The Friendliest Thing," and couldn't go through with it. He nailed that sucker with his bare hand, though, when it tried to bite the baby.

***

In Beverly Hills, California, Lowell, that schitzed-out little druggie, had just been released from the hospital. Not Dr. Hess's hospital – the kind of hospital they put you in when you've been beaten senseless because you delivered half a kilo of salt to a Hollywood mogul who was expecting something more intoxicating. And therefore, you did not get paid. And therefore, you couldn't pay "them," the guys with the tire irons.

No amount of talking could make "them" see humor in the reason why Lowell didn't get their money, except when they pointed out that the joke was on him.

Then they laughed as they broke his arms and legs, smashed his skull, took his Maserati and his TVs and his VCR, his stereo, his boom box, his personal supply of drugs, and left him bleeding and uncon-

Day Five: And There Was Glory . . .

scious. This struck them especially funny because when Lowell awoke he was really going to need a pain killer.

Back home, living with his father, Lowell dreamed of writing the letter which would set him back up in business, and take revenge on the short blonde female who'd nearly gotten him killed.

"To whom it may concern," he'd write, "What part did goddess hopeful Demeter Newman play in the unsolved murder of a Hollywood pimpette. I have in my possession a ring . . ."

Sure, he still had Honey's ring. He hadn't spent his time on the street learning to be friendly. The cubic zirconium copy he'd returned to her had cost him pennies compared to what he'd make when he took the real thing out of his safety deposit box and auctioned it to the highest bidder.

But with typical lack of follow-through, Lowell never did get the letter written, so today he borrowed his step-mother's Jaguar and went to the bank. He'd sell the ring directly to "them" to buy the freebase he'd decided he wanted in large amounts.

He could almost feel the rush, the deep sinking away from reality that he wanted right now, needed right now.

He cranked the Jaguar off the Hollywood Freeway onto Washington Boulevard looking for the bar where "they" usually hung out in the afternoon. Where the hell was Eden Avenue? Off Olympic?

He pulled to one side of the street and checked the glove compartment for a map, his hand shaking over one more hassle in the endless list of hassles which defined his life. No map. Just a copy of *The National Probe*. With Honey on the cover.

Anger welled and more self pity as he ripped open the paper. His lip curled as he inhaled the article about her, hating Honey as he hated his still-too-busy-to-be-bothered father, hated his fix-it-with-money step-mother with her diamonds as big as headlights, hated Los Angeles, hated California, hated The United States of America, hated everyone and everything, including seedy storefronts, parked cars, and the wad of gum on the fire hydrant in front of him, but first and foremost, hated Lowell, that schitzed out little druggie.

ON THE SEVENTH DAY SHE RESTED

He wadded *The National Probe* into a tight ball and threw it out the window, but some words had imprinted themselves, backwards, along his middle finger. He tried to rub the newsprint off but it refused to be obliterated. Curious, he held the digit up to the rear view mirror.

"Get Over Yourself," said Lowell's finger, faintly, as he gave himself the bird.

What's enlightenment? Feeling lighter? As though a load's been lifted? For this boy who'd used drugs to defy gravity so often there was no such high, only a sudden and unexpected acknowledgement of the Commandment he had coined. This, coupled with the logic that he'd beaten his physical addiction. His lengthy hospital stay had cleaned him up. All he had to do to keep it that way was to steer clear of "them."

He waited awhile, replaying the mirror mantra in his mind until he was sure it was going to be acceptable to him. Then he started up the Jaguar and headed home.

***

These were the small beginnings of Honey's legend, but she was unaware of them.

Mostly, after returning from the lake, she stayed in her beautifully appointed bedroom. That is, when she wasn't in her beautifully appointed bathroom, throwing up.

Flu was the diagnosis. However, had it been Dr. Hess instead of the family physician naming her disease, he might have noticed how the onslaught of this hostile bug coincided exactly with Honey's discovery of her daughter's hostile note, penned in heavy black marker on the issue of *The National Probe* with the headline: HOLY MAN FATHERS GODDESS'S CHILD.

Corinne had circled the headline and penned "YOU LIED." Then she'd packed up her things and left home.

By Jelia's best guess, she'd probably gone to live with her lover – her *lover*??? – Innocencio.

Day Five: And There Was Glory . . .

Honey listlessly read the mail Calvin Still had messengered to her bedside. He needed his columns despite her infirmity.

> Dear Demeter:
> This B. W. is nothing but a slut with a bastard child. By printing her letter you will burn in hell for ever and ever . . .

> Dear Demeter:
> Sex involves responsibility. When are girls like B. W. going to figure this out?

> Dear Demeter:
> It's all the fault of television . . .

It had only been a matter of weeks since she'd written the column which elicited the correspondence, but it felt like a lifetime ago. She set the letters aside and for the fourth time that afternoon, called the private detective she'd hired to locate her daughter.

But there was no enlightenment for her. Innocencio lived outside the system. He had no social security number, no bank account, no passport, no listed telephone number. There were no license plates registered in the name Miclantecutli. He had no known residence, no known friends, and no it wouldn't help to call the police again because there was nothing they could do. Missing persons, if they were over eighteen like Corie, and had left home of their own free will, had a right to privacy. The police wouldn't involve themselves unless something "bad" were to happen.

Honey staggered back into the bathroom, fell on her knees and worshipped the china bowl.

Nothing her husband said in those first few days was of real consolation. Neither were the frequent, concerned visits of Margo Best.

Honey's parents were no help either: though they tried to be kind, it was obvious how they felt from the looks on their faces.

It was the twins who eventually got her out of bed and, weakly, back to work.

ON THE SEVENTH DAY SHE RESTED

"She's got a car, and money, and she knows our phone number," Sean told her. "She won't do anything too stupid."

"So you might as well take a deep breath and have some faith in Corinne," Brian put in, as they presented her with two hard green tomatoes and an embryonic rutabaga from the backyard. Kids learn so fast.

Adults, however, can be slower to adapt and, although it was a middle aged member of Honey's family who eventually took her Commandments to their zenith, who became her number one convert, you wouldn't have guessed it when Zack first returned from the lake.

Animosity towards his cabana guests caused him to forget his mountain promise to give them both a hand. Upon discovery of the reason for Corinne's defection, not following the Commandment Shhhh!, he'd raged into the backyard intending to tell the two of them to get the fuck off his property.

But Sah was gone. LaVie was, too.

If Zack had remembered to Keep Breathing, he might have taken a moment to notice the weeding of the collard patch, the tidying of unruly zucchini, the re-staking of beans. He might have exclaimed that the garden had never looked trimmer. He might have asked who did all the work.

And who picked the fruit from the tree in his yard, fruit which was waiting for the Newmans by the bagful, by the bowlful, when they arrived in the city: a harvest of grey-green, opening to ruby-pink, womblike, seed-filled, sensuous ripe figs.

If he'd checked with Jelia she'd have told him. She could also have told him when Sah left; on the afternoon of the day the family went on vacation. And why: because he didn't want to cause more trouble for them. And how LaVie, sensing that she, too, might be wearing out her welcome, asked if she could tag along. She was packing up her snakes when the reporters arrived.

This information came to Zack later, along with recognition that Sah had tried to repay him for his hospitality; that the harm LaVie had done had been done without malice.

Day Five: And There Was Glory...

But that didn't assuage his own guilt over Corie's flight from the family, or lessen his fears for her or his sense of loss, or his frustration that there was nothing even a Biggie could do beyond what was being done.

As a result, he husbanded the family he had left.

He carried soup to Honey's bedside. He listened, interrupting with only the occasional joke, as she talked about Corinne, talked about herself. In his own baggypants style he supplanted Dr. Hess as her confidante. He got to know his wife and began to see her as being more like himself: a survivor.

He involved himself in the twins' summer activities, enrolling them in the latest computer course. He found them a part-time job gofering on Eddie's picture. He often drove them out to that prick Roger's and sometimes went back to get them. He helped arrange their parties, met and of course charmed, their friends.

One evening, during that summer, as he plucked a fresh fig off the spreading tree behind his home, with Honey, still fragile, doing some light hoeing nearby, and the boys splashing each other in the pool, their voices half masculine/half feminine, giggling; with Bones barking his head off at anything that moved, he realized he was happy.

Of course,to accomplish so much, he had to stop working late.

5:7

Just as wheat dragged us, kicking and screaming, into the Iron Age, The great-grand-parent of a rutabaga, the turnip, pushed us into the Industrial Revolution. And for a similar reason: turnips will fatten cattle and kine as well as humans.

It took ten thousand years for this Paleorootic information to reach 17th century Europe, but when it did the rush to grow turnips caused the fencing of the last of the public pastures in villages where people still shared land.

Whoever could afford to buy and fence the real estate did, rotating crops of turnips, barley, clover and wheat.

ON THE SEVENTH DAY SHE RESTED

The landless left farming to find work in cities or moved to pre-America, or learned to steal for a living, or got permanently drunk.

A few took to inventing the tools that were needed in an increasingly complex world. Soon the tools made it possible for landowners to farm with fewer laborers.

Factories were needed to make the tools, and the factories spread over the land. And people forgot how to grow their own vegetables and had to depend on agribusiness.

But there came a time when new tools outsmarted the old, doing so many jobs so efficiently that factories were downsized or phased out, displacing people again.

The job the new tools did best was to record and disseminate information.

***

Downtown in the heart of Los Angeles's industrial district, there are no fig trees. Warehouses crowd the streets and the sound of Mack trucks drowns out the music of the wind. Trash replaces grass and car alarms out-tweet the birds. Business abounds even in a recession.

Some people have no business downtown but they live there anyway, on the street, hoping for work, or help. Or not hoping for anything, just putting one foot in front of the other.

Sah and his new friend Lavie, sat on the pavement near the Central Wholesale Produce Market, sharing the avocado, the tomatoes and the cucumber they'd found in a dumpster; sharing information about Honey and her Commandments.

Here, among their fellow homeless, no one remarked on their odd attire: his grey robes, her wrong-for-the-streets vermillion ensemble. No one questioned her cages of snakes. Considering that they were camped next to a man who lived under a ladder with a bath mat for a roof, they were in creative company.

They were unlikely acquaintances if you thought about their aims in life: LaVie with her dreams of sex on demand and abundant real estate; Sah with his vow to extinguish all desires.

Day Five: And There Was Glory . . .

For him, poverty was an elective like his celibacy. The cement beneath him was no harder than the cave he'd inhabited for almost half his life. There was nothing he wanted for himself.

There was something he wanted for Honey, and his daughter, too, now that he knew he had one. But they were part of another man's family. And he was only an interloper, unable to erase whatever suffering he'd caused, as impotent as the eunuch priests dressed in women's skirts who, LaVie said, were eventually allowed into the female religion.

But perhaps he could help indirectly. By disseminating Honey's Commandments, the simplest version of universal precepts he'd ever heard, he thought he might be able to make things better.

Meanwhile, there was just sitting, sitting, eating, eating, feeling unbearably sad.

And listening to the scarlet woman beside him complaining, complaining.

"I just thought after *The Probe* article She'd get some followers. And everybody'd get off on her ideas. But it isn't happening," LaVie was saying. "Know what She needs? A video. MTV could make her an instant hit. Can you write songs? I mean hymns?"

"No," said Sah, placing a tomato on the bottom rung of his neighbor's ladder in case he should awaken and be hungry. "But we could write a book."

LaVie wrinkled her nose. "It says in People Magazine the only books that sell are cookbooks." She offered a piece of avocado to one of her snakes. But the asp took a pass. "Or ones that tell you how to lose weight, be successful, or find love."

As she split the morsel of avocado between herself and Sah, he split into that place in the void where puzzles are effortlessly solved.

"Demeter's Recipes For A Happy Life?" he proposed, chewing, chewing.

LaVie smiled her approval. "We're going to need some paper and a pencil."

Sah walked a few steps to a dumpster overflowing with office waste and got what they needed.

ON THE SEVENTH DAY SHE RESTED

"And a publisher," she said, eyeing a tall building rising above the city skyline, headquarters of *The Los Angeles Sun*.

***

It took superhuman effort by her early followers but, towards the end of September, on the heels of the autumnal equinox, the little book *Demeter's Recipes For A Happy Life* was everywhere.

Given a bountiful first printing by Sun Pocket Editions, it was on special display in bookstores, employing four different jacket colors based on vegetables, to catch the prospective reader's eye – Calvin Still's idea. It was in supermarkets, not only on bookracks, but – LaVie's idea – stacked in the produce section, mingled with the fall harvest.

A slim volume, rushed into print, it featured the only recent, decent photo of Honey that Calvin had been able to find, *The Probe*'s cheesecake shot of her paddling around Big Bear Lake in a bathing suit.

As to content, it began with an account of Demeter's spiritual journey written by LaVie – In brief: Small town girl thrust into big city turns ordinary beginnings into success through use of her own Commandments.

The Commandments, now entitled Recipes, were quoted in large type.

Most of the balance of the material was Sah's. He suggested ingredients and gave preparation instructions so the book could fulfill the promise of its title.

For the Vegetables, he said not only to Give and Receive them, but to chop them, cook them, and serve them with reverence; to eat them with a desire to feed more than the stomach – to feed the soul.

Even readers who weren't into revering produce or feeding their souls saw benefits in his instructions. Eating more complex carbohydrates, you'd be healthier, drop a few pounds. Things were bound to get better for a slimmer, trimmer you.

For Keep Breathing, Sah wrote that fear is the anti-ingredient, a poison that holds people back in their lives. He suggested they sit quietly,

Day Five: And There Was Glory...

breathing, for a few moments before acting on things they were afraid of, that frustrated them or made them angry; sit quietly and count their breath. Count to ten, he wrote, then do it again.

Count to ten: people latched onto this easily. It was something their own mother might have told them as they threatened to whack their kid brother over loss of a favorite toy.

For Shhhh!, Sah suggested forgetting all the toys occasionally, turning off the TV and the stereo and just listening to the sounds of the birds or the traffic, the sounds of real life. He suggested spending a whole day in silence once in a while, communicating without words. Those who tried it found that silence put the cheese sauce on the broccoli, offering quiet moments to appreciate each other, to share the private signals they missed when one eye was glued to *Inheritance*.

As for Doing The Friendliest Thing, most readers figured they were doing it already, but Sah pushed them further. He said not only to take it easy on the people, plants, and animals they encountered every day, but to lighten up on the person they saw in the mirror when they were brushing their teeth.

Then, he said, the Recipe for Get Over Yourself would gather its own ingredients, sift them, mix in the milk and honey, throw itself in the oven, and bake itself to perfection.

Until it was ready for release, the book and its authors were kept by Calvin Still out of sight of the woman whose ideas it espoused, and also from her husband, who, it seemed to Calvin, was more concerned these days with his wife's well-being than he was with making money.

Calvin also kept another secret: the amount of hate mail in the wake of *The Probe* article that had been directed to his office.

It was mainly because of the quantity and virulence of this correspondence that Lowell's father suggested repackaging Demeter somewhat, so as not to discuss her divinity in the book.

Not even the pre-historic precedence for God being female was included, though LaVie had written a detailed chapter on the subject. Lowell's father suggested it be edited out and that, for now, all reference to Honey's well-publicised higher ambition be shrugged off as "just part of a mid-life crisis." As he said, her super-human status could always be written about later, after she was established, the way it worked in other religions.

And how did Lowell's father get his oar into Honey's lake?

"She turned my kid around," he told the publisher over lunch at the California Club. "He was such a little shit I used to wish I'd used a condom. Now, suddenly he's almost a regular human. He even got a job. Well, I gave him a job."

"Are you saying she saved your son?" asked Calvin.

"I don't know. I'm an atheist, not a holy roller."

"Then I guess," said Calvin, choosing his words, "you wouldn't be willing to let me print something like that."

"Cal," said Norman Nathanson, "you can print anything you want. You can have anything you want." His eyes filled. "I'm so very, very grateful."

***

Some people said later that Honey became a biggie despite herself.

She had Sah and LaVie to write her popular book.

She had the press in her pocket, with the owner of *The Los Angeles Sun* publicising her every move, pussyfooting around her, hiring a staff to help with her column so she'd have time to travel.

She had rich parents, supportive friends – Liz Macavoy, one of Bel-Air's best known hostesses; scientist Margo Best, who was making her own meaningful contribution to society; not to mention the famous psychologist, Dr. Augustus Hess.

She had Norman Nathanson, executive producer of the world's favorite television series, doing all the major talk shows with his son, Lowell, presenting The Recipes and testifying how they'd affected their lives.

And, never forget, she had the best personal manager in show business right in the family, protecting her interests and building success.

But no one gets to be a biggie unless she wants to. Though it took believers to ease Honey out into the middle of her pond, she was the

Day Five: And There Was Glory . . .

one who slapped a fifty horsepower motor on her dinghy and turned it into a speedboat.

She was impressed with Gene – no – Sah's expansion of her Commandments. She was delighted with the format of the book. Its existence and the maelstrom of busyness into which it swept her left little time for lingering over the role that LaVie and Sah had played in Corinne's exit from the family.

And her wishes had been met. There was not one word in it about her being God.

"It's happened," she told her mother. "They're finally taking me seriously."

Even so, during all the days that followed until Corinne came home, at every moment of triumph, every booksigning party, every photo-op, every television appearance, at every high there was a low lying in wait, a recurring chill, remnant of the illness from which she seemed to have recovered. There was always the question: where's my little girl? from which she couldn't escape.

5:8

It goes to the heart of the rewrite to honor those who tamed the vegetables. But consider this: isn't it also true that the vegetables have been taming us? Tying down our great, grand, mothers? Causing untold generations of their progeny to jump through hoops?

Aren't we still the dogs of wheat here in the latter days of the Iron Age, doomed by the turnip to keep living out the upheaval of the Industrial Revolution?

Or will it be vegetables which bring us full circle, into an age beyond the Age of Information, an age of rebirth and renewal (will we have basements full of snakes?), a tastier age for our children, and their children, and their children's children, and their children's children's children, and their children's children's children's children's children's children's children to grow up in?

ON THE SEVENTH DAY SHE RESTED

***

The sun was going down earlier, the nights getting colder. Tomatoes in Southern California knew it was time to make way for the peas.

In Honey's ex-living room, Margo Best closed the window against a late September sea breeze, then returned to the sofa to re-read her autographed copy of *Demeter's Recipes For A Happy Life* which she'd left open on the coffee table.

It was too bad, she thought, that Honey's original concept had been whitewashed, that there was no mention in the handbook of a goddess.

But at least her Commandments, that is Recipes, were intact, Recipes not dissimilar from the Yoruba proverbs Margo had grown up with as a child in Trinidad; Recipes she'd been using to get through this day.

Because also on the coffee table was the letter ending Margo's grant due to inconclusive evidence of the value of her research in cancer therapy.

Of the eight patients she'd treated with hormones, four had lived and four had died.

Of the eight in the control group who unknowingly received a placebo, four had lived and four had died.

"Inconclusive" was the right word, unless you looked at the stories of the patients themselves, each a mini prime-time soap opera.

One hormone recipient, whose prognosis she'd thought to be positive, had a visit from his brother. Margo overheard their scalding argument over business. In a matter of days, her patient was dead.

And elderly woman in the control group, whom Margo expected to go, got news that her first great-grandchild had been born. The next thing Margo knew, she was ordering tickets to Denver and, within a month, was on her way to meet the next generation.

Though it wasn't the one she'd been after, Margo had reached a conclusion. That, barring murder or mayhem, people die when they're finished living, and live when they're not. As important as treatment, she'd observed, was the patient's own reason for going on in life, or going on into the big Shhhh!

Day Five: And There Was Glory...

Not that she was qualified to evaluate psychological data. It wasn't what she was testing; hadn't been recorded in a scientific way. There was little she could do, professionally, with the information.

Besides, there was nothing new about it. Any ancient shaman took into consideration the mind of the dis-eased; knew that cures were possible with chicken droppings and snake's entrails if the patient could be helped to feel comfortable about getting well.

And if not? She'd reached another conclusion: that death is a person's own business and nothing to be ashamed of.

Margo pictured The Goddess as She's sometimes seen in African and other mythologies, as Death – symbol of the inevitable dying that everyone has to do, but always with the understanding that death begets and supports life: it's an ever-changing immortality (say "ever-changing immortality" three times fast).

If people could accept this reality, she thought they might, perhaps, pass on more easily, give up their space in a crowded world; go through the change known as dying with less pain.

But if they wanted to Keep Breathing, she believed they had more to say about it than they knew.

Margo turned back to Honey's book.

The words Get Over Yourself might have been written for her. She felt less failure over the patients in her study who'd died and less responsible for saving the ones who'd lived.

But meanwhile there was her own life to consider.

What next?

Margo closed the book of Recipes and put it back on the table. She carefully folded the grant letter and placed it there, too.

That's all. She was still sitting there an hour later when the phone rang.

She let the machine take it.

It was Roger wanting to know if she'd like to join him and his channeler for dinner. Then they could all come home to bed.

***

ON THE SEVENTH DAY SHE RESTED

Jelia, too, had received an autographed copy of the book of her employer. She hadn't had time to read it. Though having time wouldn't have helped because she couldn't read English. But if she could have read English she wouldn't have opened a page. She was positive there must be something blasphemous in it.

It was at Luis's Tacos where she was moonlighting – by bus now that Corie had gone off with the car – that she found out about its contents. Luis's wife's sister had bought a copy, which she translated.

It wasn't as bad as she'd feared; took none of the glory that belonged to Others.

On the other hand, she couldn't figure out what all the *conmocion* was about. There was nothing special about the Recipes.

The Giving and Receiving of Vegetables was something she and her family routinely did in Guatemala and she and her friends routinely did in L. A.

Shhhh! was a way of life for all illegal immigrants.

Keep Breathing was something you did when Senor Newman discovered you had washed all his white underwear with one red sock.

And Get Over Yourself? This was an unwritten law for those who cleaned other people's toilets.

There was one Recipe that nagged at her: Do The Friendliest Thing.

How can I smuggle my mother and children into the United States, she asked herself, and leave my brothers and sisters behind?

5:8

The Demeter Corporation was formed to manage the unreasonable amount of money being generated by the woman for whom it was named.

Though she only received a third of the earnings from *Demeter's Recipes For A Happy Life*, ownership of which was shared by LaVie, Sah and Calvin Still, she solely held the rights to her sayings.

Day Five: And There Was Glory . . .

Merchandising deals, skillfully negotiated by Zack brought her a small fortune up front with royalties already rolling in from a Recipe poster series and Recipe teeshirts.

Recipe watches, hats, jackets, and lunchboxes were beginning to rack up respectable numbers.

Just out was the Recipe video game in which, instead of bombing or gobbling your opponent, you handed him a rutabaga. In promotional competition, one player had given out 623,144 rutabagas before succumbing to the evil Conqueror Carrot. He was currently the kid to beat.

A collection of her Recipe-based columns had also been rushed into print and a second collection was in the works for the following June.

Taken together with her rising price for public appearances and the influx of unsolicited funds which arrived daily – it seemed the American people were so used to paying their gurus, they automatically mailed money – Honey found herself in Money Drawer Five: Having Too Much.

So The Demeter Foundation was created to get tax exempt status for her excess rectangular green dollars. They could be voted towards Doing The Friendliest Thing.

In meetings with her advisors Honey said it was time to get going on the big issues: ending war, famine, and ecological ruin.

And she had a long list of people she wanted to help: victims of earthquake, hurricane, fire and flood; drugs, rape, murder, and child abuse; economic mismanagement and political self interest.

She suggested good-deal-for-everyone ways to address their problems and proposed a campaign to communicate them, but her ideas didn't always meet with the approval of The Demeter Foundation's illustrious Board of Directors.

Calvin Still led the Board in voting that her notions about war be tabled for the time being.

Though he didn't disagree with her statement that wars were generally held so that somebody could grab land and/or the assets that went with it – that war, not glorious, was actually stealing – he thought

ON THE SEVENTH DAY SHE RESTED

Honey's approach to the problem too simplistic.

She said most parents taught their kids not to steal and if they caught them doing it, they made them give back what they stole or pay for it.

He said you couldn't make a country do that.

She said the world had always done it with the losers of wars. From now on they should do it with the winners, too: make them settle up for land they'd taken from its earlier inhabitants.

As conquerors and the successors to conquerors redressed old wrongs, she said, they'd create wealthy new trading partners. Terrorism and civil war would end and everyone could start afresh.

But Calvin, Red, and Norman Nathanson said it was fine to penalize your former enemies but it wouldn't be nice to shake a finger at your friends.

Regarding famine, Honey said it was mostly caused not by nature but by war.

She proposed that a tax on weapons be levied by the world, with the money to be used to stockpile food and seed and farming equipment and the wherewithal to deliver it In the event of a shortage of vegetables.

But Zack said hunger was traditionally a music industry charity and he didn't think The Demeter Foundation should horn in on anyone's gig.

Likewise, they should probably butt out on saving the ecosystem, which had its own very rich, very opinionated lobbyists. Besides, he said, we already had the technology to clean up our act. All we had to do was use it.

Honey suggested sponsorship of a world conference on The Family to discuss what a family is and who belongs in it. This get-together would re-examine parenting, population, and birth control, including abortion, from a pre-historic point of view.

But Norman Nathanson led a majority of the others in a 'no' vote, saying that while existing governments and established religions were hoping for a return to older values he didn't think they'd be interested in going quite that far back.

Day Five: And There Was Glory . . .

On the subject of natural disasters, Red thought her notion of an international insurance fund, paid for by insurance companies, was a mite early for its time. To suggest that big insurers act like parents, oversee their own industry, and make certain the little guy didn't lose his shirt when his fly-by-night broker took a powder after Hurricane Henry, was going to make some powerful people angry.

Honey thought that murderers, rapists, child abusers, and drug dealers, as well as white collar criminals and corrupt politicians should pay for the damage they did to other people's lives. Not just with jail time but with actual dollars.

If a person knew he'd have to atone for his crime with the sweat off his brow, in or out of prison, perhaps for the rest of his life, he might think twice about committing it.

She also suggested that no convicted criminal ever receive publicity. Like a bad child, a criminal should be sent to its room, its name disgraced, its face not seen, until it could redeem itself and act like a human being.

The Board, for various reasons, felt these ideas were dangerous. With money at stake, some people would become professional victims. Liberal lawmakers would side with silenced criminals; scream suppression of free speech. And, as Red said, it would turn prisons into factories: that sounded like slave labor. Worse, it sounded like Communism.

The most controversial of Honey's ideas, the one closest to her heart, was about the unwed mothers: she wanted them all to be enrolled in real estate courses.

She proposed that The Demeter Foundation start a trust fund for their training which should include mandatory gardening lessons.

The thought of teenaged girls with babies at their breasts and hoes in their hands selling real estate – and buying it! – had certain board members rolling their eyes. But what finally quashed the idea was the certainty that financial grants to unwed mothers would compromise their welfare checks, their public housing, and their food stamps.

So the Board of Directors of The Demeter Foundation found itself,

ON THE SEVENTH DAY SHE RESTED

for the time being, at odds about what to spend its money on.

LaVie, naturally, petitioned the foundation for a temple where she could preach goddess religion. But Norman Nathanson said for the nineteenth time she was jumping the gun. He voted "no" to a church and Honey seconded the motion saying it was something she wanted no part of.

As to smaller but worthy causes, they were set aside until a research committee could be formed to evaluate requests for funds.

The one suggestion, made by Calvin Still, which was generally agreed to, was that, in the Age of Information, The Demeter Foundation should use television to get its ideas, whatever they turned out to be, across. By almost unanimous consent – Sah abstained – the Foundation purchased its own TV station.

That the station had been formerly owned by Calvin Still was just a happy coincidence.

***

Whether they gave her a church or not, LaVie couldn't help preaching in parks, on street corners, anywhere she could gather a crowd.

She came home from a sunny November day of it to find Sah planting cool season vegetables in her backyard and couldn't wait to give him a full report.

With her earnings from *The Recipes*, Lavie had purchased a small cottage in Venice to put a roof over her head and the heads of her snakes. But she couldn't get Sah to put a roof over his.

He insisted she take his portion of the money. As he said, it was a principle of the women's way that she should control wealth, and a vow of his that he should be poor.

LaVie had invited him to stay at her house, but he, so used to living in the outdoors felt claustrophobic the minute he set down his begging bowl. He wasn't that crazy about her cobra, either.

He prepared to leave.

"Where will you go?" LaVie had asked.

Day Five: And There Was Glory . . .

"Out," he replied.

So LaVie set up her old pup tent in her new backyard, hoping he'd think of it as "out." He accepted provided he could do her gardening in exchange.

But it made her feel kind of embarrassed, hogging all the income and property and everything. This "assets" part of things was beginning to bug her.

She hated seeing him out in the tent now that the nights were turning cold.

But anyhow, it was great to find him there when she returned from her missionary work. She always hurried home to tell him of her successes.

Today, she said, she'd had no trouble attracting a multitude. People were finally getting excited about the Mother of Religions in modern form.

Her ex-boyfriend Garth and his partner Vince had testified. She thought they'd soon be ready to preach.

Sah raked and nodded, working the tiny plot she laughingly called the south forty, changing it over from eggplant to spinach, as LaVie enthused about her day.

Even Mrs. Whistler had addressed the crowd, she told him, but Mrs. Whistler always left out word that, in a matriarchal system, a girl and her children lived with her mother, and that even if she got really close with one of the fathers, he still lived with *his* mother and only came over if he was invited.

Mrs. Whistler didn't want her daughters moving back in with her. She said she'd spent enough of her life cooking and scrubbing, and her girls, between them, had four unruly ankle-biters. Mrs. Whistler, LaVie said, was only telling half the story, the free love and lots of land part, but she was bringing in converts.

"Could you hand me those spinach seeds?" said Sah when she took a breather.

LaVie noticed he was staring at the ground, summoning that incredible concentration of his.

ON THE SEVENTH DAY SHE RESTED

Uh oh, she'd done it again: talked about sex when he was never, ever, going to have any, and talked about children, when his own daughter was out there somewhere, missing.

And he thought it was all his fault. And it hurt him. Every day. Maybe every minute.

That was one thing that was making her doubt her new/old religion. Well, maybe not doubt, maybe question. Sah had never really known his kid. And this system she was promoting would put a lot of fathers in the same position.

Worse, she was beginning to wonder about the blazing mattresses.

Before she met Sah she used to love the idea of wild sex with hunky young men of her choice. But these days there was only one man with whom she wanted to make love. She had to admit it. It was the bald person in her backyard.

She never wanted to go to a temple and get it on with some stranger. That would be nasty.

And what if she and Sah were lucky enough to have children?

In secret moments she pictured daughters, of course, but at least one son who would look just like him.

But what if that boy of theirs never had a chance to make anything of himself and was nothing but a sex object all his life?

Oh, why worry about details? she asked herself. Sah was oblivious to her, this celibate monk, busy planting his stupid spinach in his stupid holes in the stupid ground.

She dropped the packet of seeds she'd been handing him and fled into her house.

She tried counting her breath up to ten but it didn't work. The tears came anyway, so that when Sah came in to see what was wrong, she hid her face.

"Go away," she said. But he didn't. He took her in his arms and held her as though she were some kind of feather.

He touched her hair, her face. It looked like he was going to kiss her.

"Your vow," she warned, respectfully.

Day Five: And There Was Glory . . .

"Things change," he replied.

He did kiss her then, and Amazons applauded; birds and bugs and unborn babies bravo'd.

"I love you," she blurted, "but it's very confusing."

"Shhhh!" said Sah, putting one lip in front of the other.

𝔇𝔄𝔜 𝔖𝔦𝔛: And It Came To Pass That She Got It All

6:1

Getting back to the Industrial Revolution for a moment, it's another era that needs renaming.

The agricultural aspect, the turnip tableau, the root of the revolution, has been ignored in nomenclature.

Amazon queens are sighing, "Not again!"

Or maybe it's the turnip sighing, the beautiful, bountiful turnip, good food for everyone, whose kindness caused more fencing off of land, so that, finally, all of nature became somebody's property. And that property-owning somebody made the rules, then expected everyone else to live by them.

You can bet, however, that it wasn't a turnip's idea to put up a fence.

Then whose idea was it?

Mmm . . . food for thought.

***

Having known Honey when, you'd hardly have recognized the woman who filled the house at Carnegie Hall in New York City a few days after the harvest festival of Thanksgiving.

Simply dressed, her blonde hair pulled back with no more bangs she had a clean California look, an understated authority, as she held the stage hour after hour. She looked almost tall, holding out her arms to her audience while they wore themselves out with approval.

Day Six: And It Came To Pass That She Got It All . . .

Anecdotes about *The Recipes* and their friendly effect enthralled and amused her listeners.

And, she was able to report that in America's gardens vegetables were back in vogue.

When a woman ran up on stage in the middle of Honey's speech and weighed her down with a mighty cornucopia of them, she turned the happening into something almost sacred, inviting the giver to walk with her amongst the audience, distributing the plenty.

But the best of the Honey-you-could-take-seriously was yet to come.

"I had intended," she said, "to talk about something basic. Peeling vegetables, maybe."

There was a ripple of recognition among the cognoscenti who knew that peeling vegetables was Honey's metaphor for revealing love. That's what Lisa Huxtable had written in her insightful essay on *The Recipes* in *Now Magazine*.

"But I've been getting letters, lately, from people who say my Recipes don't deal with specific issues. Like abortion . . ."

Ripple. Ripple. Chat, chat. The divisive topic.

"But they do," said Honey.

Ripple. Ripple. Ripple.

"When I was growing up the only method of birth control was a moth-eaten condom the boy carried in his wallet. There was no sex education, and nice girls didn't talk about such things with their mothers or their friends. It's not surprising that many of us became unhappily pregnant.

"Today we have the pill and other methods. We've come a long way.

"But some of us don't know about birth control. Some of us can't afford it. Some of us are told not to use it. And sometimes it doesn't work."

Ripple.

"Animals and plants abort their young when conditions for survival are blighted. It's nature's way to save the mother so she can breed on a better day."

Ripple. Ripple.

"But some people want to deny this decision to human mothers. So let's remember, for a moment, what it was like when abortion was illegal in our country.

"It wasn't a matter of calling your doctor or checking in to a clinic. It was a harrowing search for the ex-army medic or the failed nursing student or the woman across a border who would help you."

Nodding.

"It was how to get the money."

Nodding.

"It was a scrape on a table in a back room with newspaper on the floor. It was a syringe full of lye solution or chemicals stolen from a hospital. It was no anesthetic. It was fear and filth. It was always a horror story."

Applause.

"No man has ever had to go through this."

Applause.

"Only women have."

Wild applause.

"And they've died from it. Or suffered long-lasting complications.

"So, when I hear male politicians talk about outlawing the clean, safe abortions we have today, it curdles my blood.

"When they say, 'Have the children, we have room for them,' I have to answer the way Tonto answered the Lone Ranger as five hundred Apaches in warpaint thundered over the hill: I have to say 'Who's WE white man?'"

She hardly waited for the applause and laughter to die down.

"Will WE make it possible for the unmarried sixteen or fifteen or thirteen year old mother-to-be to stay in school?

"Will WE let her know her flesh and blood if she gives her child up for adoption?

"And if she keeps the baby will WE feed and clothe the child born to a child who lives in a poverty stricken household which already features six kids?

"And even if we do all that, would WE want to be sentenced to welfare?

Day Six: And It Came To Pass That She Got It All . . .

"Will WE solve the childcare problems of the single mother who goes to work?

"Will WE challenge the stigma of being a single mother, or the child of a single mother, which is once again on the rise?

And here's one for you: are WE going to accept the woman who has a baby when her husband is not the father? What if the child is not one hundred percent the same race as the rest of the family?"

Big time ripples.

"Will WE cherish the child born of incest or rape?

"Will WE?"

Much mumbling and head shaking.

"You see what I mean?" said Honey. "And that's the crazy part. Because we DID – in other times, in more motherly cultures.

"And that's what makes me think WE COULD.

"We'd have to view the family differently. But that's already changing. Lots of us are raising kids who aren't our own. But we'd have to go further. We'd have to see the whole world and everyone in it as part of our family. We'd have to Do The Friendliest Thing. We'd have to Give and Receive more Vegetables. We'd have to Keep Breathing, turn off the noise in our heads, and listen to a bigger idea.

"We'd have to Get Over Ourselves.

"Thank you. Goodnight."

Hubbub. Hubbub. Hubbub.

***

Having known Zack Newman when, you'd hardly have recognized his attitude towards his wife. He seemed to be approaching her with, what? Respect?

Yes, that, and not a little awe; the kind of awe we reserve for mavens and movie stars and people with whom we're falling in love.

Zack had flown in to New York for her Carnegie Hall appearance, but until now they hadn't spent much time together, monopolized as she was by the press and her public.

ON THE SEVENTH DAY SHE RESTED

When they eventually found themselves alone and able to get comfortable in her suite at the hotel, Zack couldn't find enough praise for her.

"I can't get over the way you handled the abortion issue," he told her.

"That wasn't my idea," she said. "That was straight out of the oldest religion."

"Well it was great. And you were great!" he insisted

"I couldn't have done any of this without you, Zack," she responded, as she loosened his tie.

"Sure you could," he answered, as he slipped off her jacket.

"No, I couldn't," she said, unbuttoning his shirt.

"Yeah, you could," he said, helping her off with her dress.

As their argument continued, piles of clothing grew on the floor around them, revealing two lifesize, guiltless, naked people who just managed to make it as far as the bed before their mutual admiration overwhelmed them.

It was these same piles of clothing which had to be tiptoed over, later, when they went to the fridge to bring each other a bagel or a beer, and the lack of clothes which got them touching and exploring, making love again. And it was scattered slacks, a dress, some mauve snakeskin sandals, and a pair of Jockey shorts flung over a lamp that had them smiling as they fell asleep with Zack's warm hand roving over Honey's breasts.

***

Having known Corie Best when, you'd still have recognized the teenaged sneer with which she viewed an interview of her famous mother on television:

"Mrs. Newman, in your speech tonight, it was unclear to this reporter exactly where you stand. On the one hand, you advocated clean safe abortions, on the other . . .

Day Six: And It Came To Pass That She Got It All . . .

"I just think that abortion isn't very friendly to the fetus," Honey was saying, "but as long as there's a need for abortions, they're going to take place."

"And you want to eliminate the need?"

"Yes, I do. Wouldn't that be wonderful?"

"Oh, CAN it," said Corie, unable to stomach another sound bite. What did her mother know about anything, living like a queen all her life? How could she presume to understand what was needed by the disenfranchised?

Corie snapped off the television set and glared at Innocencio's dingy apartment, at the cracked wallpaper, the broken blinds, the stained twelve foot red velvet button-tufted sofa, the windowless bedroom with the sagging bed and the crumpled black satin sheets under which she was lying and sighing.

How ironic – she'd wanted to empower the disadvantaged, not be one of them.

It was hard enough being poor, but it was awful being lonely. And bored.

Innocencio was hardly ever home. Which would have been fine if she'd still been in school, but he'd given her an angry fiat: he didn't want her "hangin' out with no horny college *cabrones*."

In a way she was flattered by his wanting to possess her completely. Her deepest desire was to belong to somebody. But he was gone for weeks at a time and when he was home his hours were erratic.

Last night she'd had a useless shouting match with him, demanding to know where he'd been, but he always ended their fights the same way, by making blissful love to her until she stopped complaining.

Tonight with Innocencio gone again, she could hear an argument in the next apartment over money. Her own was running low. And she could hardly ask Innocencio to give her any.

But she did have twenty-seven dollars in her wallet and half a tank of gas in her car. She decided to get out of his depressing excuse for a hovel and find something to eat.

She would have driven up to Luis's Taco's anyway, but when she saw Jelia dishing up hot sauce, a familiar face, a face from home, she was so relieved she forgot to order food, forgot she was living with Jelia's former boyfriend, she forgot everything but her troubles which she poured out to the patient housekeeper in the parking lot of the taco stand.

"If he had a good job, maybe I wouldn't be so uptight," said Corinne. "We could find a decent place to live, get married, be happy. If only he had some money."

There was a long silence while Jelia weighed the danger in telling the girl the truth, but . . .

"Innocencio got nothin' but money," she finally said. "He is a coyote. He make a fortune smugglin' illegals into United States.

"He cash the checks for workers who got no ID. He is the post office for some who send money south of the border. For all this, like Senor Zack, he take a fee.

"He will never marry you, Corinna. He already got a wife and family livin' in a big white house in Ensenada. Just like he will never marry me, though he still take my pants off on Mulholland every chance he get.

"I'm sorry to say you such bad news," she continued softly, seeing the look of desolation on the poor child's face.

"Please," she urged. "You should please go home."

Apparently, Corie didn't see that as an option. After she sped out of the parking lot, it was a long time before anyone heard from her again.

6:2

Still unanswered is a burning question: Who's idea was it to own the land?

Should we pin it on the males of our species as Dr. Hess suggested? Or did priestess/queens put up fences of their own, draw lines in the dirt; say "These vegetables are mine not yours."

It's only a legend, so some may not take it seriously, but the sorceress Medea is said to have founded one Edenistic country – Media, now a part of Iran.

Day Six: And It Came To Pass That She Got It All . . .

The words "media," "medium," "mediate," "medicine," and "magic" are named for the ancient Medes, who became one of the four major powers of the ancient Near East.
The legend says that Medea made her son the king of the country.
Is that another story?
Maybe not.

***

In contrast to her daughter, Demeter Honey Newman couldn't wait to get home. Home to her own bed with the Porteault linens, clean and soft from many washings. Home, with its busted appliances and rutabagas in the backyard. Home to her wonderful husband and sweet boys and adorable Jelia. Home for Christmas, to the home on which she'd recently paid off the mortgage with her very own rectangular green dollars.

For the past month on her speaking tour, she'd spent as much time in airplanes as she had on the ground, looking down from great heights on the real estate currently labelled United States of America. Under her eye the brilliant colors of autumn gave way to ice and snow: mountains were capped, valleys whitened, lakes and rivers made skateable.

What a change from the days when she shopped on Rodeo, or schlepped for Arlene, or struggled with her filing system, trying to find answers to the problems of modern existence which, nowadays, could so easily be solved by quick reference to *Demeter's Recipes For A Happy Life*.

Proof: it was a hit.

And she was a hit. Wherever she went. With all but a few wild-eyed professional Demeter-haters. Whom she was ignoring.

And her own daughter who'd run off with the king of hell.

As always, thoughts of Corie, and Jelia's recent sighting, put the freeze on Honey's lake. But lately "After all I've done for her," came up a lot. And occasionally "If she messes up my life again . . .!"

ON THE SEVENTH DAY SHE RESTED

Corinne's bail-out from the family, so far a secret from the press, could be damaging if they found out.

Honey cast a wintry glance out the window of the airplane to find she was about to touch down in Southern California which kindly disregards the seasons and goes on giving out vegetables.

She'd all but missed the fall harvest from her overflowing backyard garden which, Zack reported when he picked her up at the airport, was feeding half the neighborhood.

Credit for the surplus was due to Sah, who'd offered to take care of the garden when their latest yardman got an acting job on a series. The only difficulty in having Sah as a gardener was that LaVie usually came with him. But the extent of the problem did not come home to Honey until she came home to Home.

Zack's horn honking at a tour bus which was blocking their driveway awakened her from a jet-lagged catnap.

"Why is the bus stopping in front of our house?" she asked her husband groggily.

"You're on the celebrity tour," said Zack. Then he spied LaVie. "Shit, I told her to quit doing that!"

On the front lawn, with her boa constrictor, LaVie waved at the amused tourists, wearing a sandwich board reading "HOME OF THE GREAT MOTHER." Bracketed beneath were the words "Did you know God was a woman?"

Down the lawn ran Jelia, in her apron, yelling imperatives in Spanish, trying to hide the offending sign from the tourists who, by now, were all over each other craning out one side of the bus.

At an upstairs window, the twins, looking out at the craziness, ducked back, hoping no one would notice they lived there.

Through the wrought-iron gate to the backyard Honey could see that the lawn had been tilled into furrows up to the edge of the pool, in terraces around the gazebo, in long straight lines leading to the pool cabana; in a circle around the tree. Near the gate, in a muddy path, knelt Sah, planting a handful of winter wheat.

It seemed this new backyard look was not something Zack had okayed.

Day Six: And It Came To Pass That She Got It All . . .

"What the fuck?" He was halfway out of the Rolls Royce, threatening mayhem, when Honey, aware of the busload of her fans, grabbed the waistband of his sweatpants and hauled him back into the car, urging, perhaps too loudly, that he Do The Friendliest Thing, as LaVie, in her sandwich board, with Jelia hard on her heels, now being joined by a mud spattered Sah, hurried over to greet them.

"Keep Breathing," she reminded Zack, or was she reminding herself?

We'll never know because there's a more exciting thing which merits description here: the seven-year-old boy on the tour bus, laughing his head off at the hi-jinks at Honey's house.

This may not seem like a big deal but it was, because the boy had never, ever, uttered a sound in his life.

***

Incidentally, the magical Medes were the mothers of The Magi.

6:3

"What a dreadful Christmas," Missy carped to Red, as she peeled holiday rutabagas in the kitchen of their vacation cottage at Big Bear Lake.

Honey's parents had followed their daughter, Zack, the twins, and Jelia and Bones, in their flight to the mountains from their home in Beverly Hills which, in the wake of a new *National Probe* headline, had become something of a circus.

From the moment *The Probe* hit the news-stands with its headline "DEMETER HEALS MUTE BOY," wedged between the information "ELVIS WAS AN ALIEN" and 'TWO-TOED SLOTHS INVADE LOS ANGELES," sick people began to gravitate to Honey's front door.

She'd tried to nip the migration in the bud, but when she came out of the house to address the hopeful, telling them in the kindest possible way that they were being misled, that she couldn't heal anyone, a

ON THE SEVENTH DAY SHE RESTED

woman threw down an expandable white cane and began running, tearfully, around the property, exclaiming, "I can see!"

Catching her hysteria, an overweight man announced with equal fervor that his stomach pains were gone.

"I've quit smoking!" claimed a young woman as she hurled a pack of Marlboro Lights 100s into the next door neighbors' yard.

As word spread, Honey's home was inundated by the ill and ailing, including one old lady who had herself delivered by moving van in her Ethan Allen Colonial Maple queensize bed, complete with side table, water carafe, pills and two attending private nurses.

Honey'd had no choice but to gather her household and leave: to have her parents and LaVie and Sah whom she'd long ago invited for Christmas dinner, meet them up at the lake.

"I said 'What a *DREADFUL* Christmas'," Missy repeated, but her husband didn't commiserate, absorbed, as he was, reading details about his daughter in *The National Probe*.

"It's downright depressing," Missy addressed herself to Jelia, who was preparing the gefiltefish and the butterball turkey and the brisket and the cranberry sauce.

"Si, Meesis Meesy," Jelia answered, being polite.

Jelia was a bigger-than-ever-butterball herself, Missy noticed, but she had more pressing worries.

"Poor Zack," she said, "trying to make the best of things, cutting a Christmas tree or a Hanukkah bush or whatever he calls it, when we don't have an ornament in the house.

"Then LaVie tells the boys this is the 'festival of the winter solstice' and talks them into decorating it with vegetables!

"It's positively pagan," Missy said, trying unsuccessfully to get a rise out of Red.

"Still, I have to feel sorry for LaVie: once a prominent Beverly Hills hairdresser and now . . . Someone should tell her those goatskins are awfully goaty.

"And Gene," she sniffed, though obviously nobody was paying any attention to her, "never amounted to a hill of beans. You know the two of them are living in sin? It's a blessing his parents aren't alive."

Day Six: And It Came To Pass That She Got It All . . .

She sighed again and this time it was for the twins who'd been dragged away from friends and holiday fun. With no computer at the lake they couldn't even play their favorite games. They had to make do with riding innertubes in the snow, the poor little pumpkins, pretending to have the time of their lives.

Missy managed to change that once they were all seated at the dinner table for their feast.

"Poor Corinne," she said brokenly, dabbing at her eyes with a napkin. "I hope she's got something to eat."

It was a silent night.

***

Zack did his best to break the mood of doom and gloom after dinner by suggesting a walk to the lake, an idea adopted by all except Bones who balked at the door. His sausage shape didn't lend itself to marching through snow.

The others bundled up and crunched down the path through the woods, where pine trees cast their branching shadows and birds and bugs sang even in the frosty dark. Brian and Sean bombed each other with snowballs, but the adults were still preoccupied, if not with Corinne's whereabouts, then with that other thing hanging heavily over them.

As they reached the lake, Red was the one to mention what was on their collective minds.

"Somebody planted that blind woman," he said. "She wasn't really blind."

"She might have been," Sah suggested, helping Missy circumnavigate a snowdrift in her high-heeled boots, as they all clambered down to the beach. "She might have been genuinely healed."

"Get outta here," said Zack, an involuntary shudder raising the fine hairs on his neck.

A full moon was rising, huge and round, tinted golden orange by the San Bernardino smog. The lake, not frozen, made its muted whisper at their feet.

ON THE SEVENTH DAY SHE RESTED

"In the east they explain it as the power of 'qi'," Sah said.

"Key?" said Missy.

"Think of it as a kind of plenty that abounds in the universe which we can tap into at will."

"Like 'The Force' in Star Wars?" said Sean.

"Yes," answered the recently culturally updated Sah. "Everyone has some sense of this vast and powerful good, even though we sometimes forget it belongs to us. Anyone can use the energy and take nothing away from the whole."

"Let's get moving," said Zack. Philosophical speculation bored him shitless.

"I'd rather stay here," said Honey, "Look how the moon is making a path right to us."

And it was. As it rose, it cast a glittering beam of light reflected by the water, beginning on the horizon, ending with them: their own, private, diamond path.

Zack shrugged his acquiescence, so Sah continued.

"Some of us pray, making a plea for this plenty. Some just have faith, which is the door to it. Some are so pure they're a conduit for it, like my teacher in Sri Lanka who just sits there and glows. Or certain saints, or Jesus himself, or the Buddhas and bodhisattvas."

Are you saying my daughter's like those boys?" said Red.

"People want her to be. They want her to be the intermediary, to get the plenty for them. They think they're using her magic when all the time they're using what belongs to everyone."

"Okay, that's it for me," said Zack. "I'm going for a walk." He took a few strides down the beach.

"Hey, look at this," he called back after a moment. "The moonlight's following me." He pointed to the shimmering highway which now ended at his feet.

"No, it's not," Brian argued. "It's still shining at us."

Sah suggested an experiment. He got them all to take positions up and down the beach, and sure enough, for each one the moonlight seemed to be shining directly at them. And yet it was shining on all of

Day Six: And It Came To Pass That She Got It All . . .

them at the same time. And not only them, as Sah explained, but, as the world turned, everyone.

"Fuckin'A," said Zack. "Like the Sufis, huh?"

"Cool," said Sean, though he and Brian knew it was physics.

"My God," Red exclaimed.

"Good Lord," said Missy.

"*Dios mio*," fretted Jelia.

"Great Mother," exulted LaVie.

"Yes," said Sah, agreeing with all of them.

As for Honey, she said nothing, here on the shore of her lake.

Though the moon was shining on everyone, she reasoned, it had to be shining a little brighter on her. Maybe she couldn't actually heal, but she was the only one in this crowd who'd made a blind woman see, made a Marlboro smoker quit. Even Margo, a scientist, had acknowledged that religion could cure.

Maybe she was more like Jesus, or Buddha, or God for that matter, than anyone knew. It was an incredible feeling. She basked in the moonlight. And for the first time she didn't stop LaVie from bowing and bowing and bowing.

6:4

History, mystery, mock: the snake ran up the clock . . . If only we could have a conversation with the world-wide, X-ed out, farmer/priestess/warrior/queen/oracle/judge/explorer/astronomer/archi-tect/magician/artisan/writer/healer/traders who've been lumped together as "Amazons", we could ask them important questions for the rewrite.

Such as: Did they ever have it all?

If so, what were their attitudes?

Did they keep on sharing and caring?

And why did they fall from grace?

***

ON THE SEVENTH DAY SHE RESTED

If you want to plant lettuce, you ought to be in a garden, but during California days for Bibb and buttercrunch, January and early February, Honey stayed at Big Bear Lake, hanging on to her moonbeam. Keeping Jelia with her, she dispatched the twins to stay with Red and Missy in Bel Air so as not to interrupt school. She sent Zack to Beverly Hills to arrange for a security system around their house. It should include a high iron fence around the property, electronic gates, she thought, and perhaps some slightly vicious dobermans.

"It's going to be like a prison," Zack cautioned, when he brought the twins up for the weekend.

"You want to live at Lourdes?" said his wife.

She still Did The Friendliest Thing, giving interviews by telephone, when she wasn't working on her speeches for which she was now booked a year in advance, or a sequel to The Recipes which she was drafting.

In her latest work, she Demeterized Sah's thoughts on qi, and Dr. Hess's meditation "It's Your Lake", turning it all into a useful chat on inner healing, which had such a beneficial effect on people that more cures were reported in the press.

This gave her the springboard for the good cause on which to finally spend her foundation's money: a television show of her own, to be broadcast continuously from the station which The Demeter Foundation owned. More effective than any book, or spot coverage of her speeches, her plan would allow people to tune in to her message twenty-four hours a day, giving her full access to, and influence over, the Age of Information.

Board members of The Demeter Foundation loved the idea, except Zack who had reservations about the amount of time Honey was already spending away from the family, and Sah, who on the day of the decision was planting vegetables in city parks. The others expressed their enthusiasm in meetings she held at the lake. These days, everyone, even Norman Nathanson, came to her.

Everyone including Dr. Margo Best, who showed up unexpectedly on a chilly February afternoon with a few suitcases and a sorry story.

Day Six: And It Came To Pass That She Got It All . . .

Because the twins' lives would be affected she thought Honey should be the first to know she'd left Roger.

She also thought Honey should be aware of Roger's channeler and how she fit into the picture.

"It feels funny running to you," Margo said, warming herself with her third cup of coffee, "when I used to be the other woman."

She tidied a litter of tattered sweetener packages which had built up next to her cup and arranged them neatly in a pile.

"I loved him, Honey," she said, apologetically. "There was a time when all I wanted was to stay home and have his children." She gathered up her pile of envelopes. "But Roger didn't want brown babies. Where's the garbage?"

Honey pointed to a door below the kitchen sink, allowing Margo to get up and wipe at her tears.

"I guess his parameters aren't that wide after all," she said, depositing the small pink envelopes, a damp tissue, and a stray paper towel she found on the kitchen counter, into the trash.

It also came out that this was not an opportune time for Margo to be starting over. She was out of a job, and, once she and Roger divorced, she'd have little money and no home.

"You'll have a home at Broad Beach," Honey said forcefully. "You'll have half of everything you contributed to the marriage.

"Because of two little words, there *will* be community property: *Unfit Father*."

"He's not an unfit father. He just wanted me to go to bed with a woman medium who claims to talk to dead people. And I could never expose him in front of the twins."

"It's only a bluff," said Honey. "Somebody needs to teach you how to use information.

"Oh, and about your work? I'll fund you. What do you need? A million? Two?

"But maybe you should change your focus. It seems silly to be looking into the forces of life and death and not be studying *me*."

***

ON THE SEVENTH DAY SHE RESTED

With the spiked iron fence completed, Jelia came back into town to get the house ready for Senora Newman.

Even the forbidding fence and the dogs didn't stop sick people from standing hopefully out on the sidewalk or in the back lane. Then there were the gawkers who slowed traffic to a crawl. A security guard was added to the scene. Things hadn't been this disrupted in the neighborhood since somebody painted pubic hairs on all the Greek statues on that shipping magnate's front lawn.

Jelia cleaned and scrubbed and polished, regretting now that she'd busted the Dust Buster and floor buffer and the electric broom. It was tough to get everything done by hand, especially with Innocencio's child inside her, taking her qi, making her want to do nothing but eat and sleep.

In the fifth month of development, the baby was beginning to bulge, but whenever she thought Senor Newman might be eyeing her shape, she'd laughingly wave a taco chip and stuff it in her mouth. With robots around the corner you had to be extremely crafty.

There were times when Jelia wished she were a robot. Robots never got tired. Robots didn't get fired. And robots didn't have forty-eight members of their family arriving soon from Guatemala.

It was that big bonus check Mrs. Honey had given her that helped Jelia Do The Friendliest Thing.

Now she had money for her mother, her little ones, her fourteen brothers and sisters, their wives and husbands, but she was still short for their children and the three aunts and uncles she wanted to import. She must ask Luis to take her on again, and work harder at both her jobs in order to accomplish her dreams.

And getting her family here was only the beginning. Each one of them needed to eat.

6:5

Perhaps there's something to be learned about the behavior of prehistoric queens by observing more modern monarchs, even if they got

Day Six: And It Came To Pass That She Got It All . . .

their crowns from their fathers instead of their moms.

If so, Isabella of Castile, Columbus's patroness, might be a lady to look at.

Though she tied the knot with Ferdinand of Aragon, the Duke next door, she kept her wealthier country separate, with its own laws, taxes, armies, and doubloons.

Marriage helped her secure her borders but she soon over-reached them, personally suiting up in armor, leading and camping with her troops.

In the lands she conquered, people of many faiths had lived in harmony. Isabella's Inquisition put an end to that.

She also stiffed Columbus, leaving him to die in squalor after he brought home the vegetables and information about a continent which would make the country not-yet-known-as-Spain the richest in the world.

***

Like a white rhinoceros is to not enough, Honey was to time. It was rush, rush, rush, after her return from the lake to Los Angeles, where she travelled incognito so as not to be hounded by her public. But everybody knew it was her in the jogging suit, Nikes, and dense black sunglasses, being ushered from a chauffered limousine into her television station to fine-tune the launching of herself as a permanently televised presence. She'd decided on a name for her program. It would be called "*Something To Believe In.*"

Calvin had filled the conference room with baskets of vegetables and was patiently waiting when she arrived, even though she was over an hour late. She took this as her due, being used to the red carpet treatment nowadays.

With a breezy, "Hi Cal, how goes it?" she removed her sunglasses, through which she was having trouble seeing, allowing that it was going to be satisfying to broadcast from the place where she first began to make history.

ON THE SEVENTH DAY SHE RESTED

"Norman says we can shoot my segments all together every few months so it won't cut into my travel schedule," she said, sitting next to Calvin on the couch. "Did you hear I'm going to Russia next spring?"

"The format's going to include all my ideas," she said without waiting for his answer. "We're going to have readings from *The Recipes*, testimony of people they've helped. We'll get Zack's clients as guests. I haven't talked to him about it yet, but as Miss Arlene used to say, we've gotta keep 'em entertained.

"There'll be a healing segment, phone-ins, I think Margo could be right for that, and, I haven't quite decided yet, but I might give LaVie a chance to preach.

"We won't sell advertising time," she went right on as though dictating. "We'll use the commercial minutes to promote our own products – the rutabaga hats aren't selling well. We're going to have to push them.

"We may be criticized for making too much money, but we can rationalize that, because the work we're doing is so meaningful."

"Why don't we talk about this in bed?" said Still, a man who never stopped trying.

"Put it out of your mind, Cal," she said. "I've got a good deal going with Zack. We're each successful as individuals. But when you put us together, you get a third thing, a team. Hmm, maybe I should use that on the show. One plus one makes three. I'll call it Demeter's Arithmetic."

Calvin showed his bullet teeth, deferring to her absolute power.

"I'm glad you're happy," he smiled, not meaning a word of it.

They discussed details of the renovation he was making to his old station to accommodate her; the size of Honey's dressing room; the setting for the party that The Demeter Foundation was throwing for the opening, then Calvin got up to go.

"Well, see you later My Queen. Say 'Hi' to your hubby," he offered amiably, as he left the office. "By the way," he enquired just before he closed the door, "is Zack still giving it to Rayanne?"

Day Six: And It Came To Pass That She Got It All . . .

***

Another queen, Elizabeth I of England, founded, by divine right, the first "limited" company.

She wrote the law which limited her financial liability in The East India Company to loss of goods but not to loss of human life. For the widows and orphans of the sailors who died plying her trade routes around the world, she kindly created poor-houses.

She remained a virgin in the old sense of the word. Although she took lovers – Sir Walter Raleigh woo'd her with potatoes from the Americas – she never married, making sure no man usurped her power.

As defender of her faith, Queen Elizabeth imprisoned, then beheaded, Mary Queen of Scots, a rival with a rival religion.

As for Mary, she'd shocked her subjects by marrying the lover who murdered her husband, and been driven out of Scotland into England. If she hadn't lost her head, she might not have lost her head.

***

ZACK AND RAYANNE?!? Honey was glued to the spot where Calvin left her, but everything inside her was racing, or rather, rowing frantically to escape the tsunami-sized wave he stirred up on her lake. *ZACK AND RAYANNE, ZACK AND RAYANNE, ZACK AND RAYANNE!!!*

She tried calling Margo at Broad Beach but the machine answered. *RAYANNE AND ZACK!!!* "I'll call back."

She tried her mother. *ZACK HOLDING RAYANNE.* "Hi, Mom. No, nothing special, just, I miss you." *ZACK KISSING RAYANNE.* "Yeah, I'm really busy with the show and my new book and my speeches. Did you hear I'm going to Russia next spring?" *ZACK NUDE. RAYANNE NUDE. ZACK'S WARM HAND ROVING . . .* "Yeah, I'm a big hit all over the world. Well, I'd better go." *ZACK TELLING RAYANNE HE LOVED HER?* "No Mom, I'm not crying. 'Bye."

ON THE SEVENTH DAY SHE RESTED

1. Not Getting Any.
2. Getting Some But Not Pleasing.
3. Getting Lots But From The Wrong Person.
4. Getting It Just Right But . . .

Honey exited the TV station recalling the files she'd made as Miss Arlene's secretary. Of course, she knew by now that SEX wasn't LOVE. Love had more to do with vegetables.

Yet even with celebrated vegetables to give, she still found herself in Drawer Four with all those women who used to write:

Dear Miss Arlene:
Last night I noticed my Clairol Nice'n'Easy was missing from the bathroom cabinet and found my husband using it to dye his pubic hair light ash brown. Do you think he's having an affair?

Dear Miss Arlene:
My husband keeps going out to buy milk at odd hours. He doesn't drink milk. Do you think he's having . . .

Dear Miss Arlene:
My husband lost thirty pounds, bought a toupee and hasn't been home for two weeks. Do you think . . .

She aimed her car for Beverly Hills, her busymind shuttling from the past to the future. All those nights she'd wanted Zack to put his hands on her, to give some sign he cared, she thought it was her fault, something wrong with her, when all the time Rayanne was taking his best.

Lately, everything had seemed so perfect, so wonderful, but now . . . Now that she knew? Should she cause a big scene? Admit another failure? Split up her family one more time? Wreck her public image?

No! she told herself adamantly. Absolutely not. Some things you had to make up your mind to live through, the way she had when she was pregnant with Corie, or when Roger left her with a houseful of

Day Six: And It Came To Pass That She Got It All . . .

kids and no house to house them in. She'd have to put the thing out of her mind so it couldn't break her. That's what she'd do. Forget she ever heard it.

ZACK AND RAYANNE! Alright, she'd heard it, and not one of her sayings from Keep Breathing to Get Over Yourself could stop the tears from making tracks in her peach-blossom blush-on.

Neither escapist sex with Calvin, nor the cocaine he offered, calmed her down.

Cocaine? Calvin? Let's just say she took the long way home.

***

One last queen, Catherine The Great of Russia, murdered her husband, then, in the name of religion, beat up all her neighbors, snatched their waving wheatfields, their fertile deltas, and set her lovers up as governors over them.

History records that she also took horses to bed. Hopefully, some future hungry holder of the pen will leave that information out.

***

"Calvin. Calvin. Roll over."

"Frnnffff?

"Cal, will you please roll over? You're snoring."

"Mmmm," he said in his sleep, and "Mmmmmmm!" as he started to awaken and curl himself around her again.

Still had an insatiable appetite for sex but four times was more than enough. She inched away from him in the bed, feigning exhaustion so he'd go back to sleep.

She *was* tired. Tired of searching for those elusive rutabagas. Every time she yanked one out of the ground it had a worm in it.

Maybe I'm expecting too much, she thought. Maybe I want too much.

She lay in Calvin's penthouse apartment listening to his impersonation of a death rattle.

ON THE SEVENTH DAY SHE RESTED

No, goddammit, she decided. I want my rutabagas ripe and ready, and I want them boiled to a mush, with lots of butter and sugar and salt, pureed not diced, and I want a Mack truck full of them.

As for Zack and Rayanne? Let them get their own damn lunch.

She reached for the glassine packet containing the coke, snorted a little something, awakened Calvin and took him up on his offer.

6:6

What's this? You want a story conference regarding Honey and her behavior? A rewrite, starting where she takes the long way home? You think it ought to read "the wrong way home?"

C'mon! Quit seeing everything with squinty patriarchal eyes. Get pre-historic! She just took Cal into the temple, that's all. In the old days, you would have gone along to watch, reverently observing her inspiring feats.

But maybe her motivation for choosing him and not somebody cuter should be made clear. In matters of the female temple it's important to pick a partner who's willing to attend. That way, the ceremony to be performed goes as expected.

***

"Have some toast," said Zack on a March morning to his wife, who had one eye on her draft of The Recipes II and the other on some polaroids of the progress of renovation at her television station.

"In a minute, Kid," said Honey. "I'm writing a memo to Cal to tell him to go easy on the stained glass windows."

"Stained glass windows?" said Zack, looking over the pictures. "This doesn't look like a television station. It looks like a church. Who talked you into this? Calvin? LaVie?"

Honey shrugged, "It's time."

"What's this going to be the church of?" Zack enquired. "What's your position going to be?"

204

Day Six: And It Came To Pass That She Got It All . . .

"Eat your breakfast. We'll talk about it later."

Zack obeyed this edict from on high, managing to munch an English muffin while she wrote the memo.

There were other things he'd like to discuss, but didn't know how. No sex for one.

And her snoring. She was like a living buzz saw these days. If he hadn't known better, he'd swear her nose was stopped up from coke.

She was hardly ever home, always working late with Calvin or going back out on the road. She was leaving for Canada this morning, taking the twins who were on March break.

"Oh, there's the limo," she said, snatching a cold piece of buttered toast as she jumped up from the table. "Call off the dogs will you, Kid?"

***

Zack rattled around the house with too much on his mind, alone except for Jelia, missing the twins already, missing Honey, missing Corinne, wondering what happened to the family he'd longed for when he married the girl with the brood.

There wasn't much motivation to go to the office: his wife was making so much money. Everything she touched turned to gold.

She rarely wanted his advice or assistance now. When he gave his opinion, it was usually disregarded.

His other clients? Rayanne had efficiently taken them on as Zack spent his time on Honey. She'd earned their loyalty and their trust.

He wandered out to the garden. Inside its border of harvestable kale, spinach, brussels sprouts and carrots, outside the island for the fig tree, encircling the swimming pool and the pool cabana and the gazebo, was a field of waist high, young, green, winter wheat. Despite his unease, Zack had to smile at the beauty of it. It was like stepping into your own private pasture in the middle of Beverly Hills.

That Sah was some gardener. With more time on his hands, Zack began to think he might like to try it.

ON THE SEVENTH DAY SHE RESTED

He stretched out on the remaining patch of lawn beneath the tree and watched the clouds making animal shapes in the Southern California sky. Breaking his hard and fast rule, he whistled for Bones who was sleeping nearby. He patted his stomach, inviting the dachshund to climb aboard and be petted. But Bones, annoyed at being shaken from a dream of dobermans in satin, did not comply.

Rebuffed again, Zack dozed and tried to forget his troubles, until he was jarred awake by Jelia's screams.

He ran indoors to her room to find her convulsing, watched helplessly as she passed out in a pool of blood.

The ambulance seemed to take forever. Zack hovered, felt her pulse for signs of life, fanned her ineffectually, trying to bring her around.

Shock. Keep her warm, he told himself. He started to bundle her in blankets but realized he should do something to stanch the flow of blood.

It was when he ran into her bathroom to get towels that he saw the straightened coathanger, and the note of apology taped to the statue of the Virgin Mary.

Zack's stomach seized. His knees buckled. He wanted to faint but there was no time for that. He had to take care of Hey Ya.

6:7

Whether it was Gene's genes or Honey's that accounted for Corie's strength in the face of adversity would be a hard call. Some people just naturally put one foot in front of the other.

In Corie's case, after a few days of anguishing over Innocencio, she'd done what she could to make something of her life. She'd sold her car, caught a bus north to Santa Barbara, found a nighttime waitressing job and enrolled in school.

It didn't leave much time for fun – she was hardly ever in the dormitory – but then it didn't leave much time for feeling miserable. And if she was being stubborn, even cruel, to people who cared about her, it didn't leave much time to think about that either.

Day Six: And It Came To Pass That She Got It All . . .

In the steak house where she was working, she only half-heard the television news, on the run, not wanting to slow her service to two tables of six and one table of two. She needed the tips. It was big tips added to her miniscule salary and a school loan that were paying her way.

She ordered five margaritas, a large pitcher of beer, and two white wines from the bartender, but the TV set above the bar gained her shocked attention with news of "Demeter's housekeeper lying near death from an attempted abortion."

Corie thought about the many times she'd proselytized Jelia about abortion. She hoped, she prayed, that Jelia would live.

Footage of a worried Zack coming and going from the hospital with her grandparents, and shots of the twins with Honey in Vancouver, intensified how much she missed them all.

All, except her mother. She didn't miss her. Not one bit. Her mother was a flake who'd loused up Corie's life from the get-go. She never wanted to lay eyes on the woman again.

"Demeter, you've spoken and written frequently about abortion," Corie heard a reporter say, as the bartender loaded her tray.

"You've been known to advocate safe clean abortions until they're no longer needed. And yet, it's rumored that your oldest girl is a love child."

Corie stiffened, wishing she could turn off the TV, change the channel . . . something!

"This seems to indicate that abortion is not a route you would choose for yourself," the reporter continued. "Forgive my asking this very personal question, but have you ever had an abortion?"

"Yes," said Honey, like a true queen of the universe, "when I was seventeen."

Corie nearly dropped her tray. "Take over my tables for a minute," she asked another waitress as she headed for the phone.

"Zack," she said urgently. "How can I reach my mother?"

"Mom?" she said eventually. "Mom, can I come home?"

ON THE SEVENTH DAY SHE RESTED

***

A nurse wheeled an incubator closer to the window so Zack could get a better look at Jelia's teeny weeny preemie. He was not much bigger than a plucked chicken, still purple and pissed off at his early entrance into the world, squalling and fretting, checking around for his next meal.

Since a nipple couldn't be found, his fist would have to do. He put half of it in his mouth and sucked powerfully. What an ugly little bird: illegitimate, unwanted, but here on earth anyway, toughing it out.

Zack waved two fingers at the helpless, fatherless, no-chance-in-this-world thing, not knowing that the baby couldn't see yet.

"Keep Breathing, okay?" he whispered, though, of course the baby couldn't hear him either.

Later, on his way to the airport to pick up Honey and the twins, he was still thinking about Jelia and her baby.

If only she'd told him earlier, in her beaner English, that she was having money problems, he would have been glad to give her the few thousand dollars that all this seemed to be about. He wouldn't have fired her for being pregnant.

Or would he? Perhaps he might not have felt so charitable if he hadn't been personally involved as she drifted between death and life.

At least he'd remedied that now. He'd written her a check, right there in the hospital, hoping that whatever she intended to do with the money might cheer her out of her guilt and despondency over her abortion attempt. He'd assured her she could raise the baby and keep her job. That had finally gotten a smile out of her.

Jelia's boy would be the first newborn in his household: the only newborn anyone had ever named after Zack.

This fact reminded him of the unorthodoxy of his family in which nobody, except for Honey, was even named Newman, and never would be no matter how well he played the father role. And when they all grew up and had kids of their own? What would he be? A rent-a-gramps?

Day Six: And It Came To Pass That She Got It All . . .

Honey was right, he decided, when she said we were going to have to think of the family differently. We'd have to toss out some of those old labels and come up with new ones.

How about "friend?" he thought. This is my friend Zack. This is my grand-friend Zack. This was my great-great-great friend Zack.

He liked it. A family of friends.

Zack showed his pass to the security guard at the airport VIP pick-up entrance and drove the Rolls directly onto the tarmac.

In his mellow mood he was glad to be able to welcome his wife without the intrusion of the press, which, since her statement about having had an abortion, was becoming a giant pain in the ass.

There were still reporters hanging around the house, trying to make a story out of the delivery of the Newman mail, the collection of the Newman garbage.

Zack knew that a real story was about to happen. Corie was due back this afternoon. His "friend" Corinne, he thought, warmly.

Now if only his "friend" Honey's plane would arrive on schedule, the timing would be perfect. He'd whisk her and the twins to the house, let her drop some tidbit to the press, get rid of them, then Corie could slip quietly home.

"Mr. Newman," said an emissary from the airline, tapping on the window of the car.

"Yes?"

"Mrs. Newman's plane is going to be delayed."

***

And so it happened, on that day of the vernal equinox, March 21, the official start of spring, that LaVie's ex-boyfriend Garth was the one who opened the front gate at Honey's house.

Having come there with Mrs. Whistler, who had then driven LaVie and Sah, who were standing in for Jelia, to visit her at the hospital, Garth was the first to welcome Zack's friend Corinne, who was six months pregnant.

ON THE SEVENTH DAY SHE RESTED

He was the one to answer the questions of the press when they spied her rounded belly as she hurried past them, questions ordinary people don't get asked, like: "Who's the father of Demeter's grandchild?"

"Who cares?" said Garth with all the authority of a senior goddess disciple, as Corinne sped into the house.

He told the reporters that, under Demeter, society would probably return to a matriarchal, matrilineal, matrilocal system. "Once everybody knows she's God and She can change things back the way they were.

"If you don't know what matrilineal means, it's that all the money and the land and the buildings and the perks, like who sleeps with who, go from the mother to the girls, so it doesn't really matter who the father is. It only matters who the mother is because she's the one with the goodies to hand out."

"Does this mean Demeter's hoping for a girl grandchild rather than a boy?" asked a newswoman, shoving a microphone in his face.

"That would be best," Garth stated. "But if it's a boy she wins, too. Even after he mates, he'll be spending most of his time here, with his mom and Demeter.

"The mothers of *his* children, naturally, will be over at *their* moms'.

"If he's gay, that'll be okay, because Demeter isn't counting on him to continue her line. Although it wouldn't be too good if it's a girl and *she's* gay unless she has some sisters who aren't and they have kids who are girls."

There were no more questions because every reporter ran, hightailed it, flew to their respective offices to file this amazing story which came out variously that Honey advocated illegitimacy; a new Amazon dynasty; being gay. It came out that Honey, like Hitler, was merely biding her time before foisting a ghastly new society on an unsuspecting world. But mostly it came out that Honey was one hell of a bad mother.

***

There was no hint of headlines, however, as she and Zack and the twins drove up to the house, now devoid of people with clipboards and

Day Six: And It Came To Pass That She Got It All . . .

cameras. As the boys remarked, they felt like normal people coming to their normal home on a normal afternoon in Beverly Hills.

Of course, they hadn't yet laid eyes on their half-sister the blimp.

Even then, they all tried for an ordinary evening back together. Each was deferential to the other. But about an hour into the Chinese dinner they ordered in, the twins couldn't resist saying how they felt about Corinne's pregnancy.

"You're a throwback, man," said Sean, sounding disgusted. "We wanted you to get cloned, like us."

"Or at least have a test-tube kid," added Brian.

"It's kicking," said Corinne. "C'mere, you can feel it." She took Brian's hand and placed on her stomach.

"Hey, neat," said her brother, despite himself. "Try it, Sean."

"No way," said Sean. "You're a big hypocrite, Corinne. What happened to birth control? What about abortions? You were always going to get an abortion."

There was silence at the table while the adults present, equally interested in the answer, eyed their plates and waited.

"I guess," said Corie, shyly, "I guess I wanted someone to love."

"That's funny," said Honey, taking her hand, "because that's how I felt about you."

They looked at each other then, really looked, and so much of their former animosity just plain up and left the table.

Corie played with her chopsticks for a moment, then spoke.

"Mother, this may sound sort of strange and formal, but there's something I have to say to you."

"Yes, dear?"

"Thank you for giving me life."

What a moment!

The tears!

The hugging!

The joy!

Yet, as she was experiencing it, Honey was thinking someone should be there to write it down, to take pictures, to record it.

ON THE SEVENTH DAY SHE RESTED

Which brought up another point. Where were the reporters who usually waited in front of her house? Why hadn't the press been there to welcome her home?

6:8

It's hard to control a rewrite. The characters in the story head off in all directions and ideas have red pencils of their own. Still, the whole human race keeps scribbling away, always dreaming of paradise.

***

Demeter's mother knew how to put on a gala. She made the Founder's Night fundraiser at Honey's redecorated television station an affair to remember.

Fundraiser? Didn't the Demeter Foundation have bucks-a-plenty? Sure, but Norman Nathanson insisted that the first rule of show business was to use other people's money (a new Commandment?) so Missy was called in to turn the opening into a charity event.

She A-listed it with people in glittering gowns, well-cut tuxedos, real jewels, regular goers to parties which give you a tax write-off. She invited all of Zack's clients and the richest of her daughter's newfound followers. Into this core of social heavy-weights, she mingled Honey's suppliers: licensed manufacturers and distributors with their newly donatable money. Hobnobbing ensued.

The sumptuousness of the buffet would have put a network affiliates banquet to shame. Alongside every known meat and seafood dish, were tempting concoctions of vegetables. Vegetables were included in the dessert menu, too, with pumpkin petit fours, petite sweet potato pies, and orange/carrot custard ice cream, being favorites among the partygoers.

Much talked about were Missy's vegetable centerpieces, each a variation of the arrangement on the head table which featured a thirty pound cabbage imported from Alaska especially for the do.

Day Six: And It Came To Pass That She Got It All . . .

At the head table were Demeter and her manager husband; Calvin Still; Norman Nathanson and his son Lowell (The First Miracle); the Talking Boy (The Second Miracle); Demeter's parents; and Margo Best (The Grantee) – what meaningful work was she doing?

At another table was The Unmarried Pregnant Illegitimate Daughter, and, at another, Those Two Oddballs In The Funny Clothes. Everyone knew *HE* was *HER* father. It gave the whole affair a kind of leading-edge, we're-not-afraid-of-change feeling.

Notably absent, except for Calvin Still's own people, were reporters who had been barred from the occasion because they were twisting everything lately, trying to make Demeter look bad. The folks at this gathering were used to that sort of thing. The press always hates you when you're loaded with rectangular green dollars.

The band stopped playing R.E.S.P.E.C.T., as Calvin arose to ceremonially unveil and light the sign, with its 30,000 individual bulbs, which spelled out Demeter's Recipes, then flashed off and returned in a pattern to spell out, in large letters, the name of her show, *Something To Believe In*.

After the applause died, he introduced the architect who'd turned his old studio into such a spiritual place.

The guests nodded and chewed as the architect explained that, although this was a building celebrating the simplest of precepts, he felt a certain standard of elegance was required in this sanctuary consecrated to them. Hence the sheaf-of-wheat columns with the snakes twining on them, which gave the place a templish look. Likewise the stained glass windows illustrating The Recipes in action, and all the marble statuary of Demeter with her arms held out in welcome. The Recipe theme, he reminded them, had been carried outdoors. All the landscaping had been done with vegetables.

After more appreciative applause, Calvin took over again to remind the guests that it was from this impressive place that Demeter would broadcast her healing message to the world, but that, of course, the price of such a dream would not be inexpensive.

He let this statement hang over the diners for a moment.

ON THE SEVENTH DAY SHE RESTED

"To help defray the costs," he stated, "I pledge twenty-five thousand dollars."

"Thirty-five," pledged Norman Nathanson, executive producer of Honey's future programming.

These heavy pledges got the ball rolling so that the guests were soon shouting to out-endow each other, including Roger Best who wrote a check on the spot for ten thousand.

Recently, Roger had become an avid Demeter convert. His reason, he claimed, was the latest expansion of his parameters which caused him to see that following The Recipes was the ideal way to grow as a human being.

He also saw that he'd have a home at Broad Beach if his first wife hadn't coached his second wife into throwing him out. As a changed man, he hoped to reinstate himself with Margo, a potential threat to his net worth.

After the first round of pledging, Calvin introduced the lady of the house.

"And now," he said, "here's *someone* to believe in: *DEMETER!*" He pronounced her name with a dramatic resonance which lingered as the audience hushed in anticipation. She mounted the podium. They burst into riotous applause.

"Thank you, thank you," said our heroine, her jaw working slightly as she waited out an eternity of acknowledgement.

"Shhhh!" she said finally, commanding them to quiet down.

"This is a great night for me. And a great night for the world," she said, tossing her blonde mane. "But it might never have happened without a man who's been my inspiration." She pointed to Dr. Augustus Hess. "I want to introduce him to you now.

"Gosh," she said, as he came up to join her, "I should have brought a sand box for you, so you could take your shoes and socks off and really get in the mood.

"Y'know, I've been wanting to ask – why are you always changing your socks?"

"Well, I guess you can tell me that later because I want to dive right in here.

Day Six: And It Came To Pass That She Got It All . . .

"Folks, I first met Dr. Hess when I was having my famous nervous breakdown. And he was the one who made me see that it's alright to want to be God," she turned to her mentor. "Didn't you?"

"Well . . ."

"And he's the one who told me God used to be a woman. Didn't you?"

"Yes, but . . ." Dr. Hess squirmed uncomfortably.

"He was the first to hear my Recipes, which we used to call Commandments, and now he's here with us, watching as we grow into a full-fledged religion. Tell the truth, Dr. Hess, aren't you proud?"

"Uh, maybe proud is the wrong word," said the doctor, his brows knitting above his sharp black eyes. "I think you've got a few things muddled. Can we talk for a moment?" He took her elbow and led her away from the microphone.

"Why did she dig this guy up?" said Calvin Still to Norman Nathanson. "It's embarrassing."

"Lowell knows him," Norman told Calvin. "I do, too. Maybe we can do something."

"Never mind that. Get Lowell to make a pledge. Keep this thing on track."

Lowell Nathanson wished he hadn't been around to see what happened next. As his father turned to him to enlist his aid and Calvin took over the microphone to cover for Honey, she got into a hissing argument with Dr. Hess, then stalked away from him and headed for the powder room.

It was at that moment that all Lowell's old disgust with everyone and everything re-entered his life.

Not because Honey breached her own Commandments, from Do The Friendliest Thing to Get Over Yourself. It was the tiny white glassine package of cocaine he spied as it slipped from beaded bag to Honey's palm.

That didn't stop him from pledging fifty thousand big ones, though, a sum which refocused and boggled the guests, including his father who wondered how he was going to come up with it.

Lowell didn't say. He left the party with no goodbyes.

6:9

Maybe it's just as well that the stories of so many ancient priestess/queens have been deeply buried. Myths about how some of them behaved make more recent queens look good.

There can only be one reason why they took their sons or brothers as lovers, then bumped them off once female heirs were born: they must have been tempted to believe they could own the land.

Under their system, divine right to real estate came through the mother. Line breeding was the way to keep the assets in the family, by giving an ever-increasing dose of Mom to the daughters which resulted from the mating.

But the brother/son/consort had to be sacrified so he didn't grab the golden rutabaga. No problem. They made it part of their religion.

The brothers and sons of ordinary women were insignificant, but too many young men massed together can create a threat. They needed to be pointed, like arrows, at each other, or at themselves.

See the ancient snake become a devouring dragon . . .

And, no, that's not another story.

Greed beats Motherhood like a rock beats scissors.

***

Sah and LaVie hitchhiked back to her home in Venice: while he still preferred to put one foot in front of the other, she couldn't walk that far. But not everyone wants to give a lift to a bald-headed monk and a tattoo'd girl in red leather. They had miles to be morose about the opening of Honey's glitzy new temple.

"I'm starting to guess why the oldest religion didn't last," she said to him, glumly, as they wandered away from their disappointment.

"What I'm thinking? Maybe the goddess worshippers didn't just lose it in a bunch of battles. Maybe their lady leaders went too far, hitting that snake juice? Getting drunk with power? Maybe it all got

Day Six: And It Came To Pass That She Got It All . . .

to be about getting rich instead of sharing out the vegetables. They were, y'know. The priestess/queens? Filthy rich."

LaVie kept her thumb out but the cars and trucks drove by unheeding.

"And all that sex-in-the-name-of-religion? Maybe it meant their parishioners would keep on birthing new workers? And warriors? And stay so poor with so many mouths to feed they wouldn't have time to complain? They'd have their hands full just scratching out a living."

Rounding the corner, the driver of a rusty Ford flatbed loaded with crates of produce was scratching out his own living. He sized up Sah and LaVie and decided he wouldn't mind their company. He slowed to a stop but neither of them noticed.

"One thing I know for sure," LaVie was saying. "Change doesn't come when life is, exactly, wonderful. It comes when everything sucks!"

Sah nodded. He had been there,

"I'll bet there came a day when a woman couldn't raise a willing army.

"Ordinary girls probably welcomed their conquerors. And a male God. And tried this new thing called marriage? Hoping life would get better? But instead it got worse? Because now the guys got totally greedy?"

The driver of the produce truck tapped his horn a couple of times, but LaVie had turned to earnestly face her companion.

"And that's why I'm scared, Sah," LaVie said, "because it's our turn again and I don't want us to mess up.

"It's got to be a good deal this time," she said passionately, "a good deal for everyone.

"I don't care who God is . . ." she burst into tears, "we humans have to do better!"

Sah took her to him and rubbed his cheek against her flyway red hair.

"We will," he said softly. "We will."

ON THE SEVENTH DAY SHE RESTED

The driver of the truck leaned out his window. "Hey! I gotta get these vegetables delivered," he yelled. "Are ya comin' or not?"

***

They found Lowell in his bedroom three days later. This time he'd left the planet with no goodbyes. No note accompanied his suicide from an injected overdose of cocaine, unless you counted the envelope, pinned to his arm with the syringe, addressed to The Demeter Foundation, containing fifty thousand dollars in cash.

DAY SEVEN: And On The Seventh Day
God Ended Her Work Which
She Had Made, And She Rested
On The Seventh Day From All
Her Work Which She Had Made

7:1

There are people who think that one way human beings can do better is to deliver more food into the mouths of those who are barely scratching out a living.

Some think the way to accomplish this is to have fewer mouths.

Some think the way is for more humans to have access to a piece of real estate.

Some think the way is to make the real estate produce more and better things to eat through science and technology.

These speculations will have to be sorted out before we can draw conclusions about what happened to paradise and whether we can get it back.

***

They didn't drag Honey off to jail like they did with Bianca on *Inheritance* – remember how Congresswoman Mendez accused her of embezzling tree frog funds, and slapped her in prison, where she had to dress in ugly clothes and thought she'd go crazy if someone didn't *do* something to get her out of there?

ON THE SEVENTH DAY SHE RESTED

Honey only had to appear in court. As soon as her bail was posted she was free to go until a preliminary hearing could be held to decide whether or not there was a valid case against her.

But when the press got wind that Norman Nathanson had charged her with negligent homicide, religious malpractice resulting in the death of his son, everywhere she went became a jail. She was hounded by reporters, shunned by people who'd thought she was hot a moment before.

She was further confined in her mind. The circumstances of Lowell's suicide provided mental manacles, a windowless cell, and a set of iron bars between Honey and the rest of humanity.

In the past, when she came upon trouble or things she didn't understand, her approach had been one of curiosity, even wonder. But these days, she knew too much for her own good.

She knew, for sure, that life was not Recipe-prone; that the people in it were only out for themselves; that there was no such thing as a good deal unless someone gave up all their vegetables.

This knowledge allowed her to sublimate her sorrow for Lowell and Lowell's family; to view Norman Nathanson as a man trying to add to his bank account – he'd also filed a civil suit demanding millions in damages.

When Margo, applying her own research, tried to smooth the waters of Honey's lake by suggesting that Lowell died for his own reasons, Honey, who'd been hoping for more scientific input, cancelled her grant.

When Zack, to his credit, stood solidly with his wife, hiring the lawyers, dealing with the press, she knew he was only protecting his fuck you money.

Even the loyalty of LaVie and Sah went unappreciated. They had their royalties at stake.

And what about her children when they showed their sympathy? What about her unborn grandchild? What did they have to gain or lose? Plenty, Honey decided and viewed even her nearest and dearest with suspicion.

Day Seven: And She Rested On The Seventh Day . . .

But perhaps we're jumping ahead too fast. First, let's get the goddess into court, then worry about her lack of a positive attitude.

***

Honey's lawyer, a willowy, well dressed, thirty-five year old brunette of Chinese ancestry, told the prosecutor, a fortyish third-generation Irish-American dishwater blonde, that the charges against her client were a fantasy.

Lowell Nathanson was an habitual drug abuser. Though her client could be connected with his temporary recovery from drugs, that didn't make her in any way responsible for his relapse or his death.

The prosecutor believed otherwise. She intended to prove that Lowell's recovery had more to do with Dr. Hess's treatment than with Honey's mumbo jumbo. She would show that it was her religious teachings which led him away from effective treatment and confused him to the point where he ended his life.

"Because of the money he left to The Demeter Foundation?" said Honey's lawyer, skeptically.

"No," said the prosecutor, calmly. "Because of a videotape young Mr. Nathanson made of his own suicide. He was quoting your client's so-called Commandments as he killed himself."

She crossed to a television set in the conference room in which they were meeting, flipped it and a videotape machine on, pushed the play button and waited until the screen was filled with Lowell doing his last deed.

It was almost impossible to watch him mockingly describe the vegetable origins of his final dose of poison. He claimed to be Doing The Friendliest thing as he prepared the needle. He reminded himself to Keep Breathing until he was ready to inject. "Shhhh!," he admonished the omnipresent music which was blaring in the background as he pushed the needle into his arm. Then, "Get Over Yourself," he said as the drugs hit and he lost consciousness.

Honey's lawyer lowered her eyes and drew in her breath, not audibly, just enough so that the prosecutor picked up on it and smiled,

ON THE SEVENTH DAY SHE RESTED

knowing she had a breakthrough case here, the kind of case you prayed for. The one that could make your career.

***

In the adjoining reception area, a couple of secretaries waited impatiently for the two attorneys to be finished with the conference room. They usually ate their lunch there and watched syndicated reruns of *Inheritance* on the only TV set in the office. They'd wasted almost fifteen minutes of their hour break when the two women emerged, shook hands, and parted leaving the meeting room free.

The secretaries hurried in with their brown bags, turned the set on and settled down to pleasant escape from the drudgery of office work.

"Oh, great," said one of them, tuning the set to their favorite program. "This is the one where Bianca gets revenge on Congresswoman Mendez who's trying to get into the pool man's pants, and Jodie's sleeping with Matt, and Robert tells Bianca that he's leaving her and going off to save the black-footed ferret."

"Don't tell me everything," said the other girl. "I haven't seen this one."

Just then the prosecutor put her head back into the room, apologizing for interrupting her secretary's lunch. She wanted to dictate some notes on the Newman case. "I only have half an hour. Would you mind?"

Her secretary seemed to go willingly, but her look to her girlfriend said otherwise.

"Don't worry," the friend whispered. "I'll tape it for you. You can watch when you're finished.

"So anyway," she said, as the other girl got up to go, "what do you think of the Newman case? Is she guilty or not?"

"I don't know, but I saw her on TV and I really love her hair. Plus I read her book. It was neat. She's got this church. I don't know if it's open yet but I was thinking of checking it out."

"Me, too," said her girlfriend. "If she gets off, let's both go."

Day Seven: And She Rested On The Seventh Day . . .

***

Not that Zack could sleep anyway, but his wife kept waking him up at all hours, trying to come up with a rewrite of her plight.

"Someone's putting Norman up to this," she announced one morning at 5:00 AM, a week before her preliminary hearing. She was pacing the bedroom floor, her new habit.

"He's lost his only son, Kid," her husband disagreed sleepily. "He can't handle the grief."

"There's more to it than that," Honey insisted. "Someone else is behind him."

"Who?" Zack was awake now.

"Someone in the medical establishment," she said, heading for the Duke of Aragon's campaign chest. "Somebody big. Because I'm making medicine, including psychology, obsolete."

"Uh, Honey, I don't think you're exactly making it obsolete. I mean . . . Lowell died," said Zack.

"Plenty of other people lived," she replied impatiently, doing a u-turn and marching towards their Elizabethan four poster.

"Either that or it's agribusiness whose toes I'm stepping on. Too many people are growing their own vegetables."

He didn't answer, hoping she'd come back to bed. It was almost dawn.

"Or else it's the religions," she said, on the move again, heading for the fireplace. "I'm taking dollars out of their collection plates. There are pews empty because of me." She insisted Zack reflect on this new and better piece of paranoia.

Zack found himself staring at the empty space above the fireplace where a painting used to be.

"No, it's not one group," Honey said, vying for his attention, "it's all of them. It's a giant conspiracy to ruin Demeter. Well, I'm not going to sit still for it. I'm going to *get* the bastards."

She sounded like an old rummy. Or an old god.

"We need a new painting," he mused as he turned over to go back to sleep."

Honey glared at Zack's back.

"I can see whose side you're on," she spat, heading for the bathroom where a snort of coke awaited her.

"P.S., I know about you and Rayanne," she added venomously, "and I couldn't care less."

"Awww, Kid," her husband sat back up and took notice. "It's been over for a long time," he said gently, "not that that's an excuse . . ."

"At least I've got Calvin in my corner," she interrupted his apology, closing the bathroom door with a bang.

"And he's better in bed than you are," she lied.

***

But only Calvin had Calvin in his corner. Honey found that out after she inhaled the coke, threw on a bathrobe and marched downstairs into the garden.

As it usually does, the sun was coming up. Its first few rays made the dew on the fig tree glisten.

Aside from that, the place looked like hell. The winter wheat had been harvested and all that was left was a field of stubble. There'd been no spring planting, nevertheless some vegetables had seeded themselves along the borders of the yard and were on their way to being bushy. Two volunteer beans climbed last year's stakes and a wild zucchini was taking over a corner of her old rutabaga patch. Someone had weeded around these plants and there were two pony paks of horseradish sitting out, waiting to go in the ground.

Honey ignored the promise of providence. When Bones and the dobermans snarled, she almost snarled back, not realizing that their bared teeth were for the paperboy, making his way down the back lane behind the house.

The Los Angeles Sun came close to clipping her when he tossed it over the high iron fence. It landed at her feet, falling open to reveal Calvin's real feelings.

DEMETER CONNECTED TO MADAM'S MURDER

Day Seven: And She Rested On The Seventh Day . . .

He had splashed the headline across the front page over a three column photograph of Honey's wedding ring, followed by details of a letter from the late Lowell Nahanson describing the circumstances under which it had fallen into his hands.

Calvin had, of course, edited Lowell, eliminating any reference to the late Arlene Morrigan, so the reader was left with the impression that Honey was the sort of person who prowled the city looking for strange sex. It was intimated that she might have been being blackmailed by a mysterious female panderer who met with a sordid end.

One mystery solved by Calvin's article was where Lowell got the money to back his pledge.

Honey folded the newspaper and sat down heavily under the fig tree, covering her face with her hands.

But she soon came up for air. It was nothing personal. Just business. Calvin had probably bought the ring to protect himself. Now he was bailing out of what he viewed as a sinking ship.

But she was going to win. By whatever means. She'd have her day in court. It would be easy to prove that Norman Nathanson was blaming her for his own mistakes. Then she'd blow Calvin out of the water by revealing the location of Miss Arlene's grave.

Suddenly she couldn't wait for her hearing.

But first, there was the matter of her fight with Zack. She'd better make up with him. She didn't need another enemy.

She threw away the newspaper, went back up to her ninety-two thousand dollar bedroom, and waited for Zack who was brushing his teeth in the bathroom.

Trying for a contrite look, she timed her apology with the opening of the bathroom door.

"Sweetheart, about this Calvin thing . . ." she began, but "I'm sorry" wouldn't come out of her mouth.

"We're both at fault," Zack replied, taking her off the hook. "But things haven't been good with us for quite a while," he added, sounding worn out.

He let the sentence hang.

ON THE SEVENTH DAY SHE RESTED

"Then I guess you'll be moving out," she countered, her expressionless voice belying the rate at which her heart was banging around in her chest.

Zack sighed and sat next to her on the edge of the bed.

"I hadn't taken it that far," he said, "but since you're suggesting it, I think we should do things differently. I think you should move out and leave the kids here with me."

"What? I'm their mother!"

"I'm their friend," said Zack. "And they need stability now. If things don't go well for you in court – God forbid – at least this way there'll be some continuity.

"At your hearing," he went on, "I'll support you in every way I can. No one will suspect we're not together.

"When you leave, we'll tell the children you need time to yourself. Only you and I will know we're splitting up."

***

If we're ever going to complete the rewrite, we'll have to consider the relationship of mouths to real estate.

World population, of humans that is, grew between the Paleorootic and Mesoseedic eras, from five million to roughly twenty million. By the Age of Trade and smelting metals and writing on paper, our numbers had increased to ninety million.

On the day Zack and Honey split, there were four, almost five, billion people, that's five thousand million! And we're living longer by as much as *fifty* years. Bring on the chow!

In Queen Hatshepsut's Egypt, one-half to one acre of irrigated land fed a family of five.

In Elizabethan England, four to five acres fed that family and two or three others.

In 1895, five U.S. acres fed the family and five or six others.

In Honey's lifetime four hundred and thirty-five agribusiness acres typically made a supply of food for fifty people.

This is progress?

Day Seven: And She Rested On The Seventh Day...

Using the oldest of farming systems, four hundred and thirty-five acres would feed more than two thousand!

So what are we saying here? That smaller gardens, lovingly tended, produce a lot more food? That anyone who has access to even a tiny patch of dirt could be growing vegetables in it? That Eden's in the backyard and the frontyard and the schoolyard and the churchyard and next to the factory and on the street? That there's Eden in a barrel or a windowbox?

However, in Eden you have to be nice to almost everybody because you're going to want to trade with them.

And in Eden, you have to really co-operate to grow enough wheat to bake bread.

In Eden, it's obvious that no one owns the land. We just get to use it temporarily until they plant us in it.

***

No reporters were allowed at the preliminary hearing of the case against Demeter Johnson Best Newman, a ban, it must be said, which the press brought on itself.

Scandalous news about Honey and the accompanying rectangular green dollars which could be made from it were an everyday occurrence. Headlines had followed headlines:

IS GOD A PERVERT? was one which Calvin's ring story had inspired. WILL GOD FRY? one publisher felt compelled to print even though the crime of which Honey was accused was not a capital offense, nor had a court of law yet determined whether the charges against her had merit.

Chastised for their mischief by the judge, reporters had to stand in the street waiting to discover whether there was probable cause for Honey to go to trial, as the participants in this passion play took their places in an orderly and nearly empty courtroom.

Though Norman Nathanson had laid the charges, the prosecutor did not intend to call him as a witness. But Norman sat front and center in the court, his face contorted with anger and pain, unable to even look at Honey as she sat numbly at the defendant's table.

Calvin was there, too, waiting to testify for the prosecution!

Dr. Hess had also been called. Why was he looking so calm and collected, Honey wondered. He smiled at her. The snake!

LaVie and Sah, reluctant witnesses, held hands, Honey noted with disgust, while waiting to take the stand.

Margo showed up and took a seat in the back of the room but Honey didn't acknowledge her. Towards the front sat Roger. Were they going to call him, too?

As the prosecutor hurried in to court, Honey drifted to the day when Roger rushed her, bursting with twins, to the hospital.

In the delivery room Roger stood over her in mask and gown. He was the one who'd convinced her to go through natural childbirth. There she was, having two babies without anesthetic and, well, there were no words to cover it. When Roger laid the boys on her breast, the look that passed between them was . . .

The twins. Thankfully, they weren't here to see this. Corie either.

But where was Zack? Oh, there he was, doing his good-guy number, helping to seat her parents who looked older and more fragile than she remembered them. Zack the big hero. Asking her to move out. Of the house she'd paid for! She was going to move alright. Far away. With her children. Once this charade, and the school year, were over. She was only staying at Big Bear Lake, alone, for the interim.

Honey's attorney touched her elbow, indicating that she should rise with everyone, as the bailiff introduced the woman who would judge her.

After ascertaining that she understood the meaning of the proceedings, the judge, a white-haired woman of Indian-from-India extraction, wasted no time in calling on the prosecutor to begin her opening argument.

But the prosecutor hung her head, fiddled with her files, she seemed embarrassed.

Day Seven: And She Rested On The Seventh Day . . .

"Your honor," she floundered, "It seems that my key piece of evidence, the tape of Lowell Nathanson's suicide, has been erased. My secretary was having lunch and . . . she used it to tape an episode of *Inheritance*. It's the one with Congresswoman Mendez and the poolman," she fumphered, but the judge cut her off.

At the judge's request, enough of the tape was played to make certain that the purported evidence was no more, after which she beckoned the red faced prosecutor and Honey's attorney to her chambers.

An eon went by before the three woman returned and the judge dismissed the case – but not without a caveat:

"In the opinion of the court," she directed her remarks to Honey, "there's nothing intrinsically harmful about your tenets, Give And Receive Vegetables, Keep Breathing, Do The Friendliest Thing, Shhhh!, and Get Over Yourself. They have the potential to do good.

"But it's not enough to say them, or publish them, or make money out of them. If they're going to mean anything, you have to live by them.

"It's too late now for the unfortunate Lowell Nathanson to go back to the drawing board.

"I hope it's not too late for you."

"But . . ." said Honey rising to her feet.

"BOK!" the judge sternly banged her gavel down, giving her no further opportunity to speak, no chance to exonerate herself or in any way undo the damage done her, or even to say those words she found so hard to say, "I'm sorry."

And that wasn't the only cliffhanger that day.

Unless they'd seen *Inheritance* in the original, no one found out if the poolman said "yes" to Congresswoman Mendez, or hopped back into bed with Bianca, or put on his tight pink satin shorts and jogged on home.

***

ON THE SEVENTH DAY SHE RESTED

"What should we do, Sah?" asked LaVie after the hearing, as Honey hustled out of the courtroom. "She'll probably go back to the mountains. Should we go? She might need us."

"No," said Sah. "We have other things to do. It's time we spent some of your money."

7:3

Regarding The Garden of Eden, we need to answer one more question: Will science and technology bring us something new to eat, provide a new kind of plenty?

Already talked about as a future food, a world-feeder, is amaranth: it's easy to grow and its seeds can be milled into flour.

"Ha! Ha! Ha!" The Great Mother must be laughing. Back in the day, amaranth was banned from cultivation because its growers extracted red dye from the plant to paint their faces and the faces of their snakes.

Then how about triticale, a new grain made by crossing wheat with rye?

"Ha! Ha! Ha!" They've been doing that since ancient Africa and the Med.

Then what about spirulina, an algae containing perfect protein; or winged bean, or peach palm, or cocoa yam, or quinoa?

"Hah!" Look up what the ancestors of the Mayans ate.

Maybe so, but no Mayan, no Amazon, had rolls of plastic to keep the weeds out of their gardens. That's science and technology at work.

"Now, there's a thigh slapper!" Tomatoes, rice, barley, and wheat all came to humans as weeds, which grew as well or better than the crop they were trying to grow. To keep the freely growing weed instead of the hard-to-grow crop is known as natural selection. (Are you throwing away your dandelions or putting them in your soup?)

But science promises to make foods out of inedible things like maple leaves and coal.

Day Seven: And She Rested On The Seventh Day . . .

"Ha! Ha! Ha! Ha!" This crazy idea must really kill The Goddess because there are already 80,000 edible plants in the world and we're only eating about three thousand of them.

Fine, but now we can grow plants without earth, grow them directly in water fortified with nutrients.

"Ha! Ha! Ha! Ha! Ha!" That's how it all began!

So what are we scribbling at an unknown point in the beginningless, endless rewrite? That paradise is underfoot and always has been?

Now there's something to believe in!

As for Adam and Eve, Gods and Goddesses . . . you're the one with the pen.

***

From the day Honey left for Big Bear Lake, home, for Zack, was tsuris with a capital "Ts."

It was hard watching the children struggle with their mother's absence and the absurdity of her trial.

He worried that the twins might be having trouble in school. His fears were confirmed one day when he noticed the scrapes on the knuckles of Brian's right hand.

"Have you been fighting?" he asked.

"No. Why would I?" Brian replied.

"I don't know. Because of things people have been saying about your mom?"

"Nah," said Brian, "the kids at our school are used to this kind of thing. We've got a scandal-evangelist's son, the niece of that guy who says he's Satan. . ."

"And don't forget Luana," Sean filled Zack in, "she's one of the three hundred children of the Bagwan Aswan."

"Then how did you hurt your hand?" asked Zack.

"We were moving the laser printer and I got it caught in a doorjamb," Brian said.

Despite the twins attempts at nonchalance, Zack noticed the A grades slipping to Bs, and that the boys weren't that anxious to speak to Honey when she called; only occasionally asked about her return. Zack began to wish he didn't have to think up white lies when they did.

He began to wish she was coming home, had called her a few times since her hearing. He'd gotten the answering machine at Red and Missy's cottage but hadn't left a message.

What he wanted to say, he needed to say directly. At the risk of sounding sappy, he wanted to tell her what she was missing.

With enough on their plates already, the twins were subtly looking out for their pregnant half-sister, nagging her to go to bed early so she'd be up in time for school, making sure she ate her vegetables.

Corie, in turn, seemed to feel it was up to her to look out for Jelia, who fell into recurring silences on her return from the hospital.

Together, they all looked out for Jelia's baby, who quickly replaced the computer and the television set as a primary source of fascination for the family.

And then there were Sah and LaVie, two menches, who often came over to dig in the garden or otherwise lend a hand.

Red and Missy were regulars, too, stopping by to babysit, or barbecue, or just sit around and talk.

But the biggest surprise as a frequent visitor was Roger. He showed up as often as three nights a week. Though he must have had questions about Honey and her whereabouts, he didn't press them, and the subject of the twins' custody did not come up. He'd come over, help out, or hang out, then go home to his apartment in Westwood. It wasn't just that he was lonely, either. Or that he might run into Margo.

There was something he'd said to Zack one evening when they were by themselves. They were talking about Lowell's death. Roger was pontificating, as usual:

"Lowell died for our sins – the sins of the 'me' generation," he advised, but then, "Scratch that, Zack," he apologized, "that's just more of my bullshit. But we can't let it happen to *our* kids."

That wasn't the only time Zack found himself with a lump in his throat. It happened the first time Jelia gave him her baby to hold; the

Day Seven: And She Rested On The Seventh Day...

day the twins invited Missy to try the computer; the day Corie hugged Sah, her belly bulging with his grandchild; the day Roger and Margo had a fender bender in the driveway and ended up crying together.

But the most poignant part of the story was that it could soon be over.

If Honey so decided.

She held the trump card. Motherhood. Anytime she wanted, she could bring this party to an end.

It was almost too much for Zack, waiting for her mauve snakeskin sandal to drop. Sometimes it just fucking got to him and he'd have to leave the house, but then, "Get Over Yourself," he'd say, and dive back into the fray.

In fact Get Over Yourself was lived a lot by the inmates of Zack's particular Eden, together with all the other good wishes for the human race Honey'd come up with when she was at Dr. Hess's.

Shhhh! was a favorite. Lips got zipped.

Keep Breathing just happened.

Do The Friendliest Thing was also practically a given, until one day when the tour bus pulled up to the security gate and the driver rang the bell demanding entrance.

It took some time for the bus driver, Innocencio, to make clear to Zack that this was not a tour bus at all but Jelia's family arriving in style from south of the border.

"Forty-eight people?" Zack exploded, as they started to get off the bus. "What the fuck am I supposed to do with forty-eight people?!"

But then Jelia's sisters had clung to each other. Her small son Srafin stared defiantly. Her mother, stone-faced, collected them all and began to get back on the bus.

"Call Abbey Rents," Zack said to Corinne. "See if they've got enough beds for half the beaners in Guatemala."

***

It was the largest order Honey had ever placed for coke. Actually, she'd only previously purchased one small gram, but when you

ON THE SEVENTH DAY SHE RESTED

have money to spend it's never hard to get in touch with "them." It had taken some doing, though, to arrange for half a kilo to be delivered up to Big Bear Lake.

Dressed in a ratty chenille bathrobe, she waited, with the scant remains from her glassine packet dumped out on her mother's mountain coffee table, driving her Mack Truck full speed ahead over the vicissitudes of life.

Where on earth were "they"? Why didn't they come?

Maybe they thought they'd have to listen to her longing for her husband. Or aching for her children. Or grieving over Lowell.

Perhaps they thought they'd have to hear how life was too dark for her, too hard and heavy, how she wished she could go back to the way things were before people began to take her seriously,

Maybe they thought they'd have to hear how she didn't know what to do next, which way to turn, or where to go.

Or perhaps they didn't know it was her birthday.

That's right, Honey had turned forty.

The wrinkles she had all but wished for had become a reality. Some were the marks of smiling, but the main ones, the furrow between her brows, the downturned lines at the sides of her mouth, were the result of some expectations which hadn't quite panned out, caused by people who had let her down, people she wouldn't mind seeing at the epicenter of an earthquake, or floating in a flood.

But so what if she didn't have a newspaper column any more, or a television show in the works, or a publisher eagerly awaiting her next book, or a long list of speaking engagements to fulfill, all of which had been stripped like epaulets from her uniform by the vengeful Norman Nathanson, the sanctimonious Calvin Still? What if it was better for her children to stay where they were until she had things figured out? She had plenty of rectangular green dollars. And she'd have more after the divorce. Enough to stay above it all for a long long time. It was still her lake, and in the middle of her lake there was going to be this cocaine rowboat that could make her Mack truck fly.

She picked up a straw and was hovering over the dribble of white powder she had left when the doorbell rang.

Day Seven: And She Rested On The Seventh Day . . .

"Them."

Or maybe . . . Could someone have remembered her birthday? Maybe it was the kids and Zack. Or Sah and LaVie. Or Margo. Or her parents. Or all of them.

She quickly cleared up the coffee table, whisking the wisp of coke onto the floor with the hem of her chenille wrapper.

"Be right there," she called gaily, hurrying to the door, opening it to find no one she had wished for, only Calvin Still with a charming bouquet of vegetables in hand and his two-faced face split open in a big wide bullet grin.

"I've got great news," he said, strolling in casually and striking a pose with his bouquet in front of the fireplace.

"With all that lousy publicity, I thought you'd be finished," he told her, "but all it's done is to split your followers into two camps.

"The Demeterists, led by Garth, think you purposely killed Lowell to show us death's a part of nature. The Demeterites, led by his boyfriend, Vince, think Lowell isn't dead, just resting," he smirked. "The boyfriend says when the world lives according to Demeter, Lowell will return to teach us the secrets of The Recipes."

"Lowell won't be returning," Honey responded, sadly, "and there are no secrets . . ."

"Who gives a damn?" laughed Calvin. "I know we've had our differences lately but we could be back doing business tomorrow.

"Here," he handed her his bouquet and dug into his jacket pocket for further enticement. "I brought you back your wedding ring as a token of good faith.

"You can have it all again, Honey," he said, seductively, handing her the ring. "You can have it all double. They still think you're *GOD!*"

With new admiration he put his arm around her, kissed her neck, nibbled her ear, but now Calvin was sure he'd never understand women, because of all the reactions she might have had: telling him to take a flying leap, or yelling "Yahoo!" she did the one thing a man would never do.

She wept.

Not a few tears either, wails and sobs that excluded him completely. She gave way to it as though he wasn't even in the room.

Calvin hated tears. All his ex-wives had used them to unnerve him. He helped her to a chair, left the vegetables in her lap, told her to take some time to think about his proposal, and made a hasty exit, though he'd have to drive back to the city instead of bunking with Honey as he'd planned.

She didn't get up to see him out. Sunk as she was in her misery, she stayed where she was and dripped.

After a while, still sniffling, she noticed a white spot of cocaine on the carpet beside her mother's coffee table. Spilling vegetables, she crouched to the floor. She had the straw to her nose, preparing to snort the rug, when something Lowell once said came back to her.

"God doesn't need drugs!" she quoted him, getting up from her lowly position.

"God doesn't need anything," she added, "or anybody!"

She tossed Calvin's foolish bouquet into the fireplace, ground the last of the coke into the carpet and ignored the doorbell when it rang again. And again, and again.

But why was she still crying?

Why did she go out onto the deck overlooking the lake after "they" gave up and left, fling herself onto one of her mother's lounge chairs, clutching her wedding ring, and continue to mourn so loudly that she didn't hear the phone when Zack called?

Later when she shuffled indoors to go to bed, she saw the light flashing on the answering machine and picked up the message.

But it was only a hangup.

***

In the morning she awoke, puffy-eyed, red-nostrilled, and forty years old. Yet the maturity she'd longed for in her teens still seemed to elude her.

"Why am I sitting like a lump at the lake?" she asked herself. "If people want to worship me, let them!"

Day Seven: And She Rested On The Seventh Day . . .

She hurried to dress. Where in heaven's name was her white silk Norma Kamali? Something robish, she felt, would be just about right for the return of a goddess to L. A.

7:4

Have you ever seen the face of a deity on a search and destroy mission? It's a face more than forty years old. It's an Iron Age face, angry, ugly, petulant and wrathful. That was Honey's face as she crossed the city limits into Los Angeles on that sunny Sunday in May, gnashing her teeth and planning her comeback.

The Recipes II, she'd decided, should be shelved for the time being. Instead, she'd write a new book *Demeter, The True Story*, in which she'd vindicate herself, sacrifice Norman, Calvin, and anybody else she didn't much care for, and regain her former glory.

She questioned whether to milk both the Demeterists and Demeterites or forge a link between them to build a solid base for contributions to her cause.

She'd need her TV temple, which had been closed for litigation, so she veered from the route to a hotel where she'd made reservations, to have a look at it. With her own dollars, she'd hire a staff and begin broadcasting as planned.

But why stop there? She'd start her own network, build many temples, schools of Demeterism, Demeterland!

The street with the studio on it was crowded with parked cars, so she had to park hers some distance away. Walking closer, she could see that the station was boarded up but there was activity around a white clapboard bungalow which had been used as a construction shack during renovations.

There were people coming and going from it, and what looked like a tent from the Renaissance Faire set up next to it. Outside the tent, to one side, there were cages – cages of snakes . . .

LaVie! She was already exploiting the site!

ON THE SEVENTH DAY SHE RESTED

Honey strode through a knot of people making their way from the property to the street with produce in their hands. There was no sign on the white clapboard building but if she'd stopped to think about it, she'd have realized it looked remarkably like the plain white grange in Paradise, Texas.

She stepped through the open front door and, spotting LaVie standing inside, let loose her fury.

"Who gave you permission . . .?" she began, but she was outbarked by Bones who came howling up to her.

LaVie, too, came over. "You could use a haircut," she said, but then she held her arms out. "Gee, it's good to see you."

Honey avoided her hug and demanded answers, but her tone of voice felt out of place when she saw the group of people sitting, sitting, silently with Sah, in an adjoining area.

LaVie paused to close the door to the meditation room, then, "Let me show you around," she said. There wasn't much choice but to go along.

Honey was invited down a corridor to a row of glassed-in cubicles in which people were teaching things they knew to anyone who was interested.

In one area, Jelia and her sisters were teaching Guatemalan cooking to a small but rapt group of would-be gourmets. In another, Margo was giving a lecture on DNA. Honey's mother was one of her students.

"Age of Communication," said LaVie, subtly renaming her era.

In a third, Red was giving a real estate seminar to a roomful of pregnant teenagers.

"Your idea," acknowledged LaVie. "But he's taking it one step further. On Wednesday nights he teaches the boys. Gang kids? 'At risk youth'? And Roger's teaching real estate law.

"On Monday nights Corinne recycles her prenatal classes. Keep Breathing," she laughed. "On Saturdays, I teach hairdressing? Tuesday afternoons, the twins bring their computer down and give lessons? We're getting so busy around here we've had to put the vegetable exchange in the tent."

Day Seven: And She Rested On The Seventh Day . . .

She led Honey into the spacious canvas enclosure which adjoined the building. There were folding chairs set up around a platform, which Honey assumed was for religious services, but LaVie explained it was for a series of panel discussions on promoting and maintaining good health. Medical doctors, nutritionists, a chiropractor, an acupuncturist, an herbalist, Dr. Hess, and a Hopi shaman were on the panel.

"I know, " said LaVie, "you're wondering how we get these types on the dais together. Margo just told them Eddie Murphy might be dropping by."

"We're going to have dances, too. And meetings on accepting and dealing with death? And a conference on paleobotany and anthropology? Dr. Hess is putting it together."

"Then where do you worship?" said Honey.

"It's all worship," LaVie responded. "Like, y'know, every minute?"

She walked Honey over to a long table laden with vegetables, fruits, pickles and pies, and explained that people usually brought something to it, and took something else away.

"Help yourself," she offered. "Mrs. Whistler's corn relish is off the charts." LaVie picked up a jar and held it out to the Queen Of The Universe.

"But I have nothing to give back," said Honey, suddenly ashamed.

"Sure you do," LaVie replied, pressing a jar of relish into her hands.

With that, she pushed aside a tent flap and disappeared into the outdoors, leaving The Goddess alone with the vegetables and herself.

After a while, Honey realized she wasn't coming back. Thinking that, maybe, LaVie had expected her to follow, she, too, pushed aside the canvas and walked out into the sunshine. But the hairdresser was nowhere to be seen.

There was only Zack, surrounded by her sons and daughter, on their hands and knees in the garden. They'd dug themselves a hole and were planting a little fig tree. Their backs were to her and, with water from a hose running into a bucket, they didn't hear her wistful exclamation.

ON THE SEVENTH DAY SHE RESTED

It didn't matter. Beyond her brief lament, there was too much she needed to say to them. But that could come later.

She kicked off her mauve snakeskin sandals and found herself a trowel.

Then, white silk Norma Kamali forgotten, she knelt beside them and began to fill in the rich black earth around the tree.

***

And so, on that Sunday, she rested. Or you could say Got Over Herself.

And summer followed spring, and autumn changed to winter, and Honey and Zack hardly knew it. Their garden sprouted and bloomed and produced vegetables non-stop.

In it, they raised things to eat and children, her three and Jelia's four, and Corie's daughter, who was named Rhea and never called by a nickname, and, in time, LaVie and Sah's boy and girl, and the rainbow of kids the Bests adopted.

They rebuilt the pool cabana into a real home for Jelia, her mom, and kids. They helped with work permits and jobs and housing for the busload of would-be North Americans – many of Jelia's relatives ended up in television. They debriefed the dobermans and dismantled the iron fence around their house.

They took part in the teardown of a templish TV station to make more room for vegetables, and the naming of the small white building which they called The Grange, all under the eye of LaVie, the new head of the Board of Directors of The Demeter Foundation.

There was work to be done with another board member, Calvin Still. Was it Honey? Or Zack? No, Corie who talked him into running the literacy program and the writing workshop in exchange for the rights to distribute the How-To books and videos which came out of The Grange.

There was Lowell's memorial to plan and build, a stone path through The Grange's garden.

Day Seven: And She Rested On The Seventh Day . . .

Though Norman Nathanson shunned the dedication, Sah says he's seen him, twice, walking the path, alone.

On an ordinary day at the Newman house, you might find Missy showing off her research into the chromosomal similarity between collard greens and horseradish; or Red having an argument with Jelia's mother over mulch; or Zack making Rayanne a partner in his business.

The twins might be updating Sah about cars (things change); Bones might be laying dog logs in the den (some things don't).

You might find Innocencio visiting his son and his daughter, or Margo and Roger taking them to the beach; or Honey hanging a picture in the bedroom, a blowup of a slightly out of focus photograph, taken by Dr. Hess, of herself and Zack surrounded by their family of friends, up to their poopiks in winter wheat.

As to being back in, Honey has no doubt that she finally is. The water of her lake is teeming with boaters and she floats along with them.

She hasn't single-handedly ended war, or famine, or saved the white rhinoceros, though she was, is, and always will be, a contributor to that rewrite.

Except among people who have taken her tenets to heart, and a few old devotees at The Grange, her name is no longer well known. Lately, it's "Demeter who?"

Only rarely are there reminders of once-upon-a-time, like that incident the other day . . .

"Some putz is in the driveway, bowing!" Zack told Honey. "You'd better go talk him down."

"I'm sorry, I'm out of the business," she said, arriving at the door. "But come in. Join us for dinner. I hope you like rutabagas."

ACKNOWLEDGEMENTS

I've been writing professionally since the 1970s and remember well what it was like to have to go to a library, as LaVie does in this book, to do research. I was interested in the feminine face of religion even then, but making discoveries in libraries was a slog.

That's why my first acknowledgement must be an unlimited thanks to Google. It's been my resource for a world of goddess information and for most of the vegetable data, too. Google has made this a truer and funnier book.

I want to thank author and intrepid New York literary agent, Richard Curtis, for his early enthusiasm and efforts, and Tom Maddox, author of *Halo*, for his. The late Ernest Lehman, who wrote every movie you've ever loved, sent kudos which were beyond encouraging as the book was being born. Bernie Orenstein, writer/producer of a long list of comedy television series, and now author of hilarious novels, and his wife Barbara, laughed in all the right places and endorsed the "Yiddishisms." Googling any of them, you'll find delicious reading and viewing pleasures.

Patti Millington, who designed my other covers, designed this one, too. She's also my tech miracle worker. Without Patti . . .

Claudia Ziroli-Coyl, convener of The Puna Literati book club, has been a staunch supporter and I'm grateful for her useful comments. Her fresh eye is always invaluable.

Most of all I want to thank you for taking your time to read *On The Seventh Day She Rested*, which, by the way, is available as an e-book, and in print. If you had fun with it, please spread the word.

Thanks everybody!

Made in the USA
San Bernardino, CA
22 November 2014